Praise for **Rainbow's End**

"Captures the *ambiente* of the life of a borderland household as well as any book I've read."
—*The Los Angeles Times Book Review*
("Critics' Choice" selection)

"A first novel by a well-known southwestern short-story writer, *Rainbow's End* . . . describes a society in which breathtaking beauty and deep sensitivity exist alongside violence, drug smuggling, and an illicit trade in human beings."
—*New York Newsday*

"So many good books have been coming out of Houston's Arte Público Press that I lately realized I couldn't read them all . . . Of the recent titles, the one that impresses me most is *Rainbow's End* . . . Perhaps some quick-thinking movie executive will option it. It would be worth the money . . . What can't be transferred to film is González's writing . . . The creatures of his imagination combust into their own living, full-color reality."
—*The Nation*

Praise for **Only Sons**

"Belongs on that shelf of good books about modern family relationships alongside the quirky and brilliant fictions of Anne Tyler . . . Highly recommended."
—*Multicultural Review*

"A powerful collection . . . Touching and gritty stories about father-son relationships."
—Judyth Rigler, *San Antonio Express-News*

The Quixote Cult

By Genaro González

The Quixote Cult
Only Sons
Rainbow's End

The Quixote Cult

Genaro González

Arte Público Press
Houston, Texas
1998

This volume is made possible through grants from the National Endowment for the Arts (a federal agency), Andrew W. Mellon Foundation, the Lila Wallace-Reader's Digest Fund and the City of Houston through The Cultural Arts Council of Houston, Harris County.

Recovering the past, creating the future

Arte Público Press
University of Houston
Houston, Texas 77204-2174

Cover design by Vega Design Group
Original illustration by Jose Guadalupe Posada (1851-1913)

González, Genaro.
   The Quixote cult / by Genaro González.
   p.   cm.
   ISBN 1-55885-254-9 (alk. paper)
   1. Mexican Americans—Texas—Fiction. I. Title.
PS3557.0474Q59 1998
813'.54—dc21   98-28334
                                             CIP

The author thanks the Dobie Paisano Program for a Creative Writing Fellowship, which allowed the completion of this work.

8 9 0 1 2 3 4 5 6 7   10 9 8 7 6 5 4 3 2 1

For Mariella,
a glimpse into a time
when you weren't even a gleam
in your father's eye.

1
Nothing Ever Happens, Until It Happens

It's the tail end of that tiger called the nineteen-sixties, and we're barely holding on by the tip. The summer's not even over, but the casualties already include King and Bobby Kennedy, and that's not counting the body bags from the war. Elsewhere people protest why we're in Nam instead of giving the poor here a helping hand. But this is deep south Texas, and since most of the bodies inside those bags here are brown, few Anglos bother to question things. Neither do the families and friends of the corpses. Instead the dead are quickly buried, literally as well as in the day's headlines, to make room for tomorrow's victims.

After that it's back to business. In bordertown barrios like this, the war has become as much an underground economy as smuggling dope, but in subtle ways that only an undertaker could appreciate. So if a dope dealer double-crosses another, the incident isn't resolved with guns or knives but with the insignificant, invisible pinprick of a hypodermic. He's fed an overdose and dumped into the Rio Grande: few ripples in the headlines, no glare from TV cameras.

Of course you only hear the truth if you bother to listen, and even if the Anglos across town bothered to do so, they're too far to hear. They rarely even look. All they see when they drop off their maids and handymen are our rickety houses with crowded gardens that seem to have been landscaped by aliens on acid. Anglos my age are no different, even those teenagers who think they're aware because they get stoned. Never mind that marihuana's been in the barrio for longer than anyone can remember. To hear Anglo kids talk you'd think rock groups invented it. So when the dealer with the lethal injection turns up bloated, he's blurred with their memory of the would-be wetback whose body was fished out

last week, from the same riverbank where the street that runs by our barrio ends.

I live with my stepfather's father in a frame house as decrepit as the
old man. My mother, stepfather, and half-siblings live next door. Two
years ago my parents suggested I keep an eye on the old man after his
wife died, and I've lived here since. We take our meals next door, but for
practical purposes this is my home. The old man has the roosting
instincts of a chicken, so by nightfall I have the house to myself. It's an
ideal parasitic arrangement. On the rare cold mornings we have here he's
up at dawn to light the heater and work up the circulation in his legs.
Once the place warms up I check to make sure his ass hasn't caught fire.
On summer mornings like today the task is even simpler: I just make
sure he made it through the night.

These nights there's no worrying about getting up for school, so my
friend Lucio drops by on one of his werewolf highs, all-nighters on
amphetamines. Occasionally I'll take an upper too, or smoke a toke, and
our discussions drift into dawn. By then the old man is up and dressed,
griping that we kept him up all night. That said, he makes himself comfortable and hogs the conversation. We don't mind listening to his life
story, at least not for the first half-hour. Lucio says that either the old
man's memory for who said what and when is nothing short of phe-
nomenal, or else he's a pathological liar of the first order.

This morning Lucio's insisting in a low voice, "He's got to be high
on something. Come on, De la O, what's he really roll in those Buglers?"
Then he smiles and shakes his head, like when he's reading one of those
existential absurdities he loves to ponder. "Ah, to be brown, ninety, and
senile in the sixties."

Lucio leaves, but the old man has just hit his stride. Luckily two lay
proselytizers—Mormons, or maybe Jehovah's Witnesses—make the mistake of dropping in. They take one look at him and map out their strategy
on the spot, playing on the stock anxiety of the elderly. "I ask you," says
the one with the better Spanish, "where in Heaven's name are we headed?"

"Me? Nowhere," answers the old man. "I've already been everywhere." He pats the sofa. "Now I'm right here at home."

"I mean after we're dead."

"Why, the grave, of course." He doesn't even give them time to reframe the question in its full philosophical parameters. "Look, I don't know where I'll end up, but I can tell you where I've been."

And before they can pull out their pamphlets, he's off on a marathon monologue so they can't get a word in edgewise, not the Good Word, not Yahweh or any of the other aliases God goes by. They try waiting him out, but short of the times Lucio and I sit there too stoned to move, he rarely gets a crack at a captive audience. When he finally pauses to make a hand-rolled cigarette, the monolingual guy gives the other a let's-get-lost gesture and packs his paraphernalia. They pause at the door to look me over, wondering whether I'm worth saving, then promise to return.

Right. See you on Judgment Day.

I spend the rest of the day in front of a fan, reading and daydreaming. Lucio left me a book by some California Chicanos, stuff that's hard to find here, even though three-fourths of the Rio Grande Valley is *raza*.

The old man prowls past my door, looking for a pretext to catch my ear, but I put on my headphones and pretend to listen to my stereo. I don't like tuning him out that way, but sometimes nothing else works. Later I'll make it up to him by putting some *corridos* from the Mexican Revolution, which is the only reason he lets me play my stereo in the first place.

I bought the eight-track system with my summer earnings, working at a ball-bearing plant with a cousin near Chicago. I didn't make bearings, but I did make more money than I ever could with a high-school diploma here. The foreman even asked me to stay on, since I was the only worker who didn't mind scraping the insides of their huge boiler cores for hours at a stretch. I'd go in with goggles, a face mask and coveralls, my only worry that some idiot might shut me inside by accident. The tight fit made the other workers claustrophobic, but that's where my size paid off. Besides, I didn't mind the solitude.

I don't mind it here either. It beats watching television with the family while my stepfather chooses the programs, loud and aimed at the lowest common denominator. It's unfortunate, because there's a perceptive side to him, seeing through people who take themselves too seriously. But for someone who can zero in so well on society's bullshit, he'll take the same bait without blinking.

Like a lot of lower-class wage earners, he's obsessed with money. I don't mean holding down an extra job to help your kids get ahead. In his case it's the fantasy of having children who will one day support you in style. So if a young entertainer comes on the tube five minutes won't pass by before he wonders aloud how much his parents are getting. Sometimes I'll reply that parents reap what they sow, and that a kid who gets a shot at success usually has parents who made sacrifices. That stops the conversation cold, since the only parental sacrifice he and my real father are willing to make these days is the one God asked of Abraham.

I'm not saying this for myself. I'm getting an honors scholarship at a nearby college this fall, and while he never once bothered to ask about school, what's done is done. It's not too late for his own children, though, but his attitude is that he pays the bills and feeds the family, which is more than enough. In my case even this isn't quite true, because up until I turned eighteen I received child support from my father. It wasn't much, but it covered most of my expenses. More importantly, it gave me a degree of independence.

That's why I'd rather spend my days in the old man's house. I'd rather listen to his wanderings through Mexico and Texas than listen to my stepfather's dreams of Easy Street. At least in his travels the old man's feet are on solid ground.

Last week he was telling me about the Mexican Revolution, or at least about how he had lived through it, and what I heard pushed me to do some reading.

So today when he brings up the subject I immediately add a few things I've read. He must have thought I wasn't even listening all that time, because at first he simply stares at me, unable to fathom not only how my generation could know these things but why we would even want to. Afterwards he continues cautiously, as though I might contradict him with my book-learning. When he mentions Porfirio Diaz, the dictator the revolutionaries ousted, I add aloud a detail I read. During his exile in Europe, *don* Porfirio was asked why the Revolution had erupted. After all, to the outside world Mexico appeared peaceful and prosperous. His government welcomed foreign investors, the inner circle grew fat and the rest seemed resigned to their fate. Then suddenly the whole thing blew up. History has it that when he was asked what had happened, he thought a moment then answered, "In Mexico nothing ever happens, until it happens."

The old man nods while savoring the quote. "And let me tell you, when it happened, it happened!"

It's not so much boasting as reverential awe, in that same bewildered way the dictator must have answered, each in his own way reliving some terrible force of nature.

Later I find myself going back to that quote from half a century ago, only it's south Texas I'm thinking about. Here, though, only the first part of the quote holds true: Nothing ever happens. I'm reading in Lucio's book about *raza* organizing in California and Colorado, but from the way things happen here—or never happen—you'd never suspect the majority here are Chicanos living in poverty. While farmworkers are busy organizing elsewhere, a few of us who've worked in the fields—which is most of us in the barrio—can't help but wonder why it's not happening here. In fact the union did try organizing here a while back, but the Texas Rangers quickly restored law and order; that is, they put the *raza* back in its place. The view varies depending on who's observing. The difference between the official version and what you hear from those whose heads were cracked is as stark as the difference between the barrio and the Anglo side of town.

Like any doubting Thomas, I'll believe wounds over words any day. Trouble is, everything going on around us seems to happen just beyond arm's length. Dr. King's murder this year seemed to take place in some remote country and barely made a ripple in the barrio. Of course many Anglos here had already done their best to discredit him so that brown people wouldn't get similar ideas.

Bobby Kennedy's death seemed more immediate. Much of the barrio still worships his older brother's memory, although in a melodramatic way. Bobby's death, though, did little to bring home his message of change. I remember waking up that warm morning to a bulletin blaring from our neighbors' television. *Doña* Chona was trying to piece together her fractured English into some understandable whole, and the little she picked up left her shellshocked. The biggest bombshell was hearing that the assassin was brown.

"That's all we need," I heard her say through my bedroom screen. "That's just the excuse to round us up."

By the time I was up and about she had stirred up half the barrio. When I crossed her path she was talking to Mirta, an attractive undocumented maid who worked down the street. Mirta's expressive eyes became even larger as she took in that prediction.

"Ask him," I heard her whisper. "He should know."

"*Muchacho*, you're in college, right?"

"I'm starting this fall."

"Well, I'm as dumb as any donkey, but my guess is they're going to round up the lot of us and send us to Mexico."

"Even those who were born here," said Mirta. "Like you."

I pretended to give the theory some thought while they watched me closely, as though I might try crawling out of my own skin and sneak away. Finally I answered, "I don't think so."

"You haven't lived long enough. It wouldn't be the first time. Just ask the old man."

I already knew about the repatriations during the Great Depression, but I couldn't see the gringos doing it again. Still I wouldn't put it past them so I simply said, "Well, if it happens, it happens."

Like a lot of other people here, *doña* Chona's of the mind that when choosing your path in life it should be straight, narrow and clearly marked. You can be a college student or you can be a bohemian, but you can't be both. Standing before her, I had the feeling she disapproved not of my hippie haircut, but of my wanting it both ways.

She didn't say that, though. She simply glanced at my sandals and remarked, "It's a good thing you wear *guaraches*. They'll send us so far south that's all we'll be using."

"What about my hair, *doña* Chona? Mexico's not letting in any longhairs. Or maybe I can pass for Indian . . ."

"Don't worry about that, *muchacho*. They'll be happy to scalp you. I tell you, down where they're sending us . . ."

"Ay, *doña* Chona," said Mirta, "you make it sound like we're going to Hell."

"Hell is right here, what with everyone doing as he damn pleases. At least down there *rurales* are still the law of the land."

"*Rurales?*" I asked. "Like in the days of Diaz?"

"That's right, *muchacho*. If there's one thing they enjoy more than rebels, it's hippies."

She pronounced it "jipis," the same way they write it in the Mexican crime tabloids that Lucio's father sells at his store. I suddenly remembered a recent article Lucio had pointed out, about a well-known Beat writer who was denied entry into Mexico until he "ceased being a hippie and an existentialist."

I had a hunch *doña* Chona read the same story, so I put her to the test. "What about existentialists? Are they safe?"

"I don't know what they are, so I can't say." Her face, though, made it clear she didn't like the way the word sounded.

The following morning a few families in the barrio expected us to be herded and moved out, but by noon they came to their senses. By then, though, Mirta had already returned to Mexico. It was too bad, because even though I only talked to her once or twice, I enjoyed watching her sway to the *tortilleria* and back.

2
An Underground Education

Lucio's family owns a supermarket run by his father. It's not as fancy as the stores on the Anglo side of town, but they made enough this year to buy him a new car for his graduation.

We became friends a little over a year ago. Pablo, an older college student who works part-time at the store, asked me to help out one afternoon after the Border Patrol picked up their stock boys. When Lucio dropped by Pablo told him that the Zamarripa brothers had just come across some good dope. Lucio didn't even ask how good; he simply rang up a register and took out enough for a baggie.

That's how I first got stoned, behind the store's trash bins. I also found out how Pablo comes up with those interesting themes we discussed after school. They're mostly Lucio's ideas, and during our discussion that night we ended up on the same wavelength. In truth Lucio and I had crossed paths in high school, but it never occurred to us we shared some interests. I hung around *chavos* who had more basic priorities and little in common with the affluent Anglos who read to please their parents and to crank out good report cards.

At first glance Lucio seemed a more likely candidate for that charmed circle, but even though his parents had the means to put him there, he himself seemed utterly indifferent. In my case, being dark and poor, you can't enter unless you're invited, and even then you have to put up with a considerable crap from Anglos, which I won't. But Lucio doesn't have an axe to grind—he's light enough to pass for Anglo. More importantly, he's well off, and that's what baffles my other friends. If they were in his shoes, most would have already defected.

That's the main reason I like him. He's sharp, but not like the middle-class kids in high school who tried to impress us with meaningless facts. Our world wouldn't make sense to them, because we take the same things they know or take for granted then add a twist—a word play in Spanish, or imagining the strange way an uneducated relative might react to the same bit of knowledge. For instance, yesterday Lucio interrupted a conversation that had turned unusual and pretended to ask one of those students who everyone assumed was gifted. "Now let's hear what Scott Hardwicke has to say about this . . . Scott . . . Scott?"

"He can't say dick," added Pablo, "because he has no idea what we're talking about."

In real life, though, that rarely stops Anglo kids, especially when it comes to idiotic remarks they learned on their daddy's knee, like how "poor people down here"—meaning us—avoid hard work at any price. That's why the Scott Hardwickes of the world wouldn't know what to make of Lucio's monologue a couple of nights ago on surrealism in the world of illegals, following our chat with one of his father's stock boys. Assuming those gringo kids knew what he knows about surrealism; even assuming they understood the weird world of *indocumentados* beyond their simplistic prejudice—they still couldn't appreciate the surrealism of Chicanos discussing this in a barrio alley.

Besides, we get our ideas from different places. Our parents can't introduce us to the world of literature or the arts, but in a way Lucio, Pablo and I have something better—our comic-book vendor connection. Once a month the van that delivers magazines to several stores in town drops off a bundle of comic books at the supermarket, as well as some crime-and-punishment detective magazines. Lucio's father insists that's what sells here, so that's what he stocks.

But long ago Lucio discovered that the comic book man also takes good paperbacks to other stores on his route. By now he has the ritual down pat: While the comic-book man stocks the racks with junk, we scavenge through the better stuff he leaves in the van. If we find something to feed both our minds and hormones, even better. Lucio's collected an interesting patchwork of *libros calientes*, from Henry Miller and the Olympia Press to stuff strictly for adolescents.

Today we go straight to the source of things, this month's *Playboy*. After staring long and hard at the centerfold, Lucio skims through the rest of the magazine.

"Take it home, De la O. There's a couple of good articles."

"Sure it's okay with the comic book man?" I ask, even though I already know the answer.

Lucio taps the stack with his shoe. "He's got plenty more here to jerk off to."

We quickly browse through cartons of paperbacks while Lucio asks every so often, "Heard of this guy?"

I nod every now and then, but usually because he's mentioned the name before. That's how I read about Beats, existentialists and some of the Latin American writers. Lucio has an uncanny sense for sniffing out interesting material we wouldn't read otherwise. And he has an omnivorous appetite, just as happy devouring a paperback on Lenny Bruce as one on Nietzsche, which is what he settles on today.

No sooner do we jump out the van than we bump into the comic-book guy. He glances at the magazine and grins, as though relieved we're normal after all. "You boys take it easy. Watch those pimples."

I nod but look down, sneaking the magazine under my arm while Lucio settles the bill. It's a ritual we've already worked out: His father pays for the stuff we take, no questions asked.

Sometimes I stash the sex stuff at home, in a storage room next to the old man's bedroom. But today my stepfather's already back from work, and I'd rather not risk running into him with the magazine, so we visit Lucio's friend, Nicky. His parents have an efficiency apartment behind their house, which became our hangout after their last renters trashed it. Nicky's only visible relative seems to be an older, shadowy sister who leaves us alone as long as we stay out of the main house.

Like me, Nicky appreciates privacy, but while I prefer my solitude straight, he spends his stoned. He's barely starting high school, but when it comes to drugs he's right behind Lucio, if not in front.

We're not the only ones with a stash here. The Chief is already searching for some pills he left here a month ago. The Chief is about my father's age, but since his old *vida loca* friends are either straight, stiff or doing time, he's forced to hang out with the likes of us. I suspect he enjoys playing the old hand when it comes to drugs, his way of passing the toke to the next generation.

Even though he's stoned more often than Lucio, he's survived all these years by keeping his cool, which at the moment comes in handy because Nicky's starting to lose his. Usually Nicky's on the quiet side, but with pills he gets downright belligerent. The Chief manages to keep him under control, but since downers are The Chief's drugs of choice, he's also why Nicky stays stoned in the first place.

The Chief starts explaining how he took so many capsules that he had a fistful of undigested gelatin removed from his stomach last month. He imitates a surgeon digging into a mess of entrails. I doubt the operation was that dramatic, and if it were there's no way he could have known, but it's an entertaining touch.

"So that's where you were," says Lucio. "We thought you'd OD'ed or something."

"Not with Mexican capsules. You couldn't do a *doblete* if you tried. But I'll tell you one thing. They landed me in the hospital. Don't ask me what they use, but they don't dissolve right. They stick to your insides like a lump."

Out of the blue Nicky accuses The Chief of putting down Mexico, an odd comment coming from a Chicano who calls himself Nicky. Since I occasionally bore them with Chicano issues he tries to get me on his side. But his argument makes no sense, so I keep quiet.

Even The Chief winks my way and adds, "Look who's talking." Since he and I are the only dark ones there—Nicky's almost as light as Lucio— the meaning is obvious. He throws a pinch of salt on the wound: "Nicolas."

That's Nicky's given name, except that instead of stressing the last syllable, The Chief puts it on the middle one, so that it sounds like "ass-less" in Spanish.

Nicky replies as quickly as his drugged senses allow: "If your own asshole wasn't so screwed up, Chief, you could shit the stuff out like the rest of us."

Now The Chief usually has the patience of a saint on downers. You have to if you hang out with adolescents. But even junkies draw the line somewhere, and his falls above a certain part of his anatomy.

"You're saying I've been screwed up the ass?" He says this almost privately, which only makes the remark more menacing.

Nicky's too stoned to organize a coherent answer, so Lucio does the talking. "I think he means himself, Chief. That's why those things never plug him up."

The Chief appreciates the put-down even as it goes over Nicky's head, then continues with the patter of someone whose visit is other than social. Still talking, he searches the usual nooks where Nicky stashes stuff, rubbing his mouth like a famished man.

"Imagine. All that time in the hospital without a taste."

"Why didn't you say so, Chief?" Lucio grins with the immense relief of someone too polite to broach a taboo topic on his own. "I figured you came back clean . . ."

"I did, *muchacho*, I did. I even lost my original sin. But like our Father Adam said when he was tempted with that apple, 'I wouldn't mind a taste . . .' Anyway, imagine that hypocrite doctor, lecturing me to stay clean. They're the biggest junkies of all."

"Well," says Lucio, "we kept your stash double-wrapped like old valentines."

"I knew I could trust you *muchachos* . . . Say, you know my cousin Tino?"

He's another old *pachuco*, but with a sadistic streak, and I'm tempted to blurt out the nickname Lucio and I baptized him with: Psychochuco.

"Well, imagine, he offered to keep the stuff while I was recuperating. Hell, afterwards I wouldn't even find the formula."

Lucio reaches behind a chiffonier, blocking The Chief's view but not mine, and pretends to pull out a fistful of capsules already in his hand.

"Careful, Chief." He hands him the stash. "This stuff hits you harder when you're clean."

The Chief unscrews a few capsules and taps out the powder in his palm. The small mound disappears with a quick lap of his tongue, the way I used to eat powdered Kool-Aid as a kid. He even shivers from the tart aftertaste.

He catches me staring and says, almost as an apology: "The doctor said he's not going in again after undigested capsules, so I have to watch my health. He didn't say anything about what's inside, though."

That said, he licks up the remaining residue, like an addicted anteater. "Tino says that if he had to taste this shit he'd be clean by now." He rolls two other capsules between his fingers, pauses, then pulls them apart too. "Shit, he'd snort snakeshit if it got him high."

I know he's not about to take my advice, but I give it anyway so that if they hand out any more capsules I'll have an excuse to turn them down. "That's why I stick to grass, Chief."

"Grass, eh? Then pay the Zamarripa brothers a visit."

Lucio's antennae pick up at once. "Those *vatos* always have good stuff."

"This time it's not just good. It's totally tortilla. Imagine, you blow out the smoke and it's almost blue."

"Zihuatanejo purple!" says Lucio. "I've heard it's like an opium high."

The Chief agrees then begins elaborating with a personal anecdote. There's no telling where the monologue will lead to, but I know exactly how it ends: with his favorite phrase: "*Es todo*"—That's all. He'll start these convoluted conversations, then at some point when his listeners are lost in his labyrinth he stops abruptly in midthought. "*Y pues . . . es todo.*" And that's it, end of conversation, because *es todo* means *es todo*.

After Lucio and I leave we keep interrupting each other with the phrase. When we tire of it, I take up another of The Chief's favorites: "Imagine!"

"Speaking of imagination, he's going to need lots of it to get high."

I remember that sleight of hand Lucio pulled off with the capsules, and when I ask about it he simply answers: "I switched his medication."

Something told me the old guy gave them too much credit for keeping his stash in trust. Lucio admits you can trust him with anything but your drugs. "So you and Nicky ripped him off?"

"Oh, the capsules are the originals. We just took the insides and refilled the prescription."

"With what?"

"Powdered sheetrock. It was Nicky's idea."

He doesn't say this to shift the blame. If anything, he almost wishes he had come up with the idea himself.

"I guess it can't hurt. At least it'll keep him off drugs."

"Knowing The Chief he'll end up hooked on sheetrock."

My house is on the way to his, so Lucio gives me a ride over. He's had the GTO barely three months, and it's amazing the difference a nice set of wheels makes. Not that we're up to our ears in pussy. After all, Michigan manufactures cars, not miracles. Still, women that otherwise wouldn't look at us now show some definite interest. It's nice for one's ego, but it also bothers me that something so trivial can matter so much. That's why I appreciate Lucio's own attitude toward the car. Obviously his dad bought it hoping to keep him on a short leash, but it's just as obvious he'd get by without it.

What he really enjoys, other than dope, is searching beyond the surface of things, and I suppose his getting stoned is part of this. He can be quite funny around my other friends, especially in bullshit sessions about sex. He even has the hots for one of the barrio girls, but though she seems pleasant I doubt much will come of it. His family's deadset against her because she's dirt poor even by barrio standards.

He shows a real intellectual spark when he's communicating abstractions. His arguments can get as convuluted as The Chief's conversations, but he tries to link deep thoughts to our everyday lives. A few days ago he was explaining Plato's allegory of the cave to Pablo, and as he described the cavedweller coming out, almost blinded by the light, it suddenly occurred to me that there was something personal behind the intensity of his argument. Lucio has the opposite problem. He has no difficulty seeing the world of ideas. It's life in that underground cave, the ordinary world, that disorients him.

He drops me off, handing me the paperbacks he took from the comic-book van. I'm glad I didn't get stoned, since my stepfather's home and peeking out the screen door from his own house next door. I'm also glad I didn't bring the *Playboy*, so I make it a point to cross over to his house to show I'm clean.

As I walk up the porch I wonder what he'll say about the Lenny Bruce book. Actually he couldn't tell Norman Vincent Peale from Vincent Van Gogh, so pulling the wool over his eyes is no problem. What bothers me is having to do so in the first place. His view is that rather than topple the social ladder I should be trying to climb it.

No sooner do I walk through the door than he's asking where I've been.

"At Lucio's store."

"Looking for a job?" He already knows they hire only illegal kids as stock boys, but I act dumb too.

"You mean for you?"

"No. You."

"I already worked this summer." I almost add that I earned more than he makes, but decide it's a bit cruel. "And my scholarship should cover my costs."

"Think you'll have enough for a haircut?"

"All I know is there's enough to pay my room and board here. If not I can always go elsewhere."

"There's more to life than keeping your head above water."

I nearly blurt out that he's a fine one to talk. But as with most of his remarks the sarcasm doesn't last. By now he's glancing at the paperbacks Lucio lent me.

"Anything good?"

I shake my head. "We took some stuff from the comic-book van."

"And that's all they had?"

"That's all they had worth taking."

I'm not about to mention the *Playboy*, but it occurs to me he's wondering why I didn't bring home any comic books. When I was a kid we both enjoyed reading them. In fact the first thing I liked about him was that he enjoyed comics as much I did. But those days are long gone, and now all he can do is stare at these books like they were writtten in some impenetrable code.

"Next time break into their cash register instead."

But before I can answer, his attention's on some idiotic show on television.

3

The Indecipherable Computer

A couple of days later I get a call from Lucio.

"I'm here at the Zamarripa brothers'."

I'm not surprised. As soon as The Chief mentioned they had potent dope I knew he'd be paying them a visit. I'm simply surprised he took this long.

"We're waiting for you," he adds.

"The Brothers Some-are-ripped-off? What the hell do I want—?"

Lucio chuckles in that way of his, like the "tsk-tsk" in comic books. He tells someone else at his end of the line: "Guess what my friend called you."

"Wait! Don't—"

But it's too late: he covers up the mouthpiece and continues. I'm about to hang up when he comes back on. "They say they *definitely* want to meet you now."

"First tell them the truth, that the nickname was your idea."

"They say they're going to kidnap the old man."

"They can have him. He'll talk their tattoos off."

I'm waiting for some indiscreet joke about what a nice rip-off my stereo would make. The last thing I want these guys to know is that I have something worth taking.

Lucio's still chuckling, so I suppose it's safe to go.

"I'm on my way, but tell them the truth about the nickname."

"Don't worry, De la O. They wouldn't know what it means."

Like many others in the barrio, the Zamarripas are first-generation *raza*. But while Mexicans here tend to be transient and move farther north, the family rented the first house it found and remained there.

Some years back their landlord sold the lot from under their feet and moved the house a few blocks down. The Zamarripas moved with it, immigrant grandmother and all. This year he sold that lot too, so the Zamarripas moved again. Lucio insists they could move that house to China and the Zamarripas would take the first available boat out and ask for asylum. He adds, "If I were Mao, though, I'd think twice before taking them."

I have a good idea where their new lot is located, and Lucio's car out front zeroes me in. On the outside the frame house looks like most in the barrio: old, leaning a little, and with blistered paint on the clapboards. But inside there's new furniture, the overstuffed, velour type that passes for class around these parts—Barrio Baroque, Lucio and I call it.

Two huge television sets side by side are turned on to different channels, and some other odd and even larger appliance sits at the other end of the room. Lucio's next to one of the sets, crouching in that pose you rarely see outside of the conversation circles of older *pachucos*: crouched with an elbow resting on a raised knee. He introduces me to the three brothers, who slur their names so that all I catch is their surname. Maybe they're stoned, maybe to them only their clan identity matters, or maybe it's their way of telling me that the less I know about them the better.

At any rate their brotherhood rests purely on faith, since I can't find a shred of similarity among their faces or physiques. In my confusion I notice a framed photo atop an end table, so I ask indiscreetly whether he's their father. One of the younger brothers nods.

I also notice a lit votive candle beside it, and I'm about to ask if he's dead when the oldest one answers my question before I can ask it. "He's away."

Now I wonder whether he means it literally or as the delicate way some people allude to death. Lucio probably notices I'm about to blunder with my bluntness again, so he interrupts. "The Chief said he's getting out soon."

I never heard of being paroled from Hell for good behavior, so I take it he's still alive. In fact the first and only time I heard of their old man was back when the house was on its original lot. He went to check up on his mother and found an insurance collector browbeating her about a late payment on a premium, so he promptly put a bullet between the Anglo's eyes. He didn't even argue with the bastard, just shot him out the screen door then kicked the corpse down the front walk and out to the curb. I was just a kid then, but I remember feeling avenged, since I knew how insufferable those Anglo assholes could get. The episode even did some good: For a while white collectors in the barrio were on their best behavior.

I don't notice that someone's lit up a joint until Lucio, exhaling bluish smoke, hands it to me. I take a timid hit and pass it to the youngest brother. No sooner does he take it than their mother appears with a basket of sweet bread. For a moment I panic, as if I'd suddenly been busted by my own mother. The Zamarripa brothers, though, carry on. For all I know it's an everyday occurence in the house, since the youngest brother's response—partially shielding the joint with a cupped hand—has the superficial deference of ritual.

She in turn seems like a mother who, saddled with three sociopathic sons, has turned deviance into domestic routine. "Ay, estos muchachos," she fusses, then takes the napkin covering the sweet bread and rubs at an invisible heel scuff on the coffee table.

As barrio mothers go, her behavior isn't that unusual. My relatives can find fault with everyone else's children, but for their own they spare no excuse. Take my Aunt Tila's five boys. (I shouldn't single them out as the black sheep of the family, because here I am, one of the cleaner ones, and look at the company I'm keeping.) Each one's been busted for dope dealing, burglary, auto theft—real renaissance men. You'd think tia Tila would have the exhausted look of a mother whom fate dealt a harsh hand: a widow with all sons, and every one incorrigible. Yet whenever they slip through the back door at dawn from an evening of thievery, she's already brewing them coffee, welcoming them like hunters returning with game.

My mind's wandering, and I blame the grass. The same goes for the incredible case of munchies I'm starting to get. I already have my eye on the specific sweet bread I want, and I'm waiting for one of the brothers to reach first, but they simply stare at the basket like they're waiting for the pieces to multiply. Even the youngest brother, who's even thinner than I, is staring at the plate with the intensity of a starving animal, waiting for me to make the first move.

Finally, the oldest brother explains the impasse.

"Mama means well, but she doesn't know food cuts the high."

Lucio, who's as big a dope fiend as they come, agrees. "You start eating and suddenly you're straight."

And when the youngest Zamarripa reaches for some, the other two wonder aloud whether he's afraid of getting "too tortilla."

"Hell, no!" He reaches for the toke being passed around and sucks it like it's oxygen.

For these *chavos* that's what getting stoned comes down to—a matter of manhood. The important thing isn't enjoying the high but acting like it hasn't hit you. I even wonder whether their mother's deliberately trying to sober them up with munchies, but it's not the kind of insight you air in this crowd. Besides, the oldest brother's leading up to the business at hand.

"So you're going away to college?" he asks Lucio, who nods but says nothing else. "What's the name of that place again?"

"UT." Lucio says it matter of factly, unlike the Anglos in high school who would say it like they'd gone to Heaven. Besides, in the Zamarripas' mental map one college pretty much seems like another.

"Where's that? Houston?"

"No, somewhere else."

I take Lucio's lead. "UT has campuses in several cities."

"I get it. Like state prisons. Well, if you ever go study in Huntsville, we have relatives who'll help with your homework."

The youngest one grins. "They're not graduating for a while."

I'm quite stoned, but something tells me the oldest brother has a sales pitch of some sort, probably involving dope. It turns out I'm right on the big picture but wrong on the details: He goes over to the large, strange appliance across the room, sits on it, and strikes a metallic rap with his knuckles.

"So how about it, Lucio? Take this with you and you'll never have to do homework again."

"Tell me what is first."

"Why, a computer, of course."

"Where did you get it?"

"From a business. Where else?" Their fraternal laugh makes them sound less like real brothers than a brotherhood of thieves.

"You could take it to college," says the middle one.

"My car's not big enough. Besides, what about the Border Patrol checkpoint?"

"You're a college student. Just tell them you lost the papers."

"What can they do?" I tell Lucio. "Bust you for transporting an undocumented computer?"

The brothers don't appreciate the humor. Maybe they only see someone who can sour the deal, because they turn me into their next target.

"You're staying in the Valley, aren't you? With this baby you'll never have to do homework again."

When I explain that I don't mind doing homework, his incredulous look makes me revise the remark. "I mean I don't mind it much."

He still looks at me like I'm some sort of freak, but from where I'm sitting he doesn't look too normal himself: a grown, tattooed drop-out with a hot computer he's trying to pass off as a homework helper. I could see him trying to sell a set of encyclopedias still in their boxes. But a company computer . . . We're all out of our league here, and I try hinting as much.

"I wouldn't even know how to turn the thing on."

He holds up a power cord, almost as thick as an anaconda, that could easily brown out the barrio. I get a better look at the tattoo on his bicep: ZAMARRIPA, in stylized letters. The RIP part is framed by a tombstone.

I realize I'm staring and look away, only to find the youngest brother staring at me in turn. "Say, wasn't your face in the paper the other day?"

"The paper?" asks the middle one. "Trouble, *carnal?*"

"No. I got a scholarship."

"A scholarship? So you're a computer brain, like Lucio here?" He answers his own question. "Of course! That's why they're friends!"

The oldest one gets a eureka look on his face. "Damn! We're trying to sell a computer to a pair of encyclopedias!"

Compliments like that make me uncomfortable. People who say them may mean well, but it shows they're impressed by those who memorize trivia. Right now, though, I'm glad it gets us off the hook, and I even try to add a little humor: "Lucio, see if that computer's female. Maybe we can screw it."

The joke falls flat, so we sit around and do another toke until Lucio says we have to leave. Before he can ask if they'll sell him a baggie, the oldest one offers him a free one. "Just don't let that brain go up in smoke." He looks in the direction of the computer and adds, "And be careful who you tell about this." He has a vague expression that's hard to read, as though he himself can't decide whether it's best to humor or threaten us.

I may be stoned yet I can't help but wonder why people tell you they broke the law then ask you to keep their secret. I'm sure that by now the entire barrio knows about their useless computer, and as soon as we're in the car I tell Lucio, "You know they're not going to unload that thing anywhere. They should donate it."

"Oh, sure. To who?"

"I don't know . . . Our high school, maybe."

Lucio beams a stoned smile. "Maybe they could get a wing named after them."

It was a dumb suggestion, but now I'm too tortilla to do anything but go along. "Or a detention hall."

We drive a few blocks that seem to take an eternity, then it occurs to me to ask why they took it in the first place.

"Because it was there for the taking." Lucio says it with the certainty of someone who knows exactly how they think, which may be true, but I doubt it's a two-way street. The Zamarripa brothers have no inkling of what goes on in his head. To them he's just a strange *chavo* with the means to buy anything from grass to a computer. His brain, as indecipherable as the circuits on their computer and just as useless, might as well belong to an alien.

Around the end of August Lucio packs up for college. I'll miss listening to his monologues and his rock albums, but I'm also glad he's going. Lately he's always either high or complaining that he's not.

Before leaving he hands me a small bag of Ecuadanes Simples, the downers of choice for The Chief, who insists that in the old days they were laced with heroin.

I tell Lucio I appreciate the gift, but that they're like burying your head in a ball of cotton.

"So much the better, De la O. That way you won't get it bruised."

"Better bruised than buried."

He smiles as if to say he has just the thing, then opens the car trunk and digs into the stuff he's already packed.

"Jesus, Lucio, it's a drugstore on wheels!"

"The minute I reach UT I'll put an ice-cream bell on the hood and head for the hippie district." He hands me another bag, but when I don't accept it at once he gives me a studied, hurt look. "Look, if you're just going to throw them away . . ."

That's exactly what I'm planning to do, but I also offer my own melodramatic gesture. "Are you kidding? With so many kids going to bed straight?"

He's not quite convinced but leaves the bag anyway. "So," he says by way of a farewell, "let's see who gets the higher learning."

I don't even debate the double meaning, since he'll come out ahead on both counts: Judging by the drugs he's taking along, and comparing our two schools, there's no contest. Actually, my best friend Nacho and I had also been accepted at Lucio's campus, but when my honors scholarship here came through, I stayed, and so did Nacho. We did the right thing for the time being, if for no other reason than that Lucio won't be around.

I watch him drive away, then stand by the curb a while, concerned he might simply go around the block and back. When I realize he's really gone, I feel unburdened.

There's no doubt he's an interesting and intelligent character, but you pay a price for the privilege of his friendship. If he's exploring existential nausea, he'll not only live it, he'll drag you into the experience as well. Maybe he acts like a character out of William S. Burroughs in homage to his novels, or maybe he likes the novels because they describe him so well. I don't even know how he digs up those writers. One month it's Alfred Jarre, another it's Borges, then Vallejo, or Van Gogh's letters. He loves the drug lifestyle. He quotes Rimbaud on deranging the senses. Unlike the Zamarripa brothers, getting stoned isn't a test of stoicism. Then again, it's always the seduction of the self-improvement pitches you have to watch out for.

After Lucio leaves, my other friends start coming around. Soon I'm hanging out with Nacho and Alfredo, enjoying the sort of straight stuff that Lucio considers silly. On registration day we drive up to the college with Alfredo, who already acts like someone in the know because his older brother's a senior there. We're eager to check out the *chavas*, and the first thing we notice is that they dress up like they have good jobs or, even better, daddies who have one.

Nacho's not impressed. "I'll bet their families live on tortillas and beans to pay for their wardrobe."

Alfredo tries to have the last word, even if it's his brother's. "Like Antonio says, 'The lower classes always dress up.' Anyway, it's all just show."

He's right, because other than how the *chavas* dress, college doesn't seem that different from high school.

My honors advisor helps me draw up a class schedule that includes honors courses as well as basics. When I remark that I won't have time for anything except school, he politely explains that, unlike high school, classes meet on alternate days.

Afterwards I mention my embarrassment. Nacho doesn't kid me, since he also didn't know about college schedules. He asks how many other Chicanos are in my honors group.

"I saw two or three others on a list they had."

"That's not even a fourth." He looks out at the the crowd, almost all brown. "Well, if they need a little more color, there's lots of shades here to choose from."

Alfredo, with his fair hair and skin, smiles, not only to remind us he's an exception but because he's on familiar ground. He's like most of the Anglos here, with family or friends who've gone through college and can better orient them. They're minor advantages that in time accumulate into a small avalanche that can roll right over you.

I was thinking something similar as I worked on my class schedule and overheard a white student chatting with his advisor. He seemed nice and soft-spoken, but as he pondered aloud his future he casually mentioned his family's agri-business. It was not a very large enterprise, but it had kept them in the American dream for two generations, and he expected to hear its lullaby for a while longer. I almost interrupted to add that most of my family had been in the same business even longer, only they had started from the ground up and stayed there.

I wondered whether I had ever picked cotton on his family's fields. Of course, as a kid you don't bother asking the crew boss whose field

you're working, and if he drives up to the grower's house you don't wonder whether any gringo kids are living the good life inside while your
family and friends pick up the tab.

But it also occurred to me as I listened to this guy how his own past
had cut a clear path to his future. There was something tangible and constant he could count on, property passed from one generation to the
next, which had already sketched his vision of the future. Of course, that
past he's so proud of isn't his own doing, and this notion of how your
past patterns your future is true of me too, except that the only constant
I can count on is that of utter uncertainty. I have no idea what I'll end
up doing if I ever make it through here. Economically, the best I can
hope for is to end up *unlike* my ancestors.

By the time the honors program gets going, I know a thing or two
more about life. I can outrun most Anglos and keep up with the rest, yet
several students assume I'm here because the program needed a few
brown faces. They assume they've mastered the language and even the
art of thinking just because they speak English all the time. The result is
that they write the way they talk. But when you learn a language at school
without using it at home, you tend to approach it analytically. You learn
to take it apart and put it back together as though it were a weapon. It's
similar to when Anglos first learn Spanish: They don't have to unlearn
the grammatical errors most Chicanos pick up at home.

In all honesty, I'm not too comfortable making small talk with
Anglos, since my conversational English isn't that smooth. But when we
have to discuss abstract issues I can hold my own. The trouble is, college
isn't simply cerebral exercise. The minute the middle-class students—
which is everyone else in the program—bring up their lives outside the
classroom, I end up an outsider again. Someone mentions a summer
vacation that triggers memories in the rest. A few dwell on their own
vacations, others mention assorted summer lessons or working in some
air-conditioned store. One complains, "I spent my summers at home,
bored out of my skull. So I read some plays my mom had from her high-
school days. Afterwards I started doing skits, and before I knew it I was
hooked on theater."

With that kind of conversation I'm not about to enlighten them with
my summers doing stoop labor or packing produce. Even though I've

done my best daydreaming while picking cotton on cloudy afternoons, just as I spent this summer inside factory boilers, these aren't the experiences people associate with broadening your intellectual horizons. They start believing the hype that exceptional students keep getting: One should do only things that are educational or exciting—in a word, *enriching*. I can only guess how they'd react to my reminiscing about walking back late at night from El Cine Rey after a Mexican *vampiro* movie, while the adults around you swear that such things actually happen. The irony is that these experiences are what make barrio life so interesting, provided you see them from different angles. Although I don't expect Anglos to understand this, I'm baffled by the attitude of the other *raza* in the program. The sole Chicana is dating a white guy who insists on calling her by her Spanish name. Apparently this turns him on and also helps keep her somewhat ethnically honest, but it's also obvious she gets off to having an Anglo boyfriend. The other two Chicanos are also nice, but their world seems about as distant as that of the Anglos. The father of one owns an auto parts store in my barrio, but from our conversations you'd think I was the first native he's seen up close.

Despite the strange chemistry, or maybe because of it, I've become more active in class discussions. In high school I liked to lay low, leaving the talking to students who were out to impress or win popularity contests. Most of my graduating class was surprised when I graduated high in the ranks of a class of 500, a dark horse in more ways than one.

With everything going on in the country these days, there's a lot to speak out on. But soon it becomes clear to me that even if I get the better of someone while we discuss righting wrongs, nothing changes. And sometimes nothing but ugliness and hatred comes out, on both sides.

It doesn't take much college captivity till I start hearing the call of the wild. I remember the drugs Lucio left me. Nacho or Alfredo won't take them, even though I initiated them a while back with grass. I even thought of giving them to The Chief, then realized he might tell Lucio some day.

So I end up taking them late at night, and in the morning when Alfredo and the others pick me up I greet them with a zombie stare. A few days ago I had to get out of the car and walk the last few blocks to campus. The fresh air helped, but Alfredo's brother got suspicious. And in my classes, it might as well have been The Chief lecturing, complete with monologues that end abruptly and make as much sense as his.

It's stupid and sickening, so why do I keep doing it? The answer's a lot of little answers that don't matter much by themselves but add up. Minor things, like trying to sit in class and marshal your attention on a world that's suddenly turned strange yet infinitely more interesting.

Lucio once said that anyone can go through life straight, but that only a stoned few are able to live in two dimensions at once. My stepfather, who became an alcoholic in his teens, insists that any idiot can be an addict. Maybe they're both partly right, and that keeps me coming back for more. On the one hand, there's a certain pride—a stupid snobbishness—in sitting in on a class lecture and holding your own, maybe even making a contribution or two that, at least in your own mind, is beyond the grasp of straight students. Of course you may be mangling both the lecture and your comments, but you accept that possibility with an idiot's utter indifference. Either way you lose, and either way you win; where else in life can you claim to come out even?

I even wear sunglasses in class. Not that I'm not stoned most of the time, but it keeps the other honors students guessing, and before long I get a reputation. It also doesn't take long till I get sick of the capsules. I don't mean just mentally, I mean physically ill. I suppose some *vatos* aren't cut out for *la vida loca*. In my case it's not even *el semestre loco*. I end up with a dull, constant pain in my stomach that makes me wonder whether I'll end up on the operating table like The Chief. After a while it starts sapping both my energy and my interest in the world. After I run out of capsules I end up stuck in some psychic limbo between stoned and straight. By now I don't mind the physical discomfort, at least not enough to do anything about it. Every once in a while I'll sort of sigh, as though my spirit is trying to come to its senses. But there's no feeling behind it.

Eventually, even my mother notices I'm acting more unusual than usual. Her mentioning it is in itself unusual, since she pretty much lets me go my way, standing behind my decisions without pushing me one way or another. She must sense this is serious, because she makes an appointment for me with our family doctor then insists on walking with me. It's a measure of my indifference that I don't protest that I'm not a kid anymore. When he prescribes some capsules I'm too apathetic to appreciate the irony.

A week later I'm in no better shape or spirit, so we return without an appointment. He's away on some hospital call, so we walk to another doctor nearby, an Anglo who's worked in the barrio for years. He has only one patient waiting, so you'd think the Chicano nurse who signs me in would appreciate our business. Instead she has this sour look, which I assume comes from having to double as a receptionist. But after the patient ahead of me leaves, followed another who came afterward, and I'm still not called, my mother politely asks what the problem is.

The nurse glares at me. "He's the problem. The doctor won't see people like him."

We both know what she means. There's only one other *chavo* in the barrio who wears long hair, a kid who plays in a band. My mother tries to appeal to her better nature, but the woman doesn't have one.

"If the president's son walked in with long hair, we'd show him the door too."

My mother's not one to anger easily. Like most Chicanas her age she's learned to measure her words around those in power. Still, she answers in a voice that trembles a bit but gets its point across: "Don't flatter yourself. Even the mayor's son wouldn't be caught dead in this place. And when it comes to drugs, it's the grown-ups we should worry about."

I'm just as confused by her comment as by the nurse's incoherence in trying to compose an answer. It's not until we walk out that my mother mentions a rumor she's heard several times, that the doctor and his nurse have had a relationship for years. She even apologizes for taking me there. "I wanted you to see a doctor today."

I assume she means they've been playing their own version of doctor and nurse, until she adds, "I guess a doctor can get drugs like they're groceries. And once his nurse starts, it's all over."

Suddenly I understand her remark back there about grown-ups and drugs. I even wonder whether she's making it up so that I'll feel better, except that she's not one to spread lies about others.

On the way home she suggests we stop at a friend's house, a healer. When I ask what for, she adds, almost as an afterthought, that maybe I'm suffering from *empacho*.

"When something's stuck in your stomach? I thought only children got that."

"Oh, no, grown-ups get it too."

Her friend welcomes us inside and asks if I remember her curing me of *susto* as a child. If I do, it's only in a very vague way. The parrot on the porch seems a bit familiar, but maybe I'm confusing him with those parrots the barrio shopkeepers of my childhood had as watchpets.

She has me lie on the couch while my mother relates the incident at the doctor's office. She advises in a tranquil tone, "Dear God, stay away from those two. That man can't even help himself. How can he help others?"

She pushes on a part of my abdomen with a gentle pressure, but it makes me groan. "It's *empacho*, all right. You could have gone to ten different doctors and gotten ten different diagnoses, none of them right."

While she rubs liniment on her hands I push on my stomach with my own thumbs, yet I can't find the exact spot that felt like the air had been punched out of me. She massages my stomach, starting with a subtle pressure that makes my abdomen jump every now and then. Soon the pain subsides even though she's working deeper into the muscles. She has me turn around and, using a cloth for a better grip, grabs the skin that runs along my spine. She suddenly yanks me an inch or two off the couch, and my spine makes a sound between a pop and an adhesive yanked off, but I don't feel any pain. I only hear her say softly but with utter certainty, "That was it."

She gives me a tea of some sort and makes me rest for a few minutes, adding that it was a good thing the doctor turned us away, otherwise I wouldn't have been cured. The remark reminds my mother of an episode from her own adolescence, when my grandfather took her to another Anglo doctor who took Chicano patients. They apparently caught him in a bad mood that day. Afterwards, as my grandfather went to have the prescription filled, he had the good sense to show it to an acquaintance, a *mexicano* who knew a thing or two about medicine. My mother still remembers the horror on his face when he said, "What's this man trying to do? With her symptoms, this medicine could kill her!"

It dawns on me that if it hadn't been for their bumping into that man, I wouldn't be here. I shudder just as she must have shuddered when she heard those words. As I'm lying there, listening and thinking, I also realize I'm taking an interest in the conversation. For whatever reason, I begin to feel a part of the ordinary world again.

The change isn't immediate or drastic, but it does start to happen. She instructs me to take some tea over the next few days, and the first thing I do on getting home is make sure that the herbs are available. Slowly I start convalescing.

I think of that doctor whose face I never saw and of his nurse whose features I still remember. After my outrage evaporates, I see them for what they are: a pair of sick, sorry addicts. I acknowledge my own luck, getting sick instead of hooked, and most of all getting cured by the *curandera*. That's when I savor my second, strong feeling: satisfaction at having the last laugh. Perhaps it's not the most highminded of feelings, but as a step toward recovery it's a good start.

4
Uncle Emiliano Wants You!

Soon I'm able to put back on track the studies I nearly derailed. The incident with the doctor, though, still lingers, reinforcing a lesson I already know too well: Anglos out to hurt you don't have to lynch you. They can simply ignore you, or stall until you tire and leave.

Whenever I bring up the episode with other students, though, the response is the same. Steve, a Chicano upper-classman who's run unsuccessfully for several class offices, looks at me like I can't see the obvious. "Looked in the mirror lately, De la O? You're a hippie."

I don't bother explaining that Che and the rest of the *barbudos* looked the same way. Besides, he's a fine one to talk. "My hair's not any longer than your Texas drawl."

He's so proud of his twang he can't imagine I'd make fun of it. The other students here aren't much different, except for a handful wearing buttons on the farmworkers' movement. One goes even farther, wearing a beret and an Army shirt studded with political buttons. I'm aware that activists elsewhere wear Army shirts, but this *chavo* looks like an actual veteran, older and with a subdued self-confidence. A few times he's been approached by the less serious vets who attend college simply to use up their G.I. benefits. They're obviously drawn to his fatigue shirt, but the moment they read his movement buttons they back off like vampires from a crucifix.

This afternoon I'm at the snack bar, his usual hangout, and he sits a couple of tables away. Nacho notices him too. "Say, isn't that the guy you've been wanting to talk to?"

"Yeah, but it's not like enlisting in the Army. You don't just go up and say you want to join the Revolution."

"Ask him where he got his buttons. It's not like there's a crowd waiting to talk to him."

His name's Adrian, and soon we're in the middle of an animated discussion. He even calls Nacho over, but he's a harder nut to crack. "Why's your friend so pessimistic?" Adrian asks me. "Is he a philosophy major?"

For some reason the remark offends Nacho, so I answer for him. "Reality is more like it."

"You know what Che said about reality. It's Marxist."

I ask if philosophy is *his* major.

"My minor. Yourself?"

"Psychology, probably."

"I didn't know they had that major here."

"They plan to in a couple of years."

"Sure. They promise to have a lot here in a couple of years. A decent school for the natives . . ."

"Well, I can't complain. Right now I'm taking some honors courses."

He's leery but also a bit impressed. "That new program? How is it?"

"A couple of the professors are interesting." But I know it's the students he wants to hear about. "The students are mostly white . . . they like to talk."

"He means they like to hear themselves talk," says Nacho.

Before we leave he invites us to a meeting of his group in a nearby town. I say yes right away, but Nacho wants to read the fine print.

"Now this group . . ."

"MANO. Mexican American National Organization."

"What is it, exactly?"

"We train young Chicanos to organize their colleges and communities."

"Does that mean they're nationwide?"

Adrian smiles like a salesman who's been caught exaggerating his product. "Well, we haven't organized Alaska yet. Not that much *raza* there. But we're here to stay, so if you're Chicano enough . . ."

The invitation is thrown out almost as a dare, so Nacho sees little choice but take him up on it. The arrangement works out fine with me, because he's the one with wheels.

After our first meeting I start hanging around the MANO office, not far from campus, to get a better sense of the group. The thought of an actual movement, in which people not only discuss ideas but put them into practice, sounds mysterious at first. My first meetings only add to the confusion. Everyone talks about lofty ideals, yet our actual energies are spent on issues such as helping save some program director's ass. Still, our headquarters—if you can call our improvised office that—becomes an oasis in an ideological desert. I thought I was the only oddball here who bothered asking why Chicanos end up at the back of the line, then suddenly I find others who feel the same way. Not as many as I'd like, but enough.

Movements aren't quite how history books paint them. Most accounts give you the big picture—leaders and events—but leave out the everyday people and routines. What we're doing may not be all that important to the rest of the world, but it soon becomes the center of ours. We feel our way around at first, second-guessing situations. At times everything appears improvised, yet things somehow end up apparently orchestrated.

Our office operates out of wherever we're offered space and a telephone. When I first met Adrian he was hanging his beret in a corner office of a federally funded poverty program. But now MANO's considered a loose cannon, so next week we'll have a temporary desk with the farmworkers union. One thing that gives our improvisation some coherence is the presence of the Paredes brothers, two light-complected teenagers drafted as the office workhorses. Their shaggy hair, big-boned frames, and plodding, methodical ways add to their image as a team of plowhorses, although one thing they're not is dull. When the younger one starts spending more time back in their hometown, his brother begins running our office solo and contacting activists from other groups. He doesn't impress Nacho, but I sense shrewdness beneath his disheveled appearance. On finding out that I'm interested in psychology and sociology, he immediately wants to know what I know about propoganda and crowd control.

"Not much," I confess. "I have enough problems controlling myself."

He smiles in a knowing way, and I smile back because his question contrasts with what most *chavos* ask when they find out I'm interested in psychology: whether I can hypnotize women "to do anything," or whether I can read a woman's innermost thoughts. I've gotten that last question so often that my ready reply is, "Yes, but usually you're better off not knowing.".

Since the Paredes brothers are political animals, Adrian and I start calling them Inti and Coco Peredo, after brothers who fought with Che in Bolivia. By the time their nicknames take, the younger brother has pretty much dropped out of the picture, leaving us with Coco. By then Adrian and the other Manos want Nacho and me to organize our barrio back home along with our work on campus. That's when I first ran into an unexpected paradox: The rest of our *raza* sees us as a threat, even though we see ourselves as trying to improve things all around. Altruism makes them suspicious, the thought that anyone would go out on limbs beyond those of his own family tree.

When we recruit someone, we look for his strengths. Anyone with artistic talent, say, works with Roque, who prepares posters and fliers and is planning the artwork for an upcoming newspaper. Roque's like a lot of Manos and Manas who don't fit the stereotypes. He dresses the way most people expect radicals to look, but you wouldn't guess he had an ounce of artistic talent. He's stockier and coarser than Coco, and minus even the minimal social graces. His movements suggests he'd be more at ease with construction equipment than artist's tools. But he produces.

In fact, if appearance determined talent then The Town Crier, who lives wherever our office is at the moment, has that haunted look people expect in artists, with delicate, ravaged features that make him seem saintly and possessed at the same time. You expect to walk into the office one morning and find he's come to some tragic end, overdosed or with his wrists slashed. In truth I've never seen him do drugs, not even a beer, but like Nacho says, maybe the damage has already been done.

Nacho nicknamed him The Town Crier because he aims his antennae into every conversation within earshot then broadcasts it indiscriminately. He'd make an excellent spy—provided we could keep his mouth shut. Probably my eagerness to assign him to surveillance is because everyone else here has a function or purpose. Neither Nacho nor I have a clue why he's here. My hunch is that he's some prototype Chicano radical who overdosed on ideology, and Coco lets him hang around out of pity. Nacho, though, insists the movement is too young for psychic casualties. Perhaps he finds the thought that we might end up the same way disturbing.

His own theory is more prosaic: The Crier is Coco's cousin, one he won't acknowledge publicly. That might be, since Coco sees to it that he's fed every day. Besides, no one's immune from Coco's insistence on accountability except for the Crier. Early on, after the Paredes brothers reminded me I missed a meeting, I told Nacho, "I just got here and they order me around like they own me. How come they never criticize the Crier for not following through?"

"That's because they never ask him to do anything." He added one of his father's sayings: "He has the vocation of the coyote: Eat, shit and sleep."

He's one lucky dog; on the other hand, by October Nacho and I are told to complete the groundwork for a chapter meeting in our town. It's a rush job but long overdue. Our city's the largest in this area. It isn't overwhelmingly Chicano like the surrounding towns, but in some ways that works in our favor. I've found that college kids from the more seg-regated communities have less understanding of race relations because they've had even less contact with Anglos. In my case and that of my friends we too started at all-*raza* schools but then went to mixed schools from junior high on. A little late, but old enough to start seeing the inequities, the abuses that go hand in hand with the humiliating message that the Scott Hardwickes of the world never tire of repeating: Everyone's equal in America, and if Anglos come out ahead it's because they're bet-ter and smarter. Naturally the more mediocre the Anglo, the more often he reminds us of it.

That's the tack we use to explain our philosophy for our first home meeting—helping *raza* in denial to see the obvious, no matter how painful. The meeting's attendance is only modest, but the mixture of col-lege *chavos*, high-school kids and drop-outs is impressive enough that Luli, a veteran Mana, expects good things. Adrian agrees. "This might end up being our largest chapter in the area."

The following week he invites Nacho and me to a state meeting in San Antonio. On Saturday morning I can hear his car's deep rumbling all the way from my bedroom. He's wearing his beret and gunning his GTO convertible. Before I can accuse him of materialism, Adrian points out, "This is money I saved risking my ass for Uncle Sam."

Nacho's already riding shotgun, basking in the attention of some barrio girls. "Hop in back," he says. "I bet Adrian we can't make San Antonio in under three and a half hours."

Those are the last clear words I hear until we reach the Border Patrol checkpoint some sixty miles north. Riding in back with the top down, I catch fragments of Adrian's anecdotes from Nam while his eight-track player pounds out a strange brew of *corridos* and acid rock. We're making record time, thanks to however many barrels his car has, until a pair of Anglo officers at the checkpoint turn up some MANO literature in the glove compartment. The older officer starts giving us a speech like we're plotting to bomb the Alamo and perform unnatural acts on Davy Crockett's corpse. Adrian begins a cat-and-mouse game of his own. All this time I'm trying to see things philosophically. We're all part-time parasites in the social scheme of things. In their case it involves catching illegals and drug dealers, and if it weren't for brown people in poverty they'd have to earn their pennies some other way. For that matter if it weren't for heavy-handed whites there wouldn't be a need for us Manos.

The younger officer stands around while the older guy in green keeps searching for something incriminating. It's a ritual I went through while picking cotton as a kid. Whenever the Border Patrol dropped by to check our papers, my mother simply told them she was born in Floresville, next to San Antonio. Since patrolmen receive part of their training there, the town's name had a familiar ring.

Now, to an uninvolved observer who didn't have to watch his mother (at least third-generation Texan) convince an officer she was American, such interrogations might be seen as a necessary evil. And provided the officers were courteous, one could almost overlook the insult. But here, being treated like suspected criminals and forced to listen to a lecture on patriotism, you tend to forget the other officers who acted decently. By the time he lets us go I hope some drug smuggler runs over his ass and leaves him smeared on the asphalt like an armadillo.

We reach the San Antonio motel where we're meeting, only to be told to wait our turn in the lobby while members from another region hold their strategy session. We catch the tail end of Saturday morning cartoons, then find ourselves escorted to a large room where the drapes are shut despite the weak lighting. I have trouble making out the faces of the *chavos* giving us Mano handshakes, and I don't even recognize Coco until I hear his raspy voice across the room.

Even though I'm attentive, the discussion is hard to follow. Not that the speakers are too abstract. If anything they're too mundane and trivial, throwing names around as unrecognizeable as the faces before me. Suddenly there's a brief flood of light as someone else enters the room, and almost immediately the conversation takes a new direction. The leaders start asking us things closer to home, including plans for making our organization more visible. At that point the *chavo* who walked in last suggests we protest the surplus commodities program back home. In a soft yet commanding voice he mentions that other areas use food stamps while ours still makes the needy stand outside in long lines for the leftovers that don't sell on the market. "I've been out there," he adds. "Old people have to stand for hours in the rain or the hot sun, just for some cheese or butter."

The other leaders agree it's an issue worth protesting and keeping in the public eye, although one suggests we add more emotion to the appeal.

"More emotion?" says the *chavo* from the Valley. "What's more emotional than an old lady waiting in line all morning for a chunk of government cheese?"

Before the issue degenerates into an argument another state leader gestures as though offering his blessing. "Marcos is right. An old lady practically begging for a bit of cheese . . . It's a nice image." He rises from his couch and the others follow.

In the bustle of breaking camp, Nacho presses at my side and mutters, "He thinks an old lady baking in the sun is a nice image? What kind of militants are we hanging out with, De la O?"

"Kinky ones, I think."

But for the moment I'm more intrigued by what Marcos said. At first I wondered how he knew about our local issues, but after they called him by name I remembered that several Manos back home had mentioned him before.

As we're leaving, Adrian introduces Nacho and I to a light-complected man with large glasses who seems more a bureaucrat than an activist. He is the one who made the remark about the old lady.

"Miguel Angel, these guys are helping us organize—"

"Organizers? From the Valley? We definitely need more down there."

"We have enough organizers," I answer. "What we need are a few more followers."

I don't mean the remark sarcastically, but he seems to take it that way, so I add, "Our city's less than half Chicano. It's harder to organize."

He grabs us by the shoulders and leads us down the hall, then gives us a magnified wink that seems almost obscene. "Well, start cranking out more brown babies!"

It's an awkward moment, but Nacho bullshits him right back. "Now that's the kind of organizing I like!"

He walks us back to the lobby where another group waits its turn. Coco waves goodbye, and when Adrian asks if he's going back with Marcos he quickly shakes his head and gestures him to be quiet.

"You want these guys to put me before a firing squad? Right now Marcos is getting on their case for not inviting him."

"Serves them right."

"They say they didn't know where he was," says Coco. "He's always going from place to place."

"They have ways of getting in touch." Adrian turns to Nacho and me. "Some of these guys don't consider Marcos part of the group."

"You mean he's not a Mano?" I ask.

"I mean the inner circle group. Hell, when it comes to circles, Marcos can talk rings around those guys. The thing is, he's at a whole other level. There's state." He makes a notch in the air. "National." Another notch. "International . . ."

Adrian can get carried away at times. "Don't forget the cosmic," I say.

"Listen, give us time and spaceships and we'll organize the solar system."

"Far out," says Nacho. "Manos on Mars."

On the way back I ride shotgun, and ask Adrian about the leaders we met. He outlines the hierarchy, complete with arrows in the air to highlight the occasional in-fighting. It sounds like a far cry from the plea for solidarity we make to our own people.

"Sounds like they don't have their act together."

"Oh, they're together, all right," says Adrian, laughing. "So close they're at each other's throats." He notices my concern, then points

straight ahead. "Don't worry. What's important is what we do down
there."

He's right. Already the *chavos* in that motel room seem more blurred
than their anonymous faces. Other than Marcos I didn't meet anyone I'd
go the extra distance for.

We begin planning a demonstration to publicize the plight of food-
surplus recipients. At the same time Luli, Sandra and a few other Manas
track down rumors that some women have been pressured for sex in
exchange for food commodities. If the rumors are true we can crank out
some more controversy. By now we already have a few hundred members, not counting the hardcore regulars, but we could use more people
at the protest.

Recruiting's not that difficult, at least not on campus. I try to lay low,
which is second nature for me, since the harder you try the more skittish
the students get. Instead I wear the same bait Adrian does—movement
buttons—and wait for students to make comments, usually a variation of
"You-guys-are-crazy."

That's how I end up with my first Viet Nam veteran recruits, two
chavos using up their G.I. benefits and hoping some knowledge sticks
along the way. Lizard and Nano, like many, didn't come out of high
school prepared for college. Luckily Nano has a knack for math, while
Lizard relies on what he learned in Special Forces—largely self-confidence.
Both rely on religion courses to stay one step ahead of academic proba-
tion, but Lizard has so many he could probably take his vows for the
priesthood. He has a batch of Nehru shirts tailor-made while on R&R
somewhere in Asia, and the narrow collars give him a clerical air. One
with a tie-dyed pattern makes him look like a psychedelic priest. Nano
prefers hippie beads, which go well with his serene face, further femi-
nizing his already soft features. I have a hard time imagining him in Nam
until Lizard points out he spent his tour on a ship, out of harm's way.

Both live to get stoned and have a good time, but Lizard has a tension about him, even when he's tortilla and making fun of everyone else,
which is a good deal of the time. During his tour with the Green Berets
he picked up the nickname that stuck as permanently as the tattoo that
inspired it. The tattoo was supposed to be a dragon, but most people see
a scrawny, third-world lizard. I see an iguana, but I keep the observation
to myself. After all, Lizard was the best middle-weight boxer in his boot

camp, and coming out of Special Forces that says a lot. Not that he'd get violent, least of all with me. It wouldn't prove a thing for someone whose self-confidence would border on arrogance if it weren't for his sense of humor and his openness, which comes with knowing that no one can make you eat your words. He's also honest about his motives. If you ask any number of Manos why they're involved, they'll likely give a speech about sacrificing to help our people and defend our culture. That's true, but only partly true. Most of us are in it as much for the adventure, and Lizard makes no bones about that. For him the movement's a feast of characters and interesting incidents, and afterwards he can congratulate himself for taking part in a good cause.

Coco and his kind might take exception. For them the movement involves hard work in pursuit of a higher principle, a Protestant ethic minus God, and joining MANO for reasons other than brotherhood is something of a heresy. Yet you can't erase adventure from any quest. For every old Chicano who describes leaving his beloved Mexico as a trail of tears, you hear someone like my stepfather's old man reminiscing about his migration with more than a little nostalgia. Underneath the weariness of my old man's wanderings, there's the satisfaction of a survivor.

Lizard and Nano quickly manage to bring a few other veterans into the fold. I suspect Lizard plays on both their guilt and manhood, especially with the rear-echelon Chicano vets who swap war stories back and forth, at times even stealing each other's tales. One of his recruits, though, turns out to be a genuine war hero. When I confess not having heard of him, he brings a newspaper clipping to our next meeting. His exploits read like the script of an Audie Murphy movie, and he has a limp to prove it.

Lizard didn't return without his decoration either. He got popped on the butt, scrambling up a river bank. The war hero kids him about the war wound, imitating Lizard's swagger along with a sarcastic speech about having but one *culo* to give to his country. He even does a skit about Lizard's domestic life: Each evening Lizard allegedly pulls his pants down to his ankles and lies face down on the living room floor, circled by three generations of his family plus the overweight aunt. All kneel before the wound that slashed both buttocks perpendicular to the crease of his ass, praying to the miraculous "Cruz del Culo," the cross on the ass. It's heavy-handed, but it's also one of the few times we've seen Lizard kidded with impunity. I suppose this is Lizard's way of deferring to the more decorated hero.

It's not long before I find out that Lucio and Nano are not only doing dope but dealing as well. Coco's a little slower in figuring things out, but once he does he wants them excommunicated. "If these guys get busted, Austin will have a state holiday so everyone can see us crucified along Miracle Mile."

I wonder aloud whether these aren't the very *vatos* we're supposed to be winning over.

"Maybe they're fun to be around. But Christ, De la O, they're dealing dope! Once the other Manos find out . . ."

He doesn't realize that the other Manos already know, which is partly why Lizard's so popular. He's the ideal dealer, since the Manos who get loaded don't trust most dealers any more than the dealers trust us. Lizard's one of us, though, and they can always count on him for a few free joints. Not that he isn't interesting company, but even that high-flying mania of his is fueled by a joint or two.

Coco's so worried about Lizard and Nano that he overlooks what's under his nose: Many of the Manos *like to get loaded.* He probably doesn't suspect me outright, at least not yet, since when I joined MANO I started out straight. But with Lizard and Nano around, I've lapsed. Now I'm straddling, getting stoned, supposedly to get their confidence and convince them to cut down. It's a lost cause. I'm no different from the bureaucrats who claim they're changing the system from within.

That Lizard and Nano are making easy money makes my task next to impossible. Still, it bothers me they're turning into another species of parasite. You can't condemn some agricultural grower who's gotten fat exploiting others, then look the other way when a Chicano drug dealer does the same thing. Other Manos (such as Roque) who get the free dope not only disagree with me but see a danger. Even though I'm not exactly trying to kill the goose laying the golden eggs, I am trying to put her on birth control.

Yet I enjoy the highs too, which is why after the last few meetings, after all is said and done, I've accepted their offer for a ride back home, knowing they'll bring out the obligatory toke. Even Coco's paranoia that they'll get busted disappears, since Lizard's bravado almost convinces me it'll never happen on his watch. However, I could do without Lizard's tendency to turn philosopher behind the wheel. But after tonight's meeting, our last before the demonstration we discussed in San Antonio, Lizard seems more confrontational than contemplative. Twice when Nano lingers on a joint, Lizard asks if he's reminiscing over a blow job he gave some sailor buddy. Nano simply smiles, and I do the same when Lizard says, "This stuff can kill your brain cells, De la O."

I answer in a very stoned, slow voice that I have plenty of them to burn. "But listen, Liz, if you're worried about yourself, quit while you're ahead."

I don't mean it as a boast, but that's how Nano takes it. "That's what I like about old De la O. He's not like the other brains in that honors program he's in. He also has guts."

Guts perhaps, but I wonder about the brains. I give it a bit more thought, then conclude that Coco was right. This has to stop. A few hits later, though, I'm too stoned to remember what it is that has to stop.

5
Slogans on the Streets, Silence on the Home Front

By the time our protest against the food surplus program is ready, I've already taken part in a couple of smaller demonstrations: one for the farmworkers union, another for a community project director considered too militant by his supervisors. So this isn't my first protest, but this time we'll have more than a handful of activists. It's an odd coalition, including idealistic, squeaky-clean students from the campus Catholic center as well as some questionable fellow travelers.

Rodrigo, a college junior, falls in the latter category. A while back he joined our group, made great promises, then disappeared, and I've been asked to track him down for tomorrow's demonstration. He's a veteran but by Lizard's criteria a nominal one: "He stayed aboard a Navy carrier, same as Nano. Like babies rocked in their cradles."

There's another obvious difference. Lizard spends his school days in a parody of those college *chavos* staying academically afloat for a deferment—buying time with a religion course here, a physical education course there—except that he's hanging on for his Uncle Sam stipends. Rodrigo, though, is one of those vets going through school with the single-minded focus of survivors who've already wasted too much time in barrios and jungles. Usually they watch our struggle from a safe distance, so Rodrigo is an exception and, in my view, an asset to the movement.

His ideology is hard to pin down, though. One moment he's agreeing passionately with us, the next he crosses the hall to talk shop with his mentor, a professor who stands outside his room between classes ogling coeds. A few times I've overheard them cooking up money-making schemes in shady Mexican ventures. It's Rodrigo's dual love of pesos and dollars that makes most Manos mistrust him, but for me his get-rich schemes are so bizarre that their very originality makes him interesting. One afternoon he comes to his senses and concludes that the only sure paths to wealth are stealing money or being born into it. I point out that you're only born into it when your ancestors stole it from someone else. Not that it matters much to Rodrigo, which is why his philosophy clash- es with almost everything MANO stands for. Yet there's something flattering about his support, the belief that if even one small-time capi- talist stands by you, the rest will someday convert. Besides, if he does strike it rich, he might even contribute a fat check to the cause.

Today I'm supposed to track him down and remind him of the demonstration. He's in the snack bar, romancing a gorgeous Amazon with thick, ink-black hair that makes her seem taller still. She has enough gold to put the Queen of Sheba to shame. The hairstyle and jewelry immediately peg her as both Mexican and loaded, and it occurs to me Rodrigo's discovered a gold mine as well as a third path to wealth—down the church aisle.

The moment I greet him she stares at my long hair and khaki shirt with icy condescension. When I remind him of our upcoming demon- stration he answers with a tepid commitment. When I then add that Lizard's counting on him, he suddenly seems sick. I'm probably not far from the truth because he actually begs off, insisting he's not feeling well.

His girlfriend takes on that maternal concern that even the most imperious *mexicanas* seem to have. "Ay, Rodriguito, what's wrong?"

He doesn't answer her directly but instead tries explaining to me in a combination of English and barrio slang. I can almost sense her ears pricking up under all that hair, and afterwards she stares at me as though demanding a translation, but I find his account just as incoherent.

When it's obvious I'm not about to help she excuses herself from the table with an abundance of apologies, in that classical Cantinflas talk *mexicanos* love—saying so much that you don't say shit. She insists she has to catch a bus back home even though she probably has a car the size of a small bus. I can tell she's miffed, but once she leaves, Rodrigo seems more concerned with his own apologies to Lizard. He beats around the bush then blurts it out: "Listen, De la O, don't spread this around, but I came down with this thing in Nam."

I straighten up to stretch the distance between us without making things too obvious. "You mean like the Black Syph?"

"Oh, Jesus, no! Right body part, though." It turns out he joined the Navy still uncircumcised and ended up with an infection at sea. "Not VD, you understand. It's just that sailors at sea don't bathe that often."

At odd moments like this my mind can run rampant, and I instantly imagine Rodrigo like a Hemingway character, unable to get it up with the *mexicana*. Of course, I'm right behind in that same fantasy, ready to do them the favor. Never mind that in real life she wouldn't even let me fingerfuck her shadow.

"So you're saying it left you . . . screwed up?"

"Not the way you think. They cleared up the infection. But since I'd be spending time at sea, they circumcised me. But Jesus, De la O, at my age! The cutting's no big thing, but the healing! Every time you get an erection those stitches start opening up. I'd get the slightest hard-on and they'd open up and bleed like a virgin's butt. That's what left me a little screwed up. It never healed right."

I try putting myself in his skin, so to speak, a difficult matter since I'm not circumcised. But a couple of times I've worried I'll end up with cancer of the penis, and I'm wondering whether Rodrigo can give me some advice on the matter. I'd like to confess I still have my foreskin but only end up saying, "Listen . . . I was born premature . . . checked in at three pounds . . ."

"Jesus! No wonder you're so puny."

"The point is, my family figured I wouldn't be around long enough to jack off, much less screw. To make a long story short . . . I'm not circumcised."

He studies me for a moment, realizes I'm waiting for some sort of reassurance, then adopts the slight arrogance of an expert. "Well, now, you shouldn't have any problems, unless—"

"Unless what?"

"Listen, don't take this the wrong way, but you and a few other Manos like to wear old clothes, like hippies."

"So?"

"Well . . . you guys do bathe, don't you?"

It's the kind of insult I'd expect from someone who doesn't know a thing about us instead of from another Mano, until I remember his conservative streak.

"Of course we bathe. We even scrub each other's back."

The comment is meant as a joke but I'm not sure he takes it as such. "Whatever. Anyway, sorry but I can't make it."

I relay his excuse to Lizard, who's neither amused nor sympathetic. "I knew that sell-out would try something like this," he tells Nano. His seriousness throws me off, since Lizard's usually too amoral to question anybody else's own morality. "He tells us he's on our side. But the minute we take to the streets he stays home under the covers."

"He says he won't be any good on the streets. He can't walk much."

"I'll screw him so hard he won't walk for a week."

"But he gets these flare-ups . . ."

"W-wow," says Nano with his slight stutter. "You wouldn't screw some poor asshole with h-h-hemorrhoids, would you, Liz?"

"Wait a minute, I never said he had—"

"If he doesn't have them now," says Lizard, "he will when I'm through with him. Anyway, I never heard of Navy guys needing that operation." He turns to Nano. "You guys were too busy polishing each other's knobs to ever get them dirty."

Anyone else would already be defending his honor and the Navy's, but Nano merely gives us his stoned, peace-child smile and shrugs. "Well, we'd get bored."

The next morning, however, as the march is about to start, and I'm helping to pass out leaflets outside the courthouse, Rodrigo shows up, sandwiched between Lizard and Nano. Not only that, the super-straight hustler is walking around in a stoned silence. It's as if Nixon had shown up with the Merry Pranksters, high on acid.

The rest of the crowd reflects every color of commitment, from the morbidly curious who couldn't care less about the issues, to those who depend on the food program and are risking the little they have to put a better system in place. Luli, Sandra, and Rosa get on the platform and openly accuse the program workers of asking women for sex in exchange for food. Several of the county judge's cronies have threatened to take this kind of talk to court, but the Manas call their bluff anyway. Some of the bystanders simply snicker that the women want it that way, but most get indignant. By now it's not an impersonal, unfeeling agency we're taking on, but county employees who are not only feeding from the county trough but out to satisfy other urges too.

Rodrigo, hemmed in by Lizard and Nano, claps along when they do, but he seems elsewhere. When the actual march starts, Lizard sticks a placard in his hands and guides him to the front lines, where the media is having a field day. I'm still concerned about his condition, but he seems too stoned to be suffering. Halfway through the protest he even comes to life after our marchers leading the chants up front start losing their voices. They ask for substitutes, but I for one don't volunteer. Chanting may be an orgasmic experience for some, but I'm too self-conscious to let go in public. Maybe I'm overly modest for a long hair parading past bystanders who gawk at us like we're freaks.

All of a sudden there's a piercing scream that stops several of us in our tracks. "CHI-CA-NO!"

We recover our momentum and try to trace the cry as various voices answer as one: "POWER!"

The crowd's response energizes the yell, which returns more fanatical than before: "CHI-CAA-NOO!"

"POWER!"

Nacho drops out of step to check the action up front then returns barely able to contain his disbelief. "It's fucking Rodrigo!"

"CHII-CAAA-NOOO!"

"POWER!" This time even I scream my head off, just to hear that shrill crowing again, like a demented rooster determined to do the impossible, to make the sun rise at midnight.

"CHIII-CAAAA-NOOOO!"

The pitch almost sounds painful, like those *mariachi* gritos that send chills down your spine. I wonder whether Rodrigo's health has anything to do with the intensity, or whether it's all Lizard's doing, or at least his dope. At any rate, it makes my day.

It makes my next day, too, on seeing clips from our demonstration on the local news. The centerpiece on both channels is Rodrigo's blood-curdling battle cry. I hope he's watching, and if he is, that he doesn't look back on the episode like a hungover sailor regretting last night's tattoo, his emotions of that moment now etched forever, and for all the world to see.

While things are finally falling into place in the streets, they're falling apart at my home. After the demonstration I showed up at the house with a peace sign sewed to my blue-jean crotch. My stepfather took one look at the Stars-and-Stripes pattern on the patch and hasn't spoken to me since. Later my mother pointed out that as a naturalized citizen he's afraid my antics might get him deported. I almost said that his fears were unfounded then realized he grew up in a time when deportations of that sort had indeed occurred, and over lesser matters. Even now my patch is like waving a red flag to the local rednecks. Not only does it call attention to my crotch, but since the peace sign resembles symbolic scissors, the thought crosses my mind I might end up castrated.

So I remove it, but my stepfather still won't speak to me. It's been a while since I've heard that ironic humor which complements my mother's so well that I often wonder how far they might have gotten in life if they hadn't lived under the Jose Cuervo segregation in Texas. He spends these days, though, looking out for everyday terrors, and for the weak and the powerless they can be many. It saddens me to know that, for him, I've turned into one of *them*.

He's convinced I'll bring ruin to our home. Not that there's much to ruin, not on his wages. He's a mechanic's helper at a local dealership, and before that he was a barrio cab driver. Of the two, my mother's worked harder, picking produce whenever she wasn't packing it. She started during her teens and kept at it until the summer before I started high school, when she ended up in a state tuberculosis hospital. So when I'd hear about how poor people here won't work, I'd remember those sun patches on my mother's face from working in the summer fields, the blemishes that didn't fade until well into winter. I'd remember too her lungs showing up white on the x-rays they showed us. After she lost part of one lung she asked about medical disability and was told that the packing shed owners had never contributed to her Social Security fund, though they had claimed to. Their argument was one that the case workers here are all too familiar with: She had been an independent contractor. All the case workers could suggest was that as an illiterate she try her hand as a cleaning lady, which around here means competing with undocumented maids. She replied that she'd rather be her own family's maid, especially since she had to take care of my older half-sister, who's mentally retarded.

People like to remark that in matters of intelligence my sister and I ended up far apart on the spectrum. The remark usually has a superstitious touch, as if God were an all-powerful practical joker or a cosmic bookkeeper determined to balance genetic accounts. For my stepfather, though, there's no great mystery. All things come full circle: Just as my sister sometimes utters simple truths that would not occur to the rest of us, at times I cross into the realm of idiocy.

He's not the only one who feels that way. A few days after our protest one of his friends drops by the house, beats around the bush for the better part of an hour, then blurts out: "Just exactly what's your problem, *muchacho?*"

His tone isn't confrontational. I want to answer in a similar way, except I don't know where to start. Here's a man who's been screwed over all his life and in almost every possible position, while his only crime was being Chicano . . . and he wants to know what the problem is.

"Well, it's not just my problem, *don* Regino."

My stepfather touches his head and answers for me. "His problem's here."

Don Regino takes the gesture literally and stares back and forth at stepfather and stepson. "You're protesting for long hair?"

Once more my stepfather answers for me, saying that my long hair is just a symptom. The explanation leaves *don* Regino even more confused, but my stepfather cuts off the conversation with the same type of smokescreen when people probe about my sister's retardation.

"One day you should ask papá about the Revolution in Mexico, Regino. One minute people were innocently talking politics in their house, the next minute the *rurales* rounded everyone up. Guilty and innocent alike."

Don Regino gets the hint and instead wonders aloud when we'll get the first hard norther of the season.

While my stepfather can overlook the long hair, there's something else about my head that he's at a loss to explain: what the hell's inside it. He knows from others that I've done well in school. What I lack, as near as he can figure, is common sense.

In his eyes school never counted for much. The world is full of educated paupers. That's not to say he doesn't see schooling as a tool to make money. Every so often he tries to inspire me with the example of this doctor or that lawyer, with how much money they're showering on their own parents. I point out that most of the Chicano doctors around made it because their own fathers were professionals or businessmen. And for those who got there the hard way, their own parents sacrificed considerably for their educations. If my indifference to wealth were part of a larger stupidity, he could live with it, but my alleged intelligence only makes the matter puzzling. We've had enough of these discussions to know they all end in a standoff.

Now, however, with the protests, I've gone one step farther. "*Para pendejo no se estudia*," he tells me. You don't need a degree to be an idiot. "Each dog scratches his own fleas. You should be looking out after your family, not strangers."

It's a mixed message, I think, but he doesn't realize it. On the one hand, I should scratch my own fleas. On the other hand, I mustn't forget my family. But if your family's making your life uncomfortable, I tell myself, maybe you scratch them off, along with the other fleas.

6
Baby Talk, Big-Boy Talk

Soon after midterms, I start having second thoughts about minoring in chemistry. I've always enjoyed science, but now chemistry doesn't seem that interesting. Maybe now I'm looking less at the discipline and more at the disciples. Alfredo and the other chemistry majors who dream of being affluent pharmacists spend their days in the student center, throwing formulas at each other. And although Alfredo's recently joined MANO, for the rest life seems as structured as a periodic table, and their education is calculated solely in the payoff of the profession.

Then there are those others who can't wait until graduation to make money. Steve, a bright Chicano junior whose sole ambition is to be a lawyer, never helps a poor sap with schoolwork unless there's a fee. "The trouble with you Manos," he tells me, "is that you give it away for free. People don't appreciate altruism. Even the most mediocre lawyer will tell you, 'Never do *pro bono* work unless there's a payoff down the road.'"

For Steve the pay-off is either money or a future favor. "Remember," he reminds the student he's helping at the moment, "you owe me one." When the guy leaves without even a thank-you, Steve turns to me. "That Ramirez guy is an absolute zero, but his father has more cattle than a bull with a permanent hard-on could fuck in a lifetime. And then there's their real estate. Whenever some politician needs votes his dad just digs up a few graves and points the corpses to the closest ballot box. Just like Jesus, De la O, raising the dead! If that's not being God, I don't know what is."

Moments later he still can't shake the thought. "The guy's a total loser. You know, you Manos got at least one thing right. Life isn't fucking fair."

Instead of agreeing, today I play devil's advocate. "What's unfair about it? God gave you smarts, so he had to give that poor sap something."

"Whoever's dishing out the justice in this world must be on the side of the Ramirez clan. I tell you, De la O, if I were as stupid as that guy I wouldn't be that arrogant."

"It's from all that intermarrying among his family. That's how the money stays in the same hands."

"Shit, De la O, that's not fair, for a few to hog all the goodies." Steve is like most people: He doesn't want a system that's more just, he simply wants more from the system for himself. So I tell him what he wants to hear. "But that'll only make it sweeter when we take it away, right? Whether it's your way or ours."

He looks at me the same way I check out a potential Mano, like a secret soulmate. "You really should turn to law, De la O."

"It's more fun turning against it."

"I'm serious."

"But that's all we Manos do, turn to the law, Steve. Only, once we turn to it we usually have to break it or change it. Or else get it enforced."

He regards me like an older brother casting pearls before his sibling swine. "De la O, that attitude won't even get you second-hand pussy around here. I can see you at forty, with callouses on your right hand and a face full of acne."

Afterwards, as I ask myself why I come to the center to suffer assholes like him, it occurs to me he already answered my question. It isn't to cast my net for potential Manos but to fish for potential pussy, just like the other *chavos* here. Like Lucio points out in his more primitive moments, "*Andamos sobre aquella cosa.*" We're all after that thing.

The problem isn't finding it—it's all around—the problem is finding the right fishing hole. Being in the honors program means that most of my classes are with the same women, and almost all Anglos at that. I don't have the larger waters other guys have, which is why I hang around the student center. My love life aside, the honors program has other shortcomings: In time you can almost predict what someone will say on a given topic. And what passes for wisdom often boils down to a way with words. The same kids who used to say the cutest things now make clever comments.

So I look forward to the occasional regular course, even though most of the *chavos* in them act as if it's unmanly to show interest in anything academic. So they fake boredom or arrogance, even when they're utterly lost in a lecture. At the same time a few co-eds are trading underground gossip in a corner of the classroom. Afterwards they're the first to go home and complain about their trying day at school. Since their parents usually don't know the first thing about college life, they simply keep their baby girls in nice clothes and a car. Still, I enjoy seeing them in their sexy skirts. And of all the baby dolls, there's none better than Baby herself.

Officially she's Genoveva, a name you rarely run into nowadays except in Mexican calendars that still list saints' days. Many Chicanos here feel that their given names carry a stigma thicker than any accent, so they Anglicize them, but in Baby's case it's not just cosmetic surgery, as when "Rosa" becomes "Rose," or "Linda" takes on an English inflection. "Genoveva" calls for a new, Anglo alter ego. What better new beginning, than Baby?

It's an uphill battle for those of us pushing for ethnic pride. And yet when I return to the student center and catch Baby holding court with her ladies-in-waiting, my heart and my hard-on start trading secret messages just like those *chavas* in class. She signals me to her side, since I brought along my notes for the class we're taking. But once there she continues her chatter with her friends.

"Anyway, Mommy was giving me some advice last night . . ."

Baby quotes Mommy about as often as Coco quotes Mao. I try to follow the thread that strings her mother's pearls, but I've already lapsed into memory.

Last week I saw her waiting for her Mommy outside the library. She explained that her car broke down, in case it crossed my mind she was too poor to own one, like me.

"I'd give you a ride, Baby, but—"

"I know, I know, your back's not that strong. Well, if I'm a good girl Santa might get me a new one this Christmas. In that case I could sell you my old one, cheap." I pretended to be on my way just to force her hand, and sure enough she asked: "By the way, can I borrow your lecture notes next week?"

"They really aren't that good."

"I know, it's all in your head. Well, then, can I borrow your brain?"

"It comes with the rest of my body."

She gave a rehearsed, breathless gasp. Just then her mom showed up, and I didn't have to look farther to figure out where Baby gets her great looks. The old lady's slightly suggestive air—not exactly a screw-me look, as much as don't-you-wish-you-could—only encouraged my fantasy.

By the time I drift back to Baby's conversation, she's come full circle. "So that's what Mommy always says: If you have to choose between a boyfriend with bucks and one with brains . . ." She pauses with a melodramatic flair I can easily imagine her mom doing. "Well, if you don't know by now, child, you deserve to end up with an egghead."

She gives me a slightly defiant look, though I can't tell whether it's a deliberate provocation or if she simply noticed I wasn't giving her my undivided attention. Caught off guard, I simply say, "You're wise beyond your years, Baby."

"I didn't say it. My mom did."

"Then she's wise beyond her years."

There's that perturbed look again, and suddenly I remember how in a moment of weakness she once confessed her ultimate terror: inheriting her mother's premature wrinkles. I almost apologize but decide that'll just aggravate things, until the thought occurs to me: I'm coddling the same Baby who doesn't think twice about pointing out every new pimple on anyone else's face, including mine. I'm worried about hurting her feelings over the laugh lines she's gotten from smirking at everyone else's imperfections. Fortunately, her friends direct her attention to some *chavo* checking her out, and soon she's chatting and posing like I'm not even there. It occurs to me that I'm here only because she needs my help, so I start to leave.

"Wait, De la O. You're supposed to lend me your notes."

At least today she remembers my name. Last week she claimed it was so simple it slipped her mind. She pretends to gnaw those fingernails she's spent hours cultivating, all the while glancing through my notebook with a helpless look. Yet I know she's nobody's dummy. She can get more out of them in ten minutes than most students can get in an hour. I've also seen her test results when she couldn't get my help, and there's little difference. She's quite able to hold her own. But it's almost as if her intelligence includes a license—an obligation, in fact—to make others do her bidding. If that's indeed the case, I have to hand it to her, because to get others to do your work you must first be utterly indifferent to them thinking you're incompetent.

The impression that her vision goes no farther than her make-up mirror, may say less about her talents than about how easy it is to fool us suckers. I suspect that her putting on cosmetics is a coverup in more ways than one. The real satisfaction must come from reminding herself that her beauty is there and won't let her down. It's like checking your wallet when there's a nice wad and interesting plans to go with it, or the secret pride of nursing a hard-on for an entire afternoon. So no sooner does she pull out her compact than she's utterly engrossed with herself, or at least the little she can see in that tiny mirror. Even now—skimming my notes and reading between the lines while checking her eye shadow— there's that mixture of involvement and detachment one sees in superior beings.

She catches me glancing at the clock and hugs my notes closer. "Oh, come on, De la O, don't tell me you have to go so soon." She sighs again, and although her friends know it's theatrical, they still buy it. One *chava* hints that I could have shown up sooner, while another suggests outright that a nice boy would let Baby keep the notes overnight. That Baby could study a little more on her own never crosses their minds. I answer, "I'm no nice boy. I'm one of those Manos."

Baby quickly explains, "He may be a Mano, but he's smart."

"Really?" one of them asks.

Baby nods. "That's why there's no point borrowing his notes without him here. Most of the stuff's in his head."

I smile like a kid who's praised while his rivals are reprimanded. I've learned that *chavas* like these can be cruel. I'm glad I'm not female or else they would have torn my appearance to shreds by now. But I don't take their comments to heart or try to explain myself with excuses. Usually I'm nice, but I can also be as cold as any Anglo on his high horse, and right now I'm rehearsing that haughty attitude myself. It's not that I expect them to sit around quoting Camus or contemplating Mayan concepts of time. For that kind of quirkiness there's Lucio, but even in his best moments he can't come up with a conversation as surreal and superficial as their observation on how the rock on so-and-so's engagement ring is almost as large as the fetus she's hiding.

Most of these *chavas* come from poor families, which is why their conversations strike such a false note. Baby's saving grace is that occasionally little insights slip out, like, "Oh, these boys, we just bat our eyelashes like this"—she'll offer a demonstration— "and they run up like happy puppies, eager to get their tummies petted."

It goes without saying that I'm part of the pack. The truth stings like a rolled-up newspaper, yet it shows that she's aware of the world beyond her make-up mirror. Sometimes she even tires of the games, with that unflinching honesty that comes when you realize that the only reason you seem above everyone else is because you're standing on a taller pile of society's bullshit. In those moments I encourage her to see there's more to life than being a brown Barbie doll. Once, thinking she was ripe for conversion, I suggested she check out our meetings. She started as if I had manhandled both her tits without asking.

"¡Ay, no! And sit next to those sweaty farmworkers? I'll bet they have lice and God knows what else."

I almost remarked that her own perfume could fumigate an entire union hall. I didn't, of course, even though I'm sure she's more intimate with the farmworker life than she lets on. Actually, I'd rather not know.

I let her review my notes a while longer then get ready to go after the last of her friends has left.

"Well, Genoveva, I hate to spoil our special moment . . ."

"Ay, please don't say that."

"That I've got to go?"

"You know what I mean. That name."

"Well, that name happens to be your name." I say it again, with a harsh, undiluted pronounciation that goes against the softness of "Baby."

"If you only knew how common it sounds."

"On the contrary, it's uncommon. On the other hand, your friends Cindy and Mary . . ."

"I don't mean common like you hear it all the time. I mean common like—"

"You want a common name. How about 'Baby,' like all these babies at the hospital who still don't have a first name. Baby Garcia, Baby Gonzalez . . ."

"The way you say my name sounds ugly."

"How should I say it?"

"Don't say it at all."

"But—"

"Yes, it's my name," she interrupts as though reading my mind. "It's my name." As though it's some horrible sin from her past that people won't let her live down. I wait for more, but all I get is a hard stare. Finally she says with the quiet voice of a confesser, "You sound like my grandfather calling my grandmother, all loud and rough, like they're still in some godforsaken *milpa* in Mexico."

"Was that your grandmother's name?"

For an instant I notice an innocence in her eyes, the innocence of nostalgia, of a time when she was happy to be Genoveva. Or maybe I only imagine the innocence, because it vanishes almost at once.

"What difference does it make?" she says, with the finality of someone who deals with some shame from the past by reburying it.

She gives my notes a final look while I do the same with her. I can't help but wonder why I hang around, hoping I'll change her. In the end, though, my trying to break through isn't much different from the one time she tried to talk me out of MANO, insisting I was wasting my time. Maybe it's simply that when someone we admire goes in an opposite direction from ours, we take it personally. We're each as much convinced of our own good fortune as of the other's misfortune, and can't even imagine life without our own set of assets.

I suppose all of us can't help but hope for a happy ending. The only difference is what that happy ending is for each of us. So Baby's not about to come around to my way of thinking, at least not while her beauty looks back from the mirror. How can I expect her to face up to reality when in my own way, according to what she and Steve tell me, I refuse to face up to my own?

When she hands me back my notes, I leave feeling purified and righteous, telling myself I was tempted by Miss Middle-Class America incarnate and won. No doubt she walks away with her own victory, convinced that whatever I say, in my eyes she still reigns as Miss America.

7
The Ghost of Graduations Past

The week before Thanksgiving a few high schoolers attending our meetings ask me to recruit some potential members from my old school.

"I don't know. It's bad enough we're organizing in college. What if they find out we're infiltrating high schools?"

"It's just that no one believes we're in MANO."

"Show them some buttons."

"We already did, but they said anyone could get those."

"Invite them to our meetings."

"They've heard the cops are watching. They want one of you guys to talk to them first."

I beg off, but later that week I'm asked to sign some forms at the high school for a second small scholarship I received. It's the key I need to get into the closed campus, so I set up a noon meeting with the *chavos*.

There are only a dozen or so waiting by the cafeteria, but they're serious and ready to listen. I talk till I'm hoarse then realize I took up their lunch hour.

"We already ate," says one, pointing to the small crowd leaving the cafeteria.

It's probably not true. They're the kind of kids who rarely eat at the cafeteria, but not because of the usual middle-class kid's complaint that "it's the same old stuff I get at home." For at least half of these guys daily lunch money is a minor luxury. The cafeteria menu is probably a welcome break from their diet at home.

I notice I'm being watched by a teacher on duty, my former biology teacher. I assume he's noticed because I was one of his best pupils, but after he keeps staring without smiling I too turn suspicious. Finally I excuse myself and walk up to him. "Remember me? De la O!" He was always saying, "Another hundred for the zero kid," so I add, "The zero kid!"

"What happened to you?" He stares, as astonished as if I had covered myself with tattoos.

I know he means my hair and activist buttons, but I simply say, "Oh, nothing much. I decided to stay in the Valley after all . . ."

"Excuse me." He jerks up his arm without checking his watch. "I'm already late."

The nervous fear that was in me leaves with him. I go to the main office to sign the scholarship forms. Of course, they make me wait. Soon two of my old Spanish teachers pass by on their way to the lounge. The older one recognizes me at once and begins upbraiding me in a half-serious sort of way. The other one barely acknowledges me. She even urges the older one to hurry, but this one's not through with me yet.

"I always told him not to hang around those delinquents from the colonias, and now look at him." She slowly shakes her head like it's a genuine damn shame. "I think you do these things on purpose, just to waste God-given talent." She turns to her friend, addressing her like everyone else does. "Señorita, was he that way in your class, too?"

"The same." Her voice sounds flat by contrast. "He hasn't changed a bit."

"Oh, but he has! Just look at that hair."

"I'm trying to look like Che."

A secretary gestures me that my forms are ready. We exchange quick good-byes while Miss Señorita, as we used to call her, gives me one last, knowing look, as if to say, I knew you'd come to this.

On the way back I think about the class I took with her. I actually liked her, but I never took that extra step to join her circle of teacher's pets. Instead I hung around the usual outsiders that my other Spanish teacher mentioned. On one occasion Miss Señorita had us do an oral presentation on Latin American heroes. I ended up reporting on Fidel Castro. Using a couple of Lucio's paperbacks, I told the class how his revolution had improved the lot of the poorest Cubans. I didn't pay much mind to my teacher's reaction, but I was expecting some praise for getting off the usual dead-men track. Instead she responded with a petty attack on Castro: his staying in a cheap Harlem hotel while addressing the UN; his audacity to appear in a televised, nationwide interview dressed in "pajamas," referring to his military fatigues.

One of my lowlife friends even whispered, "Jesus, what did Castro ever do to her? Pop her and drop her?"

When graduation rolled around I had the highest grade point average of the guys. My grades had always been high, but since everyone always mentioned the same Anglos, I assumed their grades were better. Now these guys were almost as pissed as their parents; worse still, few knew who I was. I wasn't even the dark horse pulling in front; to them I hadn't even been in the running. I was another generic raza student they passed in the halls.

At that point they had to decide where to stick me in the graduation ceremony. The real speeches were set aside for those already polished in the art of pollyanna, including a safe and sanitized "Spanish" student. Through some ironic celestial joke I was asked to lead the convocation prayer, even though I suspected that God either didn't exist or else was Anglo. I didn't care for speeches in the first place, so I went along.

When my high school counselor advised me about college, she steered me away from other universities and suggested our local college, on the grounds that leaving home might be too unsettling. I asked in all innocence why she was helping other students get information on colleges outside our area. Suddenly she became an expert on Chicano culture, saying she was refering to my "people." I acted dumb and said that since I came from a broken home, my people were already scattered about. That bit of information didn't fit, so she turned a deaf ear.

As it turned out, she overestimated the togetherness of Chicano families just as I underestimated the epidemic of deafness all around me that season, including my own. I ignored her advice and applied elsewhere anyway. The financial-aid paperwork included a family earnings statement, and since my father was in town at the time, running some packing sheds, I left the form with one of my aunts for him to sign. But when I went to pick it up she told me he had refused to sign, saying his high earnings might jeopardize my financial aid. He probably thought the papers were a trap to have him help out with my education. So I went to my stepfather, who also refused to sign, even after I assured him he wouldn't be liable for my loans. I was ready to join the Army until an older friend already in college talked me out of it.

"That's suicide! Haven't you heard? There's a war going on, *vato*. And besides, someone like you would go crazy following orders."

He pointed out that my main reason for considering the Army was self-pity, then pushed me to complete the forms. He even offered to forge my stepfather's signature. "Not your dad's, though. If he can do this to his son, I don't want to mess with him. And if it's true he's that well off, he probably has an attorney on retainer."

In the end the forgery was unnecessary. My mother, who had dropped out of the third grade as an illiterate, convinced my stepfather's relatives to intercede, and in the end he reluctantly came around. I was accepted at the same school as Lucio. While the financial aid arrangements were still up in the air, I took a local honors scholarship. Too much blood, most of it bad and much of it mine, had already been spilled, and I felt drained. The first casualty was the son I had once been. So in the end, as if fulfilling a perverse prophecy, I had followed my high school counselor's advice: I stayed home because of my family, but not for the reason she had given. Far from it.

8
Tripping Down to the Big Mango

Lucio comes home for the holidays with plans for a Thanksgiving trip to Mexico City. He wants me and Pablo, the part-time checker at his father's store, to come along. He's never expressed an interest in Mexico except as a source of drugs. Now he's talking about adventures like the kind Kerouac had down there, so I'm sure his college friends have sold him on the idea.

Pablo's lukewarm until Lucio personalizes the sales pitch: "I heard some Olympics athletes stayed over for follow-up games."

Pablo, who talks about last month's games in Mexico City as though they were still going on, says he hasn't seen anything of the sort in the sports pages.

"Well, that's what I heard at UT." Lucio shrugs to show that's all he knows. Even though Pablo older and already a junior in college, in some ways he still looks up to Lucio.

That evening Pablo has us talk to his *compadre*, who's been to Mexico City several times. Pablo immediately asks him about any events carried over from the Olympics.

"Not that I've read about," he says. "Then again, people want to forget about October. Who knows, maybe now's the time to keep the public distracted."

Pablo wonders aloud who would want to forget the Olympics.

I ask, "Didn't their National Guard open fire on some demonstators?"

Compadre simply shakes his head, implying it was no big thing. "They just popped a few people, that's all. College kids. Troublemakers."

He glances at me out of the corner of his eyes. "Leave those Chicano buttons on this side. And keep that hair tucked under your collar."

Something tells me he knows a lot more than he's letting on, but by now our main concern is finding bus seats during Thanksgiving. Then I remember a bus trip I once took during the holidays with the old man to his hometown in Mexico. That was when I found out that Mexicans didn't celebrate Thanksgiving. Once that matter is settled, I start getting excited about the trip. I know full well that Lucio's invitation is partly because of his father's insistence that Pablo and I go along to keep Lucio half way straight. But since he's footing the bill, that's all that matters. And since I intend to stay straight the whole trip, setting the example should be no great sacrifice. The one thing that bothers me, up to the afternoon we're ready to leave, is Lucio's lying to Pablo about the Olympics.

"So what's going to happen," I ask Lucio, "when we get there and Pablo finds out there's nothing going on?"

"I never said I was sure. Anyway, we'll take in a fight at the Coliseo."

"Why not tell him that from the start?"

"Because the Olympics are what's pushing him, even if it's just left-overs. He talked all summer about going but never did. Now he wants to believe those athletes are still there. They're his ghosts, just like yours are the places where Villa and Zapata walked, and mine where Burroughs and the other Beats hung out."

Then he adds, "I saw some Bunuel films at UT. *The Mexican Bus Ride*, and"—he pauses to make sure his Spanish comes out straight— "*La ilusion viaja en tranvia*. Just think, we'll be doing both in one trip! Bus rides and illusions."

I argue that for Pablo the return trip will be more disappointment than illusion, but Lucio insists, "What difference does it make? What's important is that he's coming along. He can help out if there's trouble."

"What do you mean?"

"Well, you never know."

In fact I don't really know until we board the bus across the border. No sooner do we take our seats in back than Lucio shows a small bag of pills held by the elastic of one sock. Above the other I see the tips of several joints.

"Camus must be rolling in his grave at the absurdity," he says. "Some guy risks his ass crossing this shit over the river, just so that we can cross it right back."

I point out a more immediate absurdity. "You've heard those horror stories about Mexican prisons?"

"That's why I bought the stuff in the States." He pretends to peer into the dim light of the bus. "You think I'd trust any of these maniacs?"

What I mean, of course, is that all that trouble could be avoided—provided we traveled clean. But that provision is either too tall an order for Lucio or else too trifling. He'd sooner go insane trying to unravel Wittgenstein than swallow an ounce of common sense. I try hard to keep the little I have left, even as a part of me enjoys the excitement too.

At our first rest stop, Lucio swallows a couple of uppers. Pablo drops one too, saying he doesn't want to miss out on anything during the trip even though it's already turning dark. I simply mention that the last time I took pills I ended up going to a *curandera*. The anecdote amuses them to no end. I hold out until we reach Monterrey, where I end up like the man who takes a potion and sacrifices his sanity in order to fit in with the madmen around him. Besides, I tell myself, the quicker we use up the stuff the sooner we'll be home free.

Once the uppers kick in I sit next to a *mexicano* who's also headed for Mexico City and who ends up as my sounding board for the night. He's about my age, but with a calm maturity that makes him pause every so often for the right word, which only makes me more self-conscious about my own non-stop speech on speed. I make an effort to do more listening and less talking, but not before confessing that I'm a Chicano activist.

It truly is a confession. Before we left, the *compadre* warned me against discussing politics. "Their revolution's been over for fifty years," I told the *compadre* back home. "The bad guys won."

"Maybe, but the government doesn't like being reminded," he said, "especially by outsiders."

"I'm no outsider."

"You will be, in Mexico. Anyway, the place is still a powderkeg." He left me with a look that hinted I asked too many questions.

If I do, it's a habit I can't break. I start asking the young *mexicano* about last month's protests. He speaks reluctantly, with the same ner-

vousness the *compadre* gave the matter. Finally he starts talking about his
involvement in the student movement in the capital. He explains how,
some weeks back, students and workers in Mexico City tried using the
international spotlight on the Olympic Games to highlight their grievances. "We didn't think the government should spend that kind of
money with so much poverty around. I was amazed at the public support we got, considering how fanatical our people get about sports. At
first the government ignored us, then they started calling us unpatriot-
ic."

"Sounds familiar."

"In the beginning it was hard work but also fun, the same way you
talk about your own movement. We organized, talked to students and
workers. We'd demonstrate, then the government would demonstrate
back."

"You mean the government threw its own protests?"

"It's nothing new. Every time elections roll around they round up
villagers and truck them over to their candidates' rallies. They did the
same thing in the city, except now you had bureaucrats herded to demonstrations on buses. The *distrito federal* is one huge, bureaucratic beehive,
so they were everywhere. They weren't crazy about going, but they also
weren't crazy enough to lose their jobs. So they'd board, bleating like sarcastic sheep all the way. 'Ba-aa! Please don't make us go! Baaa-aaaaaa!'

"That's how it went for a while. We'd take to the streets one day,
then the next day it was the government's turn. But with the Olympics
around the corner, they were afraid we'd embarrass them before the
world, so they called a meeting at La Plaza De las Tres Culturas. 'For a
meaningful dialogue,' they said. We brought housewives and children,
workers and the elderly. The government brought its gunmen and
grenadiers. Then they closed the gates, corralled everyone inside and
opened fire. Pistols, rifles, machine guns, you name it. Even a helicopter
hovered overhead, illuminating the crowd, and later I heard it too
opened fire. I couldn't tell, though, I was running like everyone else, terrified I'd die. There was screaming all around, and I tried to yell, 'Stop
the screaming!' as though that might somehow stop the shooting. But
the moment I opened my mouth I started screaming too. Or at least I
felt something in my chest. I couldn't even hear myself scream. I kept
stumbling toward the gates when suddenly a barrage of bullets hurled a

woman against some railings, like a scrap of iron yanked to a magnet. It happened so fast I couldn't tell whether she was a young girl or an old woman, I only knew she seemed so frail. An instant later she was too disfigured to tell. I started sobbing, when I noticed a man on the other side of the gates, waving his arms like a madman for someone to let him in. For a moment I imagined he was my father. He seemed desperate to get in. Here people were forming human pyramids trying to get out of that hell and there he was, dying to get in."

He turns quiet for a moment, and I ask, "So then it wasn't like the papers said, about a few protesters being shot?"

He shakes his head in anger. "Hundreds died. Even people in the high-rises surrounding the park were hit. Afterwards they were pulling out bodies from the elevators and halls."

"You were lucky, then." My mouth, already dry from the amphetamines, now feels parched.

"They say the lucky ones were those who ended up in the morgue or in mass graves. The rest of my friends are either in Lecumberri Prison or will be there soon."

"So why are you going back? Sounds like it's still dangerous."

"They took in my younger sister for questioning. That was three days ago. I'm the one they want. Not that I think it'll save her, but I have no choice."

We say very little after that. No wonder Pablo and his *compadre* told me to keep quiet about politics.

We arrive the following morning and end up on the fourth floor of a hotel without a working elevator. For once I'm glad Lucio brought uppers, but after staying up for the second straight day and night, we collapse on the beds.

The next day we stroll around Chapultepec Park, where Lucio decides that the weekend crowd is ideal cover for smoking some joints. We're supposed to take turns smoking cigarettes to camouflage the smell, but I balk, arguing with a perverse prudishness that I'll never smoke a straight cigarette. Later Pablo lights up our last joint while on a *chalupa* we rent out in Lake Xochimilco. Luckily our guide not only looks the other way but has the decency to lower the side awnings.

Lucio finds the episode entertaining, like something out of a Beat novel. "Imagine when the guy gets home. 'Honey, you'll never guess what happened while I was pushing the *chalupa* this afternoon.'"

"I don't think the guys here call their wives *honey*," says Pablo.

Though I'm enjoying the trip in a nervous way, I know full well that if we're busted it's Lucio, with his well-off dad, who's most likely to return home.

A couple of blocks from a main avenue, I come face to face with silent reminders of the massacre. Posters of Zapata, with his piercing, accusative stare, are plastered so tightly on the walls that nothing short of razors could scrape away their message: "Yesterday they assassinated Zapata. Today they assassinate students. Why?"

I try not to think much about the *chavo* I met on the bus, or the fate of his sister, until it's time for us to leave. We're taking a cab to the bus station when I ask the driver, "There's a prison around here. Le . . . Lechu . . ."

The cab driver, somewhat startled, answers, "Lecumberri?"

"That's the one. Where is it?"

He doesn't give a direct answer, but simply says, "That's where they locked up rebels in the days of Porfirio Diaz."

"Is it close by?"

"Close by? It's closed! Anyway, you don't want to go there."

"But if it's closed, what's the harm?"

"People insist the place is haunted, that you can still hear ghosts from the old days. And you know what they say about the dead."

I don't know what they say, nor do I bother to ask. I suppose it's the same thing they say here about the missing—nothing.

9
Pruning the Family Tree, Grafts and All

Returning from Mexico, I get the usual inquiries from Manos and a couple of Anglo coeds in my honors group, asking how everything went. I'd like to tell them it was an enlightening experience, but in truth I'm only more uncertain, trying to sort out the good *mexicanos* from the bad. It's obvious where the students who protested in the streets stood, but the government and press seem to want it both ways. The official publicity during the Olympics appeared to push for the same things MANO stands for: pride in our culture and a suspicion of gringos. And when some black athletes were criticized by the American press for protesting U. S. racism, many of the Mexican papers took their side. Even as I walked along the main avenues of Mexico City, I was impressed by all the monuments to revolutionaries. Government offices displayed posters in their windows of Zapata, Villa, and lesser-known heroes. I remember thinking, *This is fantastic.*

Now I'm beginning to think it was propaganda, just as the Mexican media's support for American minorities was using somebody's else's crap to clean their own hands. It was nothing more than papering over the cracks. The revolutionary posters look down on the paperwork of bureaucrats who talk of radical reform, then stall. From the little I know of the Mexican Revolution, Zapata was gunned down just as the posters on the street said—by the same ones who now murder students.

So I'm not as enthusiastic as other Manos about Mexico, at least its government. Even when I ask those same Manos what their older relatives have to say about the Revolution, what I get is a romanticized version. "My grandfather? He was an officer with Villa's Dorados. And my grandmother was an Adelita with Zapata." Since Villa's front was in northern Mexico and Zapata's in the south, you try to imagine that sort of long-distance marriage, each catching a supply train to meet halfway in Matehuala for the weekend.

At first, being naive, I was impressed by suuch accounts. But after hearing similar lines sixty different times, you can't help but wonder: Against those odds, how come the *federales* finally won? Who was left on the side of the bad guys? Moreover, so many of our grandfathers were right-hand men for Villa that I doubt the man was the Centaur of the North; he must have been an octopus.

The trouble with revising history is, it's hard to stop with modest gains. Once you realize that Indian blood is something to be proud of, you decide that yours is premium Aztec grade. One goes for the best-known brand, and makes it blue blood for good measure. Of course, even the average Aztec was a peasant who toiled for the religious elite, but why stop there when the titles of chieftains are out there for the taking? Who'll prove otherwise? Just one look at those Mexican calendars with a sullen, muscular warrior defending his Aztec maiden, and your undernourished ego whispers, "This is me."

Yet mention Villa's exploits to my maternal grandfather, and he'll counter with anecdotes of incredible cruelty from the man and his underlings, which is partly why he left Mexico. Being dirt-poor proved no immunity from indiscriminate sadism.

We create myths of our ideal ancestors as well. My father was smuggled out of Mexico as a newborn after his mother died in childbirth. After he finished his Army tour and applied for G.I. benefits, a bureaucratic background check showed that he was neither American-born nor a De la O. An uncle he occasionally visited in Mexico was his real father. The discovery didn't help bring them closer.

So my family portrait, like our history, doesn't fit the neat frame the movement wants to create for us. Yet we, like many families, perpetuate our own myths and half-truths as much as the gringos do. We insist that our family roots in the Southwest go back hundreds of years. That's true for a few but not for most. That's why if someone tells my grandfather, who never owned property until he got here, about "our land" being stolen by the gringos, he won't get the same indignation as from the landholding families whose lands were actually taken.

You even have Manos who want it both ways. "Why, the Alvirez clan has lived in these parts for three hundred years. Longer, if you count our Indian blood."

"So then they didn't fight in the Revolution?"

"Oh, they did. All the Alvirez menfolk went to Mexico to help Villa."

"Wow. Talk about swimming against the current."

"That's our family motto: A man's got to do what a man's got to do."

Actually, a Mano has to do whatever it takes to look good—even when our romanticizing the Revolution is lost on the *mexicanos* who actually lived during that time. While life under the Anglo yoke has not left them with fond memories, the despots in Mexico were an equivalent evil. And given the famine and killing in Mexico at the time, for some the United States was the lesser evil. A grand-uncle who recently heard me glorifying the Revolution sat me down to set the record straight, at least about his own experience.

He was too young to fight, so he became a human deadweight: He gave the troop hangman a helping hand whenever "justice" lingered too long. Any traitor who twitched too long on the noose made the captain squeamish, so he'd yell for the piñata boy, and my grand-uncle would run over, tackle the victim's legs with a death grip, and hang on for dear life until the man stopped kicking. If the bootheels were too high, he snared them with a short lasso then dangled underneath, jerking his own legs to humor the men until the captain gave the slit-throat sign to signal a job well done.

They called him *el nino de las piñatas*. After each hanging they congratulated him on another birthday. By that yardstick, the captain once calculated the piñata boy was already pushing eighty.

At first he enjoyed his work, especially when the captain would make a second slitting gesture, this time above his head, to cut the corpse down and let him pick the dead man's pockets. He would add, like a doting uncle fond of hiding treats for his nephews, "See if he left you a going-away gift." Most did, since the men were often the former overlords in the region. He almost never saw the thick tongues and popped eyes that the regiment's mimic entertained the troops with afterwards, only their anonymous boots, the same boots that had once been at the throats of the poor.

One day another officer arrived at camp with orders from a Colonel So-and-So to hang the captain for treason. The captain, who was the colonel's *compadre*, chalked up the charges to their mutual and macabre sense of humor. He even played along with the practical joke by hoisting a rope over the closest mesquite and slipping the noose around his own neck. He then called the piñata boy to his feet, like a mascot that brought good luck.

That same instant the officer thanked him for lightening his load and immediately signaled two of his men to yank him high off the ground, while the rest kept the captain's men at bay. Another of the officer's men put a pistol to the boy's head and forced him to hang on to his captain's boots. In the haste no one had tied the captain's trouser bottoms, so in his death throes he let go his last shit on earth. It might even have been a fitting final touch—fertilizing the very soil he had fought for—except that the load landed on the piñata boy's head.

"Good God!" howled the officer. "You hit the jackpot this time!"

"He tore open that piñata, sure as shit!" said the soldier with the pistol, laughing so hard that he accidentally fired a shot past my grand-uncle's ear, causing him to piss in his trousers.

He deserted the troop that same night, but the stench stayed in his hair and followed him until he reached the border. There he scrubbed himself compulsively with lye soap, until his hair fell out in clumps. By the time new growth came out, the stench was a thing of the past. But the memory remains to this day, even though the years have added a self-mocking irony. "The Revolution freed some peasants," he tells me. "Some of us paid for it with their blood, others with our piss."

Memories like his are why MANO's simple view of our history—good guys versus bad—usually gets us nowhere with the older *raza* except out the door. So we're left with the younger generation to organize, but even here things aren't any easier. The younger immigrants who come here to make it are here to help themselves to the American cornucopia, not to help others. In their eyes America can do no wrong, especially when they compare their lot to what they left back home. They don't recognize the racism until later, but even then they're reluctant to protest. Many remain Mexican citizens, partly because gringos try to keep it that way, partly to show they haven't turned their backs on Mexico entirely, and partly as a way to hedge their bets in case they're forced to go back.

Yet by remaining Mexican citizens they also remain powerless here. On top of all that, they come from a country where being political can be suicidal, so they leave activism to those of us born here.

But we native-born *raza* have our own dilemnas, including questions about our loyalty. Whenever Anglos hear us speaking Spanish they must feel something like how Lizard says he felt in Nam, never really knowing which Vietnamese were friends and which foes. They probably figure that if there were trouble on the border we'd either head south or else stay put and do a variation of "What-do-you-mean-*we*, white-man?" when the Mexicans show up.

Sadly, Chicanos around here often respond to this doubt by trying even harder for acceptance. Esteban becomes Steve, Genoveva becomes Baby. Yet the ghosts continue to haunt them, whispering through the trace of an accent. So Esteban/Steve and Genoveva/Baby try to cover up their accent by layering another on top, as if a Texas drawl is the high point of one's achievements. For many it is.

10
Some Family Ties Tighten, Others Unravel

As soon as the semester's over, Lucio's back for Christmas break. He blew off a couple of introductory courses, yet impressed his philosophy instructor so much that he wants him to audit a graduate seminar in the spring. He's been hanging out with hippies at his university and some older heroin addicts from the barrio. When he hints he's already shot up a time or two, I can see the invitation coming and duck.

He doesn't drop by my house much. Even at his father's store he stops only long enough to raid the cash register. Lucio's also rediscovered an old playmate who shares his fascination with fire: his cousin Alvaro, who's already weathered an addiction episode or two in his brief life.

The first time I met Alvaro I assumed he had just gotten stoned. Later I realized he's gotten high so often that it's left him with his mouth slightly agape, making him seem more abstracted than alert. Add to this the primitive features he shares with Lucio, not just how he looks but how he looks at you: his protruding brow gives the impression he'd be at home in a cave of Cro-Magnons and survive quite well, with an intelligence behind that predatory gaze. My friend Nacho, who's his neighbor, says Alvaro reminds him of a village idiot, but appearances can be deceiving. This summer he stopped an ice-cream truck then badgered the driver until he got a free cone. It was a mistake the guy regretted the rest of the summer; since then Alvaro hounded him for free ice cream almost every afternoon.

Alvaro's off-focus expression makes for an ideal disguise. It certainly served him well earlier this month. He began buying downers in

Mexican pharmacies, to cut out the middle-man, then smuggling them across. Buses crossing the border are packed with shoppers this time of year, so he could slip through customs without a problem. And since passengers have to deboard momentarily at the bridge, he began stuffing a bag of corn chips with capsules, crumpling it on the bus floor like litter, then passing through customs.

The tactic worked until the official who checked packages left on the bus caught on. He confronted Alvaro at the turnstile, dangling the bag in his face. "You forgot to finish your Fritos, my friend."

Realizing that his fingerprints on the bag were the only evidence against him, he reached for it with a curious nonchalance. The customs man who let him take it expected some, melodramatic gesture, perhaps a suicidal attempt to swallow a fistful of the stuff. Instead Alvaro peeked inside the bag. "Looks like some poor old lady left her medicine."

The way Alvaro described the episode, the man suddenly saw his blunder and snatched it back. But it was already too late: Now no one could prove that Alvaro's fingerprints had been on the bag before he took it.

He mentions the incident simply to sum up his sole concern: Now he needs a new angle to feed his habit.

I don't see either one until after Christmas, when Alvaro suddenly shows up late one night at the old man's house with the news that Lucio has eloped with his girlfriend. What's bothering him is that Lucio's parents have concluded that he is involved in the elopement.

"My uncle says he'll press charges if I don't tell him where they are. Kidnapping! Can you believe that? My own uncle!"

Maybe he expects me to side with him morally, but while Alvaro has many sides I have yet to find a moral one.

"I told my uncle I hung out with you all day yesterday. If he comes around, you say the same thing ."

"What about if he brings cops?"

"What about it? You stick to our story."

He's so freaked out on fear and whatever he's taken that there's no talking to him, so before he wakes up the old man I steer him in another direction.

"And what's the girl's father saying?"

"Who? Oh, he can't say shit. She doesn't have one."

"And her mother?"

"What do you think? She's making an even bigger stink than *tio*, even though she got just what she wanted." He catches my quizzical look and adds, "Jesus, De la O, haven't you seen her shack?"

I have. The few times I went with Lucio the place seemed spartan, even by barrio standards. I never asked about the father's absence, but her mother seemed nice enough. And Lucio's girlfriend, considering she's only thirteen, has that pragmatic attitude that comes from caring for a brood of younger brothers. In fact her down-to-earth approach doesn't go with what happened unless you see it through Alvaro's cynical eyes: that maybe she saw Lucio as a ticket out for her family, as well as herself.

"I wonder where Lucio's at now."

"Never mind. He's doing fine."

Now there's no longer any doubt he was in on it. He leaves insisting he only meant to help out, but he probably had an idea of the mess that lay ahead. Whether he screwed up Lucio's life intentionally is beside the point. Lucio himself often quotes Sartre to the effect that intentions count for nothing.

I don't dwell too much on Lucio's problems because I have enough of my own. Today one of my aunts called to let me know my father's in town. In truth he's been around for the last two weeks but hasn't bothered to let me know until now, and this year I'm tempted to boycott our annual Christmas charade. He lives at the opposite end of the state—the Panhandle—and for the last few holiday seasons he's come down and played the same game of hide-and-go-seek in public: he visits friends and relatives for a week or two, then on the last hour of the last day, he'll schedule a brief get-together with me.

A cousin who told him about my long hair says he disapproves. I don't know what that means, but it's an obvious excuse I have for not seeing him. The irony is that after all the times he's made it clear he'd rather not see me, I'm the one who has to put an end to it. I'll end up as the ungrateful son, but it bothers me more that I've gone along with our meaningless meetings.

Like clockwork, he pulls up in front of the old man's house on the day he's leaving. Since he won't talk to my mother or stepfather, he has one of my uncles walk up to the screen door and call out: "Your father's here to see you."

Before he has time to turn, and before I have time to think twice, I answer that I don't want to see him. He's the uncle I'm closest to on my father's side, and I hate to put him in the middle, but now is not the time for explanations. He simply says, "*Bueno.*" Not *bueno* as in "good" but as in "well, that's that," the way one faces up to bad news.

In the days that follow I wait for fallout from my father's side of the family, but there's only silence. Except for someone saying he doesn't want them to mention my name in his presence. Since he's the son who made good, hiring his relatives in the packing sheds he runs, his words carry weight, and it's a safe bet that I'm seen as an ingrate. Another brother abandoned his own children after stabbing some guy to death in Mexico. He went into hiding in Houston under an assumed identity and never looked back, not even when his two daughters ended up as addicted prostitutes in Nuevo Laredo. Maybe that's why my father's minimal acknowledgment of me appears magnanimous by comparison.

At least that's how his family sees it, and it's not that different with my other relatives. When my maternal grandfather hears about it, he doesn't know what to think. He's known of my father's indifference in the last few years, but he still insists that after all is said and done, a father's a father. My stepfather is also upset, although it's probably not for the same reason. Perhaps he figures that if I can turn my back on my own flesh and blood, I'd do the same on him. He doesn't realize that through the years, for whatever differences we've had, he's as much my father as my actual one. My mother even explains to him how my father's sabotaging my college loans—even though I might have ended up in Nam—was the last straw, but the account only makes him more nervous. After all, he tried the exact same thing.

Afterwards I tell Nacho, who's known about my problems with my father since we both applied for financial aid. He's surprised, but he also saw it coming. For my other childhood friends, though, my actions seem less ambiguous, and unmistakably a mistake. Most of the Manos aren't as extreme but still suggest I went too far. Their response is predictable, given the single-minded myth we promote about close Chicano families.

The two Manos who offer a hand are the ones I'm closest to at the office, Coco and Gabi. Neither is on the best of terms with his own father. Coco's is an old union organizer from the Mexican *sindicatos* who's amused that the public sees us as radicals. His dream is to live out his days in Cuba, by which time he's betting we'll have sold out anyway. Gabi, who's the most supportive in the group, doesn't have anything terrible to say about his father, but neither does he have anything good, which in itself says a lot. When I complain how, oddly enough, all of this has estranged me from my stepfather, he offers to share his room in a house near campus.

I take him up on the offer, then try to explain the move to my mother. Since she's caught in the middle, she realizes more than anyone else the growing friction between my stepfather and I. I minimize my moving away by pointing out I'll only be living in the next town, but of course that's just it. If the distance required my leaving home then my stepfather could save face with his friends and relatives. This way everyone will be asking questions.

I'm already packing at the old man's house when she walks in and reminds me that within a month's time they'll be expanding their own house. Ever since I can remember, a run-down shack in the rear of the old man's lot has housed the bathroom and shower for both homes. The place has cold running water, and while hot water's not necessary most of the year, you still have to watch out for the toads that hide in the shower, seeking the damp darkness. But now, partly with my summer earnings, they're adding indoor plumbing to their own home, including a bathroom and water heater. She's hoping this will make me reconsider. It won't, yet I feel embarrassed for the both of us. I don't have the heart to remind her that I've used such showers since junior high school. I can't quite tell her without minimizing this milestone in her family's life. I'd get the same feeling as a kid whenever my stepfather brought me comic books I had already outgrown—an awkward gratitude, and at the same time the sadness of knowing you've already outgrown that reality.

After I finish packing, Lucio shows up. They say a strong dose of reality can either fix you up or mess you up as much as any drug, and it's already taking the latter toll on Lucio. It's hard to tell whether he's still in a state of shock or simply on downers. By the time he returns to college with his child bride, I've already moved into Gabi's place.

11

The Unbeatable Foe

Once the spring semester starts, Lizard asks me to sit in on his English class to help him prepare a term paper. Afterwards I check the syllabus and drop by whenever the instructor has an interesting topic. It's not a world literature class, but from the teacher's globetrotting references you'd think otherwise. He also stresses that literature can help us make sense of our own lives, an appeal that's lost on a wavy-haired *chavo* who complains that the instructor talks above our heads.

"What's he supposed to do?" I ask. "Treat us like babies?"

"He should talk about things we know. This stuff isn't part of our lives. Why doesn't he talk about the barrio?"

"Because he doesn't know," I answer, "and he doesn't pretend to. Besides, why come to college to hear what we already know?"

Later, when the instructor starts talking about *don* Quixote, I remember that the *chavo* to my right is surnamed Cervantes. I'm not the only one who makes the connection: Whenever the instructor mentions the author, a couple of the guy's friends snicker in his direction.

Suddenly the instructor stops and checks his class list. "By the way, we have our very own Cervantes," he says, singling out the student like an incognito celebrity.

The student, flattered yet flustered, looks away but only draws more attention. The instructor then continues on his tangent, but a few other *chavos* begin murmuring, "*Que joto*"—what a queer.

By the time the teacher asks what the student thinks of Quixote's quest, the underground teasing has turned into such a private hell that all he can say is, "He was crazy."

"The character or the author?"

"Both, but the author was worse. I mean, it's crazy enough to write about someone who's not real. But then to make him crazy . . ."

The instructor assumes he's exploring the ambiguity of insanity because he presses on. "What do you mean by *crazy*?"

Realizing that more is expected of him, he turns sullen. "Crazy. You know. *Loco*."

Almost everyone laughs when he says "loco," and so does he, glad to be back in the fold. When the wavy-haired guy glances my way, I assume he's expecting me to approve of the Spanish touch. Instead he turns back to the teacher. "He's as crazy as those do-gooders trying to change things here."

A girl in back adds, "What those Manos ought to change are their clothes."

"Why change with all the cheap perfume in the air?" I answer before I can think twice. I take up the theme of craziness and run with it. I have nothing new to say, other than offer a personal twist: How ideas that seem normal to Anglos may seem strange to us. I think I hear a grunt of approval then realize it's only a groan.

The instructor and I go back and forth with the theme, but by now his heart's not in it. Maybe he's still confused by the unexpected apathy of the other students, especially the Cervantes *chavo*. He can't see, though, that when someone's lived in the shadows for too long the spotlight makes him skittish.

Still, he tries to come up with discussions our *raza* can relate to, even though the windmills of Extremadura are a long way from the barrios and cottonfields of south Texas. And while I don't care much for Chicanos who cuddle too close to Spain and ignore their own backyard, this teacher's at least trying to connect those two worlds. What's important is that he doesn't just write us off. He expects us to contribute our thoughts. The next time we meet, he's back on his Rocinante, and this time, almost everyone listens to his excerpts from Quixote, with that mesmerized look of children hearing a bedtime story. But the discussion afterwards is still minimal until a Chicana behind me says she read the novel a while back, in Spanish. One or two students glance at the instructor's thick book then back at her with a mixture of awe and disbelief. "I had trouble following it," she admits, "and not just because of the old-fashioned Spanish. I'm used to novels where everything's tied together. A plot that follows . . .well . . . a plot."

"Like in Dickens," says the instructor.

"There you go. But this book was lots of disconnected episodes, and one character after another. There wasn't much . . ."—she tries retrieving the right word with a motion of her hands—". . . much continuity. But afterwards I realized that life is like that."

While she's talking I'm checking her out. She's one of these *chavas* you don't notice at once, but once you do you wonder why you hadn't. The instructor's nodding like crazy: "You used the term *episodes*, and you're right, and about how the book's structure relates to everyday life. Life is episodic. You spend a semester sitting next to someone who becomes a familiar face, but by the following semester you never see him again. Or you spend some time with your boyfriend before class, and you remember that. It may even seem more real to you now than this boring lecture."

"Sure. Most people plow through life, from one episode to another. That's what makes life worth living."

She adds a few more comments, and the instructor seems quite pleased. For my part I can't stop thinking about what the *chava* said, maybe because I've been looking at my own life lately. I agree about the randomness in our lives, how up to a point the unexpected is enjoyable, but how there's also a need to find a meaningful pattern, maybe even a justification. She's right: We want continuity and security, but also a little adventure.

After class I hang outside the door, but the instructor beats me to her. Cervantes and his side-kick are hanging around too. At first I suspect they're also waiting for her, until I realize they're actually discussing Quixote. I hear Cervantes suggest, "Maybe you should read the book first."

"Did you see how thick that book was?" He shudders. "No, *vato*, I'd have to be crazier than that Quixote."

"Maybe we should all read it," says Cervantes. "Let's suggest it to the prof. Anyway, if that girl in class read it . . ."

"Let her. If she's got nothing better to do . . . Besides, she doesn't need a Quixote. She needs this." He makes a screwing motion with his hands and hips."A good *cogida*."

"Who? Nena? She's never even had a boyfriend."

"Well," says Cervantes, "she has one now."

For a moment I'm certain he's talking about me, so I look away. Then I realize he's peeking inside the classroom. After they go their separate ways, I wait around for a minute or two but finally leave too.

12
Kid Quixote

The next time her class meets, Nena and I start up a conversation.
The more she talks, the more I'm impressed. "Since you're so smart," I
say, "why aren't you on our side?"

"You mean your group? Well, I believe in some of the things you
stand for. But when you guys get on the news with that radical talk . . ."

"You're not for that?"

She shakes her head. "And neither are you. Face it, we're college students."

"At least we get people's attention."

"Oh, that you do. You should hear what my dad says he'll do if he
ever catches you guys out in the open."

"Tell him we'll be out in the open at the end of the month. We're
having another demonstration then. Ask him to show up, if he has the
nerve."

She seems amused by the macho histrionics on both sides. "I tell
him that since he likes to talk trouble he should join you guys."

"What would he say if he saw us talking?"

"He'd probably say what a nice boy you are." Her slight smile is a
reminder not to take myself too seriously. "After all, how many guys here
take the time to sit in on a class?"

I mention I've been skipping my other classes so she won't think I'm
such a nice guy, but I also confess I'm helping out a friend with a term
paper.

"That's even nicer," she says. "Helping out a friend."

"Since we're such nice kids, what's the harm in joining?"

"Oh, there's no harm. I just need to work on some projects. You remember our last class? The professor got me interested in Cervantes."

She proceeds to tell me about his life: How his arm was crippled in an historic naval battle against the Turks; how he was taken prisoner, enslaved and tried to escape; how he finally won his freedom through a ransom; and how he wrote his masterpiece while in his sixties and in debtor's prison. "Some say he didn't actually work on the novel in prison. But it's a nice touch, no?"

She doesn't tell me this like some of my friends and a few honors students throw knowledge around, trying to impress each other. She's happy to share what she's learned, and it's contagious.

Reaching the MANO office, I share it with the *chavos* there. At first I get only a lukewarm welcome. Too often someone's clobbering our heads with Spanish literature to put down our "mongrel" Spanish. Soon, though, Roque and Gabi get into the spirit, and even Lizard shows his interest by keeping his sarcasm to a minimum. Coco, as usual, seems out of his element whenever our conversations drift towards the creative realm. Still he watches us intently, fascinated that other Manos could find such talk fascinating.

Only Alfredo doesn't show interest, which is odd since he always reminds us of his Castillian blood. His light complexion, helped by the fact that he never worked in the fields, adds to his affected aristocratic air. He's at one corner of the room, making little asides about my sudden expertise on Cervantes. When I ask him a thing or two about the author he covers up his ignorance by putting me on the defensive.

"De la O sounds more interested in whoever told him all this."

Before I can answer Roque does it for me. "Ay, what's wrong, precious? A little jealous?"

He minds Roque's remark as much as my laughing aloud. He not only seems foppish but is obsessed with proving he isn't. I'm still smiling when he asks, "What's your problem, De la O?"

"You're the one with the problem . . . precious."

Neither of us is looking for a fight, but if I had to choose one *chavo* to go one round with, he's the one. But like Lizard says, all it takes is the other guy landing one good, lucky punch; it would be even more humiliating coming from Alfredo's effeminate fist.

Lizard's looking for a little excitement himself. "And in this corner, weighing in at . . . Say, how much do you weigh, De la O?"

"He doesn't," says Roque, who constantly reminds Alfredo and I how scrawny we are. "In fact, his name's De la Zero, not De la O."

"Did you say 'Zorro'?" I'm hoping that with a little humor the fight will fizzle out.

"Zero, you little coyote," Roque responds. "As in *nada*. As for Alfredo, he's in the minus category . . ."

"Seriously," Lizard asks me again. "One twenty?"

He's almost on the button. "Twenty-eight."

"Weighing in at one twenty-eight . . . the lightweight challenger in the brown butt . . . Kid Quixote!"

I cross myself like those Mexican boxers praying for the strength to slaughter the other guy, then start weaving and bobbing. I'm trying to burn off some anxiety, since by now I'm convinced I'm not getting off without giving and getting a few punches. When Coco steps between us and stretches his arms I assume he's about to referee. Instead he reminds us in his gruff voice that we have work to do.

"See?" says Coco. "That's what happens when you talk about useless stuff. You stray from the struggle."

"Then we should do this more often," says Roque. "We'd have more action and less talk."

"If it's action you want," says Coco, "then help me load some boxes of books on Kevin's wagon. Marcos needs them today, and Kevin needs his car back."

Whenever we need a car we turn to Kevin, a lanky Anglo from up north who works with a federal project in the barrio. He owns an old woodie wagon with exterior paneling, the kind you see in beach movies. The roof rack comes in handy for hauling placards to demonstrations and must have been used for surfboards once, since there's even faded lettering on the driver's side: S RF N' USA.

Gabi, like the other Manos, argues that it's the perfect patriotic camouflage. "Who's going to stop All-American beach boys?"

"No one, except that we look more like All-Mexican wetbacks."

"Speak for yourself, De la O. These are just tans."

"Kevin has a tan." I place my arm alongside his. "The rest of us have a problem. What we have goes over the legal tan in this state. When we're in that wagon we don't look like surfers. We just look suspicious as shit."

"Would you rather walk?"

"No, but I don't want to end up in jail either. One day the cops are going to think we stole that car."

"They haven't stopped us yet," says Roque. "But if you think we look strange, just imagine the Chicano family Kevin bought it from. They were migrants, with six kids. They bought it used on the West Coast."

"That's different. A hard-core migrant doesn't even realize he sticks out. He's beyond being paranoid. All he can see is, 'Mira, mi vida, it even has paneling on the outside.'"

"If you're not going to help," interrupts Coco, "don't bother the rest with your stories."

Afterwards we drop by Kevin's house in the barrio, a delapidated lean-to that reminds me of the Zamarripa's. With the little he gets from the VISTA program, it's about all he can afford, but he manages to have good books around, as well as plenty of Mexican beer. At first I figured he had a drinking problem, until I realized it's for whenever Manos drop by.

We're barely in the house when he calls out from his bedroom, "There's Tecate in the fridge."

Three farmworker organizers in the living room have already helped themselves to beer and books, and by the time Kevin walks in Roque's already buried his beard in a *Playboy*. Gabi and I are sharing a new book on Che, and I look up long enough to ask where he gets this stuff.

"Oh, around," Kevin answers abstractly while trying to read a car repair manual, something totally out of his league. He studies the same page for several minutes, but the only thing he gets for his troubles is a pained expression. Here's a guy who, like Lucio, can go through *Being and Nothingness* like it's, well, nothing, yet he's helplessly stalled on an illustrated, step-by-step tune-up. I'm no master mechanic myself, so the only thing I'm good for is consolation. "Those photos always look like they were taken in a cave."

From across the room Roque unfolds this month's centerfold. "Not these." Roque unfolds a centerfold. "Just look at this little cave."

"I thought you didn't like them that thin," I tell him.

Kevin gives the centerfold a distracted glance. "Excuse me if I don't salute her with a hard-on. I'm trying to figure out someone else's insides."

"Who?" asks Gabi.

"Roci."

Gabi looks up like he didn't hear right. "You have photos of Rosa Rosales' insides?"

Kevin almost blushes. "No, not Rosa the Mana. Roci, my car. It's short for Rocinante."

He returns to his book, confident he's cleared things up, but Gabi glances up again.

"Rosie who?"

Kevin assumes the problem is with his accent. "Ro-ci-nan-te? Isn't that how you say it? You know. Don Quixote's horse?"

Roque grunts agreement as though upset at himself for forgetting something so obvious. Instead of leaving well enough alone, though, I ask Kevin why he named his car Rocinante.

"Well, whenever we pile out of the wagon at a protest, with placards in our hands like lances, we're like . . . What's the plural of Quixote in Spanish?"

"¡Que jotos!" What queers.

Everyone laughs at Roque's remark except for Kevin, who obediently repeats, "Qui-jo-tos. Is that like cojones?"

His question paralyzes the laughter, and Roque looks at me for a clue.

"That's what Spaniards call huevos," I explain. "Like when Hemingway writes about—"

"If you mean huevos," Roque interrupts, "then say huevos."

Kevin realizes he's hit another nerve. "Well, it's used in Spain . . ."

"This isn't Spain," says Roque. "This is Aztlan."

"You see," I tell Kevin, "jotos is slang for—"

"Quit sucking up to him," says Roque. "Let the gringo genius figure it out, just like we had to."

Everyone's uncomfortable and the silence only makes it worse, until Gabi points out: "Look, here we are drinking Kevin's beer and borrowing his car, yet nobody stands up for him."

The instant he says it the rest of us are shamed out of our silence. But nobody has the nerve to raid the refrigerator until Kevin personally brings Roque a beer. Roque returns the peace gesture by quietly sketching Kevin's profile.

As the minutes pass I reflect on how Kevin became more entangled the more he tried to get things right; and how Roque, rather than admit his ignorance, added hostility with each passing remark. Like most of us, Roque likes his battle lines drawn in black-and-white, and our hanging around an occasional Anglo doesn't fit into the idea of a holy war. I decide to kid Roque a bit.

"Are you sketching Kevin's *cojones?* Or his white ass?"

It's the type of teasing that can backfire, but I'm wondering whether we've learned our lesson.

Without even glancing up, Roque takes the *Playboy* beside him with his idle hand and flings it my way. "It's better than sketching your ass, assuming I could find it."

"You won't," says one of the other Manos. "De la O's a freak of nature: An asshole without an ass."

"It runs in his family," adds Roque. "Now you know what the 'O' stands for."

13
Day Care Radicals

I moved into Gabi's place believing he was paying rent, but now it turns out that a middle-class college Mano who lives there is picking up the tab. He insists we call him by his full name. He even refers to himself in the third person. "Always remember," he says soon after I move in, "the days you lived under Danny Moreno's roof."

"What's this about 'days'?" I ask Gabi afterwards. "A hint my days here are numbered?"

"He wants us to remember, in case he's famous one day."

As far as middle-class guys go, he's all right. Lizard calls him Danny Marrano–porker–because of his weight, but if it bothers him he's not saying. He doesn't even mind when Gabi and I borrow his political buttons, since he just takes them back eventually. Just don't fuck with his food: He regards his tortillas the same way Aztecs regarded maize, as sacred.

Living here has its advantages. For one thing I don't have to account for my whereabouts. For another, I can sit around all night talking about the movement, women, or music with whoever drops by, although that quickly gets old. It doesn't dawn on me that I'm disrupting the others' routines until Coco's brother moves in. Suddenly it's my turn to accommodate someone else glad to live unfettered among other Manos.

By then the excitement of living an unsheltered life has dropped several degrees. The bedroom I share with Gabi doubles as a party room, with black light posters covering the walls. Danny doesn't do dope but does drink occasionally, so the room's a retreat for those who do either. Several times I've arrived to find the black lights on and incense burning, a sure sign that a party's in the works.

Tonight though, with no warning at all, I wake up in my underwear to find several students huddled in a corner, getting stoned around a candle. It spooks the hell out of me. Gabi wakes up just as they grin our way. Their eyes, teeth and a couple of white peasant shirts stand out disembodied and brilliant in the black light, like a Posada print of carousing skeletons. It appears they've been contemplating us for some time. I go back to sleep after they leave, only to dream I'm witnessing my own wake. I jerk awake to find I wasn't the only one who's spooked. Gabi's up too, trying to get those staring skulls out of his mind.

Neither of us can get back to sleep so I start remembering aloud the times I tagged along with my stepfather's old man whenever he visited his relatives in Mexico. My job was to make sure he made the right bus transfers and didn't stray off once he got there. The reason for the trip was usually a wedding or a funeral, so we'd end up at an all-purpose hall owned by a certain Chon. He called the old man his cousin, but then again everyone in town seemed related. Officially the place was a funeral parlor, but cousin Chon was forced to moonlight, promoting dances and organizing wedding banquets. Since families usually held wakes in their own homes, the parlor was used mostly for delayed funerals where family members came in from the U. S. or the farther ends of Mexico. During my third trip I fell fast asleep on one of the benches, until several drunken relatives turned too loud. I woke up startled and disoriented. For those first few moments I could not for the life of me tell whether I was at a wedding or a wake.

I tell Gabi that's the same feeling I had earlier, on waking up and finding those partygoers sucking solemnly on a toke, but by now he's fallen asleep, like a child lulled by a bedtime story. I can still see cousin Chon decorating the place, and even though in a town that small the upcoming occasion was obvious, someone always stopped by to ask, "So what kind of burial are we having, cousin Chon?" If cousin Chon answered that the lucky stiff was staying in the hole all night, it meant a wedding. If he said that the stiff was staying put, period, it meant a burial.

We Manos are always going on about our culture, framing it in epic panoramas like the Conquest and the Revolution. But in the end it's not the abstractions that stay with you but the specifics, like cousin Chon's all-purpose funeral home and wedding hall.

I suspect that's why Danny wants us around. Having grown up in the equivalent of a middle-class situation comedy, he wants an authentic barrio experience, though he wants it abridged and in language he can understand. What bothers me is that Danny expects this knowledge to fall in his lap, without his taking the time to live through things, to piece fragmented experiences into a whole. Some of the pieces don't fit, or you end up with gaps or leftover parts, but it's still the only way your ethnicity makes any sense.

When I start hinting as much to Danny, he becomes a bit peeved that he can't be a vicarious *vato* and begins wondering aloud why he has us there in the first place. He seems to think it's all a matter of memorizing a formula that we're keeping from him. He also starts hinting we've overstayed our welcome.

One day he drops the ultimate bomb: "Oh, by the way, the FBI paid us a visit."

"The *FBI?*" says Gabi. "What the—?"

"They asked questions about Marcos. They also wanted to know who else lived here."

There's something suspicious about his understated tone, since he usually he gets histrionic over the most trivial things. By this time, though, Rosa Rosales and a couple of other Manas have started a daycare center for migrant kids in a nearby barrio. The building they're renting has two stories, but by law the second floor is off limits to the children. Rather than leave the upper part idle, Rosa lets us use it as a MANO office. Coco and Roque quickly move their books and printing equipment into one of the rooms: Gabi and I move our asses into another. By the end of the month Coco and Roque are also staying there on and off.

The center is just across the street from the county jail, separated by a street and a large empty lot. The running joke is that if we're ever arrested they can walk us to our cells. I'm surprised there's not a regulation against daycare centers being that close to a jail, but Gabi suspects the authorities look the other way when it comes to migrant children. If that's the case then Rosa, Luli and those of us living here are perfectly willing to look the other way as well.

Luli coordinates the kids' meals and every so often takes some leftover food upstairs. We help out with errands here and there. Roque

entertains the kids with his guitar while Luli teaches them *corridos* from
the farmworkers' movement. What with our hanging around and the
Manas brainwashing the kids with movement music, I suggest they
change the name of the center from "The Little Rascals" to "The Little
Radicals."

"Or maybe The *Raza* Rascals," adds Sandra.

Rosa, the better businesswoman of the two, says, "Let's face it, parents would take out their kids in a minute. MANO may be trying to help
them, but all they can see is that we'll get them in trouble with the growers."

That's one reason we keep a low profile, leaving early and staying
away until school's over. A second reason is that at times the police seem
to be swarming the streets. Roque insists it's normal since we're a stone's
throw from the county jail, but at times, things can get a bit tense. We're
helping Rosa and Luli unload some groceries from their car when a
patrol car cruises by. Gabi holds the driver's stare, so he quickly swings
back for a closer look. He inspects us for a moment, and we hold our
ground to show we have nothing to hide. Finally he gestures toward the
building. "Aren't you boys a little old for this?"

"For school? You're never too old to learn."

He slowly gets out of the car at the same time that Rosa returns from
inside. She pretends to reprimand us. "What's keeping you freeloaders?
Bring that meat inside before it spoils."

The two cops glance at each other. The driver says, "Excuse me,
Miss . . ."

"Rosa. Rosa Rosales." She glances at the Anglo cop. "That's Rose
Rosebushes, for those of us culturally deprived."

"Do you work at this—?"

"It's a daycare center. I run it."

Even behind his sunglasses we can sense the Chicano cop staring
with suspicion at her peasant blouse and Adelita braids. But before he
can ask anything else she adds: "You're *dona* Herlinda's boy, aren't you?"

All of a sudden he's no longer an anonymous arm of the law. He's a
known quantity—a local kid to boot—and her unmasking him leaves him
speechless and fidgeting with his sunglasses.

We're almost at the door when his Anglo sidekick calls out: "Say! I
know a good barber in town."

The remark is aimed at Roque and me, but Rosa has a ready reply. "Then go see him," she says, returning the guy's grin. "He's sure to do a better job than the crewcut you have." She glances at the Chicano cop and adds, "You have kids? Bring them over. Maybe they'll learn about themselves."

After that I become a bit paranoid around patrol cars, although the cops don't bother us again.

A week later, however, I'm returning from classes when I hear what sounds like a megaphone. The closer I get to the daycare center, the more it sounds like a pep rally, until I turn the corner and see a half-dozen police cars parked along the south side of the center. Lights are flashing and cops swarming along the gate, trying to keep the barrio crowd at bay.

Part of me alternates between caution and panic, arguing that if they've stormed the center then going out there is tantamount to turning myself in. I'm wondering what I'll tell the cops if they see me. I keep on walking, though, getting strength from thinking of Peter and the other Apostles fleeing after Jesus was arrested. As a kid I thought they were cowards for having deserted him, and that I would have had the courage to stay.

That thought keeps me going until I'm close enough to realize that the center of the commotion is actually the county jail. By then I'm catching bits and pieces of rumors that some prisoners unsuccessfully attempted a jailbreak. The cops are trying to work out some sort of deal with them. For the time being, the police are keeping a safe distance across the street.

Fortunately, most of the daycare kids have been picked up by their parents. Rosa's waiting for word on whether to move the rest, but she's not getting straight answers from the cops, who have their own problems. One officer tells some bystanders that the jailbreakers are holding another prisoner hostage. An older lady close by begins weeping inconsolably because her nephews are inside, but the cop reassures her, "The one they're holding hostage is a wetback kid. He was helping two brothers who turned against him when the alarms went off." Suddenly it dawns on him her nephews might be the hostage-takers. "Listen, your last name's not Zamarripa, is it?"

No sooner does she say no than I turn to Coco. "Did he say *Zamarripa*? The Brothers Zamarripa?"

Before Coco can say anything, the cop asks me if I know them, and I have this vague yet real fear that I'll end up dragged into this shit.

"I've heard of them. I mean, if they're the same Zamarripa brothers . . ."

"You think you could talk to them?"

I picture myself on a bullhorn"—I'M THE GUY YOU TRIED TO UNLOAD THE COMPUTER ON!—"while half the town sees me and the other half overhears. I shake my head and explain, "I've only heard of them. I don't even know if they're the same ones."

The cop stares at me for a moment then leaves. Coco whispers: "You know the guys?"

I recall something Lucio told me: That they had asked about me after he told them I was now a Mano. I pass along to Coco what they supposedly said:

"A friend talked to them during the Christmas break. They asked if MANO wanted to buy a bazooka."

"A *bazooka?*"

"That's right. You could say they're into overkill."

Coco glances around to make sure no cops are close by. "Right now they could use that bazooka themselves, to blast their way out of there."

A while later the same cop says he heard the kid begging both sides not to harm him. A sheriff's deputy takes the bullhorn and hams it up, jumping from threats to pleas like an angry parent hoping to scare a child away from danger. The tinny bullhorn only adds to his shrillness.

"WE'VE GOT THE PLACE SURROUNDED! YOU DON'T HAVE A CHANCE, ZAMARRIPA! YOU EITHER, ZAMARRIPA!"

Another deputy tries to reason with the brothers, but it's obvious he's not used to treating prisooners as equals. He's trying hard to come across like the voice of reason, but Gabi says he wouldn't be surprised if he suddenly yelled, *Fuck it! Let's just pop everyone!*

"Poor *mojadito,*" Gabi adds.

I feel sorry for the kid too. No matter what he was in for, he's in a lot more trouble now.

Back inside Luli wants to know more about the Brothers Zamarripa, so I tell her about our only encounter. I suspect she sees them as part of our struggle, since I find myself romanticizing their screw-ups too. We're not that different from black militants who treat pimps and pushers like they're a guerrilla vanguard. But the closer you get to these guys the less they look like revolutionaries. Sometimes people have a hard time telling the difference between heroes and assholes.

I'm not sure how the standoff ends, but by nightfall all but the hard-core voyeurs have gone home. A lone constable's car is all that's left. Finally the car radio squawks out orders to return to headquarters. That leaves only a couple of Chicano deputies hanging around in plainclothes, which for them means cowboy boots and hats.

As soon as they too leave, I step out for a final look and see some-one scuttling from inside the daycare center dumpster. At first I assume it's a ragpicker collecting cardboard to sell in Mexico. He seems to see me and retreats: "De la O? Is that you?"

For a moment I'm not sure what to answer. "Yeah! Who . . .?"

"Are all the cops gone?"

I'm still trying to place the disembodied voice. "Who the—?"

"It's me."

"Roque?"

He sprints out from behind the dumpster. "Jesus! Those cops scared the crap out of me."

I can guess as much from his expression: terrified. At last he admits he was getting stoned behind the trashbin when the cops came on the scene. He jumped into the dumpster at the first sound of the bullhorn and stayed there until now.

"You mean you've been inside there? All this time?"

"How long was I in there? All I know is that when I came out I was almost straight."

"Where'd you get the dope?"

"From Lizard. Last night we got stoned out here. He left me a couple of quackies, and I figured this was the best place to stash them. I mean, I don't want to burn Luli and the other Manas."

I feel like pointing out that if he had been caught the damage would have been just as bad. Now is not the time, though, not with that unfo-cused stare. But when he asks me to help him polish off the second quackie, I tell him anyway. The thought seems to sober him up a degree or two. "Don't scare me with shit like that, De la O."

"It's the truth, Roque. If they bust your ass, they'll have tanks out here."

"I know, I know, only don't say it. Dope really brings out the paranoia in me."

I point out that if paranoia is what he wants, he doesn't need dope.
A few police cars flashing their lights can do wonders.

As we're going upstairs, I can't help feeling like a hypocrite: I'm a
fine one to talk about staying straight. On the other hand, maybe knowing you're a hypocrite is the first step towards wisdom.

14
A Baptism by the River

The demonstration I told Nena about is scheduled to take place in Del Rio, a couple of hundred miles up the Rio Grande. Newspapers throughout the state begin reporting on plans for it after a MANO leader is quoted saying that gringos are our leading cause of death, and that we should strike first in self-defense. The remark stirs up a storm.

Up to now my honors program director has supported our right to protest, but he's concerned with our escalating rhetoric. During one of our talks after class he mentions that the administration has asked about me. "They've caught you on the television news once or twice, and they're a little nervous."

"Who's 'they'?"

He says little else, except that he'll back me provided we don't turn violent.

A few days later Danny, another Chicano in the program, asks to tag along to the demonstration. The request catches me off guard, since he's a nice, bright, middle-class *chavo* whose friends are almost all Anglos. We've had some cordial conversations—some on the movement, some more where he's wondered aloud what it's like to get stoned. If he's hoping to get stoned on the trip, he's in for a disappointment. I've made it clear there'll be no dope.

I invite him along for the ride but point out there's no telling what might happen once we're there. "Some of the shopkeepers say they'll be on the rooftops with rifles, protecting their stores."

"Great. I want some photos for the college paper."

"Our college paper? Good luck, Danny. Their idea of news is that greased pig contest our school has every fall."

"Well, maybe I can put in a shot of those pigs on the rooftops."

Driving in Lizard's car, we pick him up at his house, on the Anglo side of town. He sits in back, between Roque and a highschool Mano, while I ride between Nano and Lizard, who carry on a conspiratorial conversation.

"Look, Liz," I finally interrupt, "we promised not to take any stuff to the demonstration."

"We're not. It'll go up in smoke before we get there."

Danny's Spanish is weak, and his slang is worse, so our argument goes over his head.

I shake my head. "We promised."

Lizard's hoping the others will back him up, but they know better and keep quiet. "In that case I have to stop over at my cousin Chente's."

"What for?"

"To leave the grocery bag with him."

He obviously planned to do some dealing at the demonstration, so when we get to his cousin's I tail him to the trunk to make sure he unloads everything. As he takes out the bag something metallic catches the gleam of the street lamps.

"What's this?"

"A grenade." It's as though I asked about a spare tire.

"A *grenade?*"

"It's tear gas, not a frag."

"Jesus, Liz, what if the damn thing explodes?"

"That only happens when John Wayne pulls out the pin with his teeth. Try that in real life and all you'll put out is your teeth."

"You're the one acting like John Wayne Junior."

"It's protection, De la O. In case some cops pull us over on some dark country road."

"We're not taking any country roads. Besides, what good's a grenade in the trunk if we're stopped?"

He picks it up as if weighing his options. "We could carry it up front, but you never know about these things."

"I thought you said they're safe."

"Come on, De la O, nothing in life is sure-thing safe. You'd know that if you'd been to Nam." He starts lobbing and snatching it in mid-air just to see the look on my face. "Especially grenades. After all, they're for killing."

"Look, Liz, if the cops stop us and you pull out this mother, we'll definitely end up killed. What good is tear gas then?"

"At least they'll cry over our corpses."

But I won't give up, so he tosses it in the grocery bag filled with grass. His cousin Chente greets us with open arms that immediately embrace the bag. "Ah, I was running out of groceries." He peeks in. "Especially produce." His smile melts, though, when he fishes out the grenade. "And what the hell is this?"

Lizard grins to where I can see his crow's feet. "It's cologne, for the cops."

He disappears into the kitchen while his cousin checks us out one at a time. All of us except Danny pass the test. Chente stares at the clean-cut clothes and the face without a trace of street smarts. Suddenly Lizard reappears sucking on a glowing joint. Chente glares at him, then at Danny, who's oblivious to everything except the joint. Lizard offers him a hit from across the room and Danny gestures with a nervous, unconvincing *no*. At the same time, though, he glances my way for permission.

Chente's figured out I'm responsible for bringing him along, so I explain that Danny's dying to get stoned. My hunch works: Danny doesn't disagree, and the chance to baptize a novice is too tempting for Chente.

"Roll him a jumbo, for Christ's sake," he tells Lizard. "And none of that shake you just brought. Take my good stuff."

In his khakis and pointed tangerine shoes, Chente seems an improbable *padrino* for Danny, who'd be more at home with a flower-child godfather. But Chente patiently takes him step by step through the ritual that *pachucos* follow with the compulsion of priests: Having him hold in the smoke, then talking in a low, strangled voice to keep the smoke bottled inside. He follows Danny's every expression, and when that first stoned smile appears, he smiles as well.

I'm not sampling the goods, which revives Chente's suspicions, but either it's potent weed or else Danny's one of those fortunate souls who gets stoned on his first try. Afterwards Chente brings him pork rinds and a *Playboy*. Even though he can barely keep his eyes open Danny savors the magazine but saves his best review for the munchies. "These are great! What are they?"

"*Chicharrones*," says Chente.

After a quiet spell he asks me softly, "That guy—what's his name?"

"Chente. He's your godfather now, Danny."

He doesn't really understand but adds, "He's OK."

"He feels the same way about you. But for a while he couldn't figure out what planet you came from."

Being quite stoned, he finds the extraterrestrial comparison hilarious, but a moment later Lizard interrupts his bliss.

"I hear they're expecting *rinches* at the demonstration."

Danny's mind must still be on aliens because his eyes suddenly get huge as half-dollars. "What are those?"

"Texas Rangers."

The news soothes him, and it dawns on me that Danny didn't grow up with the same *Ranger Horror Stories* the rest of us did. To him they're patrol boys sent to keep our march safe and orderly. I try explaining the Rangers' reputation as goons for the gringos, but he's either too stoned or else his attitudes too cemented, so I give up.

Roque takes up the cause. "This friend lives out by their headquarters, so he's seen their firepower . . ."

"Whose?"

"The Rangers," answers Roque. "He says that every time they clean their armory . . ."

"Who says?"

"My *friend*, damn it! He says they have fifty-caliber machine guns mounted on Jeeps."

"Those things can flip over a Jeep if you're not careful," says Lizard. "They're anti-aircraft guns."

Danny's response is as slow as it is serious. "Oh . . . but the marchers aren't bringing in fighter planes . . . right?"

Roque smiles and rolls his eyes. "Right. Anyway, who needs an airplane when we're flying high already? Right, Danny?"

Danny nods, eyes closed.

15
Canon Fodder

We reach our destination, Del Rio, after midnight and without incident. At the rendezvous area, its open acreage already packed with cars and vans, we've been promised a hot breakfast come morning. I have my doubts, but for outsiders in an unknown town and in the middle of the night, there's safety in numbers.

I wake up to find Lizard taking a leak behind the van next to us. Danny, who spent the entire drive fast asleep, wakes up soon after, disoriented but alert, and embarrassed when Nano asks, "How was the trip?"

He manages to pick up bits and pieces of Lizard's attempt to bring along the grenade. It must still be on his mind when Nano tells him, "The moment we reach the protest site, you pull out your Canon and start shooting."

He looks at me, almost apologizing. "You never said we had to bring weapons."

I can't decide whether to laugh or play up to his image of our militancy. When we reach the convention center where the demonstration is scheduled to start, he's eager for photos, but some of his subjects aren't. A few times he points his camera only to have the bystanders scatter, as if an assassin had them in his sights. I explain that he looks and dresses like a poster boy for the FBI, then add, "Don't feel bad. I'm at the other extreme. A pop-up target for their shooting range."

I steer him toward the low-echelon Manos who aren't as skittish. They're the more colorful ones anyway, serapes and field jackets studded with buttons for every conceivable cause under Aztlan's sun, along with an occasional cosmic cause for good measure. Danny clicks away while the more exhibitionist Manos strike their best Che poses. Afterwards I point out the state leaders, who stand out in their own way by their ordinariness. It's their way of telling the rest of us they don't need trinkets or talismans. They have the real magic, the witchcraft that works: power.

Yet they too play the game on their own terms to show they're one of us. These leaders walk around with a single political button. Otherwise it would be like being the barrio's most devout Catholic but refusing to wear a cross: Nobody takes you seriously. Our *raza* wouldn't acknowledge Christ himself unless he sported a crucifix. That's why everybody notices this button because no one else has it. Soon the button freaks start crowding around, anxious to get the one item missing from their collections.

Naturally you don't have it, agree the leaders, we just had it made. No sooner do they promise to distribute some through their middlemen, the mid-level leaders, than the masses go place their orders.

After Danny tires of the two extremes he zeroes in on the mid-level leaders, who seem nervous that the photos may end up in an official file, to be yanked out one day by a bureaucrat. Right now they want a little exposure, enough to say they've been there—but without leaving fingerprints, photos, or other incriminating evidence. They've learned the lesson of public figures who in the intoxication of the moment posed for a warm *abrazo* with Castro or a stiff handshake with Nixon, then had the photos come back to haunt them.

Our state leaders, a different species altogether, don't lose sleep over their notoriety. They know that if their faces are publicized enough times in the press they end up as well-known as any celebrity. So unless they accuse Jim Bowie of unnatural acts with an armadillo during his bedridden days at the Alamo, their sins are forgiven. In time they're eclipsed by the next new crop of radicals. At least that's what Marcos insists: Most of us will end up as consultants on how to deal with a new generation of malcontents. Besides, he adds, converting your critics is a feather in the system's cap. The same people you fought against have the satisfaction of saying, "Remember so-and-so? Well, he works for us now . . . He finally came to his senses."

We get a hint of what it's like to make it when we're herded inside the convention center for a few speeches from the leaders. It's an odd feeling, finally looking out from the inside, instead of protesting outside the gates. By the time the speakers are ready to address the crowd, it's charged up on chants.

Marcos steps up to the podium with a militant message at once cerebral and visceral. His voice, as always, is low-key, but that only adds to the emotion he's keeping in check. The speakers who follow try to outdo each other's radical rhetoric, until one offers the ultimate one-upmanship: *Exterminate the gringo.* He's been quoted to that effect before, in an off-the-record interview, but now he's gone public, and when he does the crowd goes crazy.

I remember him vaguely from last year, when Adrian introduced us at the meeting in San Antonio. I had my reservations back then, and I still have them. There's something inauthentic about him, and his wearing khakis and sunglasses only adds to the inconsistency. He strikes me as the middle-class, best friend Danny might have had growing up. In fact, Danny's applauding him the whole time, even though, if the *chavo* is to be believed, he'd blow away all of Danny's white friends.

By the end of his speech, though, nobody's asking whether the rhetoric fits. The press devours his speech. A well-organized demonstration afterwards goes unreported beneath the next day's headlines on greasing the gringo.

By the time we get back home, people are already asking whether we've set a date to storm the Alamo. Since there's no such thing as bad publicity, our next local meeting draws our largest attendance yet. Before we start, some high school Manos ask Coco, Gabi, and me to join them outside. One of the boys sits on Rocinante's hood and gives a nervous smile. "Remember what you guys said at that meeting in Del Rio? About killing the gringo?"

"We didn't say it," Coco's quick to add, "and the guy who did actually meant . . ."

But by now another kid's reached inside their car and pulled out a shirt stiff with dried blood. He puts it inches from Coco's face, with the fierce, proud smile of someone who passed an initiation rite. The thought immmediately hits me, *Oh, shit, don't tell me these chavos . . .*

"We ran into some gringos at this burger place last night," he begins.

"You didn't *kill* anyone?"

"No," says another boy. He sounds confused, as if wondering whether they failed for not going far enough.

"Good!" Coco almost shouts. "You did good!" He glances at the bloody shirt and corrects himself. "I mean, it's good you didn't kill anyone."

Gabi's mouth gapes. "What happened? Did they pick a fight?"

"Well, we're going in, right? We're wearing some *raza* buttons and these gringos are coming out, right? One of them whispers, 'Ooh, radicals, I'm so scared.' And when we look back, the others have that look they always give us."

The one with the bloody shirt adds, "This time we gave something back. And we took this as a souvenir."

We go through the meeting like it's set with land mines, after Coco warns me in a low voice, "Careful what you say. If anyone leaves here and does serious shit, they'll nail us with inciting to riot." Yet we also know what the new recruits came to hear. Some look so hard-core I even doubt they're drop-outs; they probably spent their childhoods in produce fields here or in Mexico. They're the actual *vatos* we say we're fighting for.

Some weeks later, I mention the incident to Lucio. He stops me cold by saying, "First you tell everyone you're out to make the world safe from gringos. Then you put these kids down for doing what you fantasize about."

I don't admit it, but he has a point. When that kid mentioned "that look they always give us," I understood. And when he brought out his souvenir, I felt repulsed, as if he'd shown me a shrunken head. Yet I also felt a secret, tribal pride. That part of me almost sighed with pleasure at being avenged.

16
Give Me Land and Liberty, or Death by Overdose

After the demonstration in Del Rio, Lizard skips the next few meetings. One afternoon Nacho and I run into him at a gas station, where he invites us to one of his parties that night. We show up expecting half the drug dealers in town, and a few from outside the Valley, and we're not disappointed.

We're barely inside his place when someone offers us a toke. Nacho's isn't about to return to his parents' house stoned, and I have my own reasons for staying straight, so we end up drinking beer.

"I wonder if Villa and Zapata ever had to go through this."

"What?" asks Nacho. "All-night parties?"

"Smoking dope with the locals to get them on their side."

The smoke must be getting to me; I add: "Camilo Cienfuegos killed cats and had Che and the other rebels eat them. Like a test."

"Maybe he hated cats." Nacho sounds like he's getting high too. "Anyway, I'd rather try a dead cat than the *tecata* they're doing in the next room."

"*Heroin?* No wonder they're not pressuring us to smoke. They're too screwed up on the serious stuff. Just remember to give a little nod now and then, and we'll be fine."

My nodding attracts the attention of an exotic woman across the room, but she doesn't acknowledge us until Lizard walks past.

"Tita," he warns her before wandering to another room, "these two are radicals. Don't let them put a protest sign in your hand."

She gives me one of those smoldering glances that people sometimes affect, only her gypsy eyes look like the real thing. "*Tierra y libertad*," she says with a smile, throwing back a slogan we lifted from Zapata. "So, you're one of those."

"No. I'm one of you."

She takes my hand. She feels feverish. I expect her to read my palm, but instead she examines the length of my inner arm. "No, you don't even have a vaccine scar."

"What I meant is that we're both *raza*."

"I'm just teasing." She shoves her own arm a few inches from my face, to where I can almost graze the down on her forearm. Then she tenses it until her veins stand out. "Look. *Ando fuerte*."

When addicts say they're strong it means they're clean, but in Tita's case it's true only in the technical sense. She may be off heroin but she's high on something else. Yet I'm aware only of her delicious animal heat and the animation in her eyes. On that basis she's one healthy specimen. She even has an attractive tan, and when I mention it she takes the compliment in stride: "Usually it's nicer, except I was in the shade."

Suddenly everything falls in place. Clean and out of the sun: She recently did time. Someone with more common sense would be backing off by now, but somehow her remark draws me closer. I try hard to imagine her in prison, and can only picture her making it with another female convict.

Nacho is thinking the same thing. "So, Tita, it must be, uh, lonely in there."

"Listen, *vato*, the last thing I was in there was lonely. We're squeezed in tits to clits."

"I think he means sex."

"Oh, that type of lonely. Well, I'll tell you, you fight the urge, but sooner or later you just fold your arms and open your legs. At that point you tell yourself, *Necesito sexo–dar, o que me den*."

I need sex–giving, or getting. I try to read between the lines: She's dying to make up for lost time with guys? She's dying for a dyke? I look in those eyes again, at once intimate and remote, and I feel I'm by a campfire at night beneath a cold, starlit sky. I'm so tangled up in the thought that I don't ask the obvious. Nacho, though, does. "So what were you in for, Tita?"

She shows us a tattoo on her arm the way some veterans show off their war wounds.

"They locked you up for a tattoo?"

I can sense she's insulted, so I examine the tattoo closer, and I notice that the crossbones underneath the skull are actually hypodermics. She adds in a matter-of-fact boast: "*Chiva y muerte.*"

I'd rather not know the details, but I keep the conversation going. "Heroin and homicide. Hmm. I never knew they had a special category."

Her street sense of survival probably tells her to keep quiet, since she develops a sudden interest in the movement, rambling on until she settles on an issue that, to hear her talk, has caused her sleepless nights: "So tell me, which Chicano band is the best?"

The question throws me off completely. But maybe for *raza* like her this is what the movement boils down to: a battle of the bands. And since we Manos are such outspoken defenders of our culture, who better to ask?

"I don't know," is all I can say. "It depends on how I'm feeling."

She stares at me. After a moment, though, she nods. "Me too. Sometimes I feel like kicking ass, sometimes like getting my own ass kicked. And sometimes I feel like both at once."

I can't place the look in her eyes, I only know it's a place I've never been to and hope I never will. Then she shuts them and does a slow-motion nod, the nostalgic reflex of ex-addicts.

After a while one of her girlfriends comes up and whispers something. She gets up, then takes my palm and writes her phone number on it with a red pen, pressing so hard it feels like I'm getting a tattoo of my own.

On our way home Nacho asks whether I'm going to call her.

"You think I should?"

"No. She's mainline trouble. But you'll call her anyway."

"Shit, you'd do the same thing."

"That's why I can read you like a book."

"Speaking of books, something tells me she gave me the number of some funeral home from the phone book."

Nacho's nod shows he's been on the receiving end of a similar prank.

Naturally I call her the next day, after checking the Yellow Pages for funeral home listings. The motel clerk who answers sounds annoyed when I ask him to ring her room.

"She left this morning without checking out," he says, "and without settling her bill. Are you a friend of hers?"

"No, nothing like that." I half-expected a weird scenario with Tita at some point, although not as early as this. Still, I'm prepared enough to improvise. "In fact, we're after her too."

"You are? You a cop?"

"Uh . . . special squad. Heroin and homicide."

"You hesitated."

"We're undercover."

He's absolutely quiet for a moment. "Anyway, call us in a couple of days. We might have something," I say. I give him a number from the open phone book in front of me, of a funeral home in the barrio.

17
Number One's Not Enough

When Lizard shows up for our next meeting, something he hasn't done in weeks, Nacho decides he's simply returning our social call. I prefer to think he's getting back on track, and my hunch grows after hearing his brief but effective speech to several new high school students.

Much of our time with these kids is spent talking about things like how to deal with a teacher or student who starts mouthing off against our *raza*. Lizard stresses to them that, while we can give them some pointers, ultimately they have to fend for themselves. He offers a few experiences from his own tour in Nam. "Back there you had to look out for number one, same thing you have to do here. Because when it's you versus the enemy, there's only one person you can depend on: Number One."

He adds more examples until a quiet kid raises his hand and asks timidly: "Who's Number One?"

For a moment there's an uneasy silence, and even one or two other faces who thought they already knew the answer don't seem that sure anymore. But before everyone else starts to smile and snicker, Lizard fields his question so matter-of-factly that no one dares ridicule the kid.

The following day, I remark to Coco that we're getting another good organizer in our barrio. Coco frowns in concentration, then gives up. "Who?"

"Lizard."

"Are you serious, De la O?"

"Look, I know he's been hit-or-miss lately, but he's starting to get his shit together."

"Get it together? It's been running out of his mouth. The last time he was here he was ranting like a madman. Not even the Town Crier could figure him out."

"What was he saying?" I ask.

"He was quoting someone. Naturally he was higher than a crow. He was going on and on about living dangerously. Jesus! He's already up to his eyeballs in drugs, and there's talk he's smuggled guns into Mexico. How much more danger does he want?"

"He's a tightrope walker."

"*Tightrope walker* is right. He was already so high he kept saying he was Superman."

"I gave him some stuff to read."

"You gave him comic books?"

"No. Zarathustra."

"Sara *who?*"

"It's philosophy. *Real* philosophy, not stuff from the movement." Coco couldn't care less about Nietzsche, so I simply add that Zarathustra was born laughing.

"Well, that sums up Lizard's own philosophy. The few times he's been at a meeting, he sits back and makes fun of everyone in the room. It's not loud, but it's disruptive."

"But he's starting to change."

"Oh, like last night?"

Obviously Coco was not impressed by Lizard's speech. Yet I add that while we could have been more articulate, we wouldn't have had the same authority.

"Authority? Is that why one of the kids offered him a joint afterwards?"

"That's the point. They'd never ask me, much less you." I let the barb sink in to puncture his fantasy as an organizer of the masses.

"Well, take when that kid at the end asked who number one was. Maybe that's why Lizard's answer didn't impress me. The question was dumb to begin with."

"Look, Coco, most kids in the barrio don't have the chance to pick up on Anglo slang. They don't have our books or opportunities . . ." I try guiding his gaze around the office, but he won't follow, so I take a more personal tack. "Anyway, there's not much difference between asking, 'Who's Number One?' and 'Sara who?'"

I even add something I'm a bit embarrassed to admit: Lucio, Pablo, and I used to read a little of Freud but weren't sure how to pronounce his name. I wasn't about to ask my high school teachers for fear they'd gasp and say, "You mean you don't *know?*"

"Maybe it wasn't the kid's question that bothered me," Coco interrupts, "as much as Lizard's reply. Here we're working toward a common goal, then Lizard tells this kid to screw everyone else. Kids like that are already ripe for selfishness. Never had a damn thing . . . Suddenly, with a little money, they're worse than gringos."

There's some truth in what he says. The drug dealers I've met through Lizard all fall into two categories: Either they've been amoral, psychopathic parasites from the start, or else they started as insecure kids who, with a little status, quickly turned into tyrants.

Maybe that explains my friendship with Lizard. He's wavering between two worlds, protester and parasite, and I'd like to tip the scales to our side, just for the satisfaction of signing him up. Of course, in the company of other dealers he's quick to disown our cause.

"So you think Lizard's finally growing up?"

"He grew up and got old already, in Nam."

"You know what I mean." He stuffs some papers into an accordion folder for a meeting with some *colonia* organizers. "Maybe we'll make a Marxist of him yet."

I get the feeling he's saying it mostly to mend the fences of our own friendship. But I also catch him glancing at a poster of Che, so I answer, "Just like our friend Guevara."

He reaches the door, then looks back with a strained smile. "Keep an eye on Lizard. And keep him off drugs."

I have enough as it is staying away from them myself, though—especially around Lizard.

18
Saint Che and Other Icons

It's easy to see why Coco idolizes Che. His image appears everywhere—at militant rallies, in radical magazines, on posters—a black inkblot against a red background, combining communism and Christmas. He's the socialist Santa. Joy to the Third World. Then there's that other poster of a stark black-and-white photo, equally at home on a fashion magazine as on an album cover, sporting a Beat beard and long hair long before it became the rage.

The Catholic students from the Newman Center respond to that stare. "Say," they'll ask us, "who's he?"

"Che," we answer: "He was killed in the jungles of South America, fighting for the poor."

Che Guevara. The name says it all: He's one of us. By the time they realize he's not Chicano, the nickname's already done its number. So we tell ourselves there's a hint of Indian in his sparse mustache, the same pattern on paintings of two other cultural icons, Cauhtemoc and Juan Diego. He's our ultimate Rorshach. We see in him whatever we want to. Roque draws his eyes somewhat slanted; he could pass for Zapata's cousin. He also tans him up like a lifelong migrant. "But he wasn't dark," insists Loza, who's one of us even though he's pushing forty. "He was pale as any Anglo."

"Of course he's pale," says Gabi. "He's been dead since 'sixty-seven."

"I mean when he was alive. Plus, he had this high voice. I knew him, you know."

Coco smiles as if to say, Yes, we all know. And while his radical ideas don't quite mesh with Loza's military demeanor, even Coco seems a bit envious that Loza actually got to meet his hero.

Gabi hit the nail on the head, though: Che's dead, enshrined in amber. Die relatively young and in the line of duty, and you're headed for socialist sainthood. It helps if you leave a good-looking corpse, or at least news photos of one. It helps that Che got an endorsement from Jean-Paul Sartre, who's into revolutionary fantasies like the rest of us.

Lucio's fantasy of Che fits into his own lifestyle: "Now seriously, De la O, you can't tell me he and Castro weren't getting stoned in the Sierra." Some day I'll have to pose that question to Loza, whose anecdotes of Che lean towards the critical. That's fine with the rest of us, along with Loza's tendency to show up for a while, then go underground. These quirks keep his accounts from becoming sacharine or getting stale. His occasional anecdotes give us the illusion that we're linked to a larger struggle, without having to put our own life or liberty on the line.

One morning, though, I end up a little closer to that reality. I'm between classes—although I'm skipping non-honors classes so often that it's more a figure of speech—sitting in the student union with Lizard and a few other friends, when my cousin Niche shows up. He's a high school dropout and about the last person I'd expect to see here. His assorted tattoos and gold incisor convince Baby's friends at a nearby table to keep a close eye on their purses.

I feel somewhat on the spot but also enjoy the attention. The other students imagine us Manos as hanging around with the salt of the barrio, and you can't get much saltier than Niche. He doesn't mind the scrutiny either. Some *vatos* feel insecure around college students and go out of their way to act tough, but not Niche. Maybe he's too stoned to care. He even flirts with a co-ed at the next table, then acknowledges Lizard with a nod that seems to say, It's a small world.

I'm wondering what brought him here: It's as bizarre as having my mother show up with my lunch. Finally he leans over and mentions something about a deal we Manos can't pass up. Baby and her party start straining their ears in our direction, so I take him outside.

"Now what's this all about?" This is what I get for trying to mix college, the movement and a bit of *la vida loca*.

Niche, though, seems in no hurry to get down to business. He looks around and asks in awe, "*Chingado*, cousin, how many students you have here?"

"Oh, about five thousand."

"I thought I'd never find you. I asked for De la O, but nobody knew you. I said you were this walking encyclopedia, but still nothing. Then I mentioned your hair and bingo! Not that many around here, eh?"

I comment that long hair is as rare around here as his tattoos. I also ask where he's parked, and he points to the administration lot. "That's the only place that had space. I had no idea so many people went to college."

"You mean you parked in a reserved space? Was there some lettering on it?"

"Shit, there's lettering everywhere. You college guys love—"

"Jesus, Niche, I hope you didn't park in some dean's space."

"What'll they do? Kick me out of college?" His gold incisor gleams for an instant. "I'll just say I'm making a delivery."

His car, a battered, lipstick-red convertible, stands out like it had BUST-ME license plates. I'm hurrying to get us out when Roque yells for us to wait. It's obvious from his labored breathing that he followed us from the snack bar and is determined to tag along. No sooner do we leave campus than he strikes up a conversation with Niche. "So, you're a De la O too?"

"That's right, except I spell the O different."

Roque glances at me to see if he's being put on. "How's that?"

"With a small 'o'."

Niche turns on that gleaming smile, and Roque returns it without understanding much except why he thinks Niche's here. "So . . . that talk back there, about a deal we couldn't pass up . . ."

"He's one of you guys?" Niche asks me.

"One of our best, believe it or not."

Roque's too tenacious to let the teasing throw him off the scent. "So . . . You got any samples?"

"Let's wait till we get to my friend's ranch. It's a half-hour away. The real stuff is there."

"A half-hour is a long ways away. You have anything in the meantime?"

Niche reaches under his seat, the same way Lizard does, and pulls out what seem like a few fat joints. It's not until he plops them in my hand that I realize they're bullets—enormous ones, the kind you'd kill caribou with. Roque's still dying to see, so I toss a cartridge over my shoulder. "Here, light one up and blow your mind."

"What the *fuck*?"

"You guys are always talking about revolution," says Niche. "But you can't start one without weapons. My friend can help you out."

"You mean with stuff like *this*?" says Roque. The ammunition looks so menacing you don't even have to shoot it; throwing it's enough.

"That's what those gringos deserve, right?" He raises a fist: Our message is getting through.

We head outside the city limits, even past agricultural fields, until we're out in cattle country. Other than an occasional GOATS FOR SALE sign, we see only stray dogs that were dumped out here and somehow survived.

Niche's friend has an odd home, an Anglo ranch-style house with a miniature junkyard out front, like the landscaping that *raza* in lean-to homes have. He has the same schizoid taste in clothes: exotic-skin boots under second-hand overalls. We follow the friend out to the back acres, past a couple of expensive pick-ups and a four-wheel drive. I'd figure he'd have them out front instead of the junked cars, unless he has something to hide.

When we reach the end of a caliche path he gets out and pretends to survey a herd of distant goats. Gazing in the distance, he asks Niche, "What did your friends here have in mind?"

"The small one like me is my cousin."

The man glances towards a herd of cattle. "Minor livestock? Or major?"

"Let's start with the small-caliber stuff," says Niche.

The man walks to a nearby shed and returns with two automatic rifles. He jams a cartridge clip into each, chambers a round, then hands me one as calmly as if culling a kid goat I'm buying for a family feast. He could probably pull the trigger on the second rifle before I could pull out a badge. On the other hand, I think, he might be a narc himself; just last month we discovered that a guy provoking us to jump on cars at the Del Rio rally was ATF: Alcohol, Tobacco, and Firearms. The possibility scares me as much as this guy being a real gunrunner. It's all I can do to hold the gun steady.

He invites me to fire a few rounds, pointing with his chin to a stray mutt staring from a nearby irrigation ditch.

Roque echoes my own sentiments: "Shit, talk about being in the wrong place at the wrong time."

I take my time, pretending to get a careful bead, then shake my head. "What if somebody hears us?"

He seems puzzled. "Who? Other strays?"

Niche, dying to shoot, grabs the gun and walks a few yards out for a better shot. He sights in a pair of animals in the horizon, and before I can say anything there's a burst of pain like something drilling its way out of my skull. What startles me even more, though, is the sight of Niche yanked off his feet for a second or so. He's actually lifted off the ground then droppped like a human piñata. He returns with the maniacal grin of a survivor, a rollercoaster rider ready for another round.

"I didn't even come close to popping those dogs! That's how fucked up I am!"

"I think they're somebody's goats, Niche."

"Christ, cousin! I'm more tortilla than I thought!"

Roque grabs the gun like a kid impatient for his turn with a toy. By now the guy has figured we're not exactly seasoned guerrillas on an arms-buying spree. Still, I don't want to insult him, so I promise to consult with our top Manos. By the time we're ready to leave, Niche is boasting he can get us a tank from the National Guard armory in his *barrio*.

I give his friend a sheepish smile. "I don't think we're ready for tanks yet."

"No problem," says Niche. "You can stash it here on the ranch." His friend agrees so seriously that he has to be humoring Niche. Or at least I hope so.

"I could rent you a few back acres. Just keep the damn thing camouflaged in the brush."

On the way back Niche goes out of his way to relate to the movement, even though we'll never see his ass at one of our meetings or demonstrations. "I've been reading your newspapers, cousin. I even thought of shortening Niche to Che, but my girlfriend says my last name's already too short."

"I'm sure if Che were alive, he'd be honored."

Niche almost lets go the wheel. "He's *dead?* Are you *shitting* me?" For a guy who moments before was intermediary to an arms deal, he takes the news hard. "*When?*"

"He was killed a couple of years ago," says Roque, "helping peasants in South America."

The new information quickly sobers him. "Getting your ass killed . . . I don't know if I'd go that far." What he does do is give us a long speech about how things are so tough that he's forced to sell dope. "I mean, what else can a poor boy do, cousin?"

I feel like saying he could get an honest job instead of ending up another parasite like Lizard's buddies. But I don't say anything because I recognize his rhetoric: It's distorted, but the source is us.

He drops us off at the MANO office. No sooner am I inside than I examine slowly our posters of Che, Pancho Villa in bandoliers, and a Black Panther wearing a beret and cradling a shotgun. Then I glance at one I've never looked at much because it seemed unassuming and somehow out of place. It's Cesar Chavez, the farmworker organizer: no guns, no berets, no revolution, just the courage of his convictions.

19
Love So Heavy It Hurts to Lift

Roque's come up with some artwork for our next newspaper, but Coco's not satisfied with his drawings for Rosa's article on *soldaderas* of the Mexican Revolution. Something is missing.

For his part Roque points to a voluptuous Adelita on a Mexican calendar. "Why does everyone think all *revolucionarias* looked like Raquel Welch?"

Coco shows Roque his drawings. "Yours are the other extreme. They look like . . ." He looks my way. "Like De la O in drag."

As I see it, the source of the bickering is our Manos-without-women existence. At first living here at the center seemed like the best of both worlds: On your own, but also working with other Manos. I figured we'd be around Manas too, what with Rosa and the rest running the center. But since we've agreed to stay out of their way for most of the day, we see little of the women, and when we do return they can't wait to get home and rest.

The so-called revolutionary life has turned into another routine, and when we get together to crank out a newspaper, it comes close to a cloistered life. Marcos, during one of his visits, comments that the center is starting to smell of celibacy.

"What did Marcos mean?" Gabi asks me afterwards.

"He meant we've been hanging around Coco so long he's starting to look good."

Marcos suggests we go out and recruit new members from the Catholic center on campus. Since several of the Manas originally started there, we quickly catch the drift. That same week we arrange a joint meeting at their campus center.

Halfway through the meeting, a trio of tall *chavas* walks in late and with nervous smiles. Their shared attractiveness suggests they're related; what's more, it also strikes me as vaguely familiar. They hunker next to Luli and Rosa in a way that works against their efforts to remain inconspicuous and only ends up calling attention to their size.

Throughout the meeting I keep glancing their way, especially at the one with the blackest hair. Even from a distance, it's obvious she's one big girl. At first I put on the psychological elevator shoes that's part of every short Chicano's wardrobe: Everything evens out in bed. But the minute the meeting's over and she comes closer, my floating heart sinks to my knees. She's too big for me, period. A tall order is one thing, an insurmountable one is another.

Roque takes one look at her face and, like me, he's a goner. But he's not intimidated by her dimensions. If anything, her size is an asset in his eyes. He likes them on the hefty side. "If I can lift her I don't want her" is his motto. Since he's on the heavy side himself, he's talking serious tonnage.

So when Luli starts guiding the trio toward us, he practically pushes me in front. "Come on, De la O, it's now or never."

"Why should *I* go?" I say.

"To help me do the talking."

I know what he means, and I hate it. My friends and cousins used to drag me in front of others then demand, "Say something smart." Besides, it's one thing to bullshit people with information, but it's quite another to come up with a come-on line that doesn't sound corny, and then to say it to a lovely woman's face.

So at the last second, when we're face to face, I fall back on the lamest line in the world. "So, Luli, aren't you going to introduce these lovely women?"

It works, though, because Luli would never expect me to say it. It sounds like something Lizard would say, and if he had, she'd be grinning in his face. Roque picks up the conversation, so I say little after that. What I do mostly is look at the girl, who's introduced as Alma. One of her upper front teeth is crooked, something most attractive women would either fix or conceal. Instead she smiles spontaneously and without a shred of self-consciousness.

When she and Roque hit it off I feel a pang or two of regret, but I'm glad she's interested in another Mano. And while I can't say that Roque's like a brother, I'm glad he's pairing up with a *chava* as nice as her. Like many of the Catholic kids, she comes from a better-off family; even the ones who live in the barrio often live in the nicer homes. They're also hooked on the idea that helping one's fellow man is a duty.

One of the other new girls asks whether Luli called me De la O. When I answer yes, she explains, "Our cousin knows you."

"We almost talked her into coming," says Alma. "But that Nena's always busy reading."

"*Nena?*"

I start describing the *chava* who told me about Quixote, and soon realize I'm describing some of the same physical features in her cousins. That's why their faces looked familiar. Alma agrees to bring her next time.

True to her word, Alma brings her along the following week. Nena also shows up at another Catholic center meeting a couple of weeks later. When we invite anyone who's interested to attend our own MANO meeting later that week, Alma shows up-she and Roque are now almost always together-but Nena doesn't. I drop by her apartment every now and then, but I don't ask why she didn't join us, nor does she bring up the issue.

Still, we become good friends. She's decided to minor in Spanish, so she's reading Latin American writers. At first I'm able to keep up with her, but soon it's obvious she's much deeper into it than I'll ever be. She confesses that a few of the Mexican students sometimes bullshit their way through without reading much, simply because they're more fluent.

Soon after Alma and the other Catholic students start helping us, things start to change around the office. Marcos calls them Manas from Heaven. Coco appreciates the work they do, but he's worried about their influence on Roque's art style. Roque's female figures no longer swing between brunettes with outrageous curves and scrawny Third World transvestites. Now they look like a cross between the models on Soviet posters—Russian tanks, Nacho calls them—and the stocky specimens on Mexican murals. I don't know much about art, but it's not hard to see that Roque's new style has been influenced by Alma: Massive and proletariat.

Picking up Roque's most recent sketch, Coco says to no one in particular:

"What the hell is this?"

"It's a woman," says Rosa. "You never saw one before?"

"I mean we need somebody slim. Not some big mama."

Sandra, who's well on her way to becoming a big mama herself, overhears the remark and calls Coco on it. "What have you got against big mamas?"

Coco looks at the six other *chavos* in the office, expecting us to save him, but we act as if we didn't hear the remark. "I meant big Manas."

"Those too," says Rosa. "That's even closer to home."

He pretends to study Roque's illustrations again. "Well . . . if that's what you all want . . ."

He glances at us again, but I'm not about to join his doomed cause. Coco seems to balance for a while following his false step, then he takes another, more timid one. "So I guess that's what everyone wants . . ."

"Do you hear anyone else complaining?" says Sandra. She ends the discussion: "That's what we want, then."

20
Chiches on Che

The spring semester's almost over when Luli asks whether Nacho and I would like to work in Michigan for the summer. "A Chicano who's directing a program out of Lansing needs some activists he can trust. He says some of the growers are ripping off farmworkers. He asked me to look around, and since you guys work well together . . ."

"We've been friends since high school," says Nacho. "And both of us were migrants."

Nacho quickly picks up the scent of money, even before Luli adds that we'd be investigating civil rights abuses for the state. We take her up on the offer almost at once. The following week she calls up the project director and we close the deal over the phone.

What I like about Luli is that she expects nothing in return, except that I cut my hair and shave my beard. "It's a state job," she explains, almost embarrassed. I can live with the trade-off, since it'll mean some summer money and a trip out of state.

We don't even talk again until after an evening meeting, when she and a few other Manas linger at one end of the office to discuss their own agenda. Most of the other Manos have left except for Inti, who's telling his brother about his problems organizing in their home town. Coco, though, appears distracted by the Manas' conversation across the room. His interest becomes contagious, until the rest of us are keeping one ear on the women. Finally Inti speaks up: "What's the problem?"

"No problem," says Luli, "but since you asked . . . we were checking out the posters on the walls and wondering when we'll have someone to relate to."

Inti obviously regrets having asked, but since he's already set out the complaint box he points to several posters in the room. "There's Che, Cesar, Zapata. Take your pick."

"That's the trouble. They've already been picked for us."

"Meaning?"

"Meaning they're all men," says Sandra.

Coco's either truly perplexed or else blinded by the urge to come to his brother's defense. "So they're men. What's wrong with that?"

"Nothing, if you're a man. But what about the women in the movement? Where are they?"

"You're right here, in front of me."

Luli nods. "*We* don't get *credit*."

"Neither do I," says Coco. "You don't see my face on those posters."

Alma barely stifles a smile. "Well, you're no Che."

"What's that mean?"

"Don't take it personally, Coco. I'm just saying you're no Che," says Alma. "We're not talking about our own faces up there. What we're saying is that Chicanas aren't being recognized for what we are."

Inti, seeing his brother outnumbered, sides with him. "And what exactly are you?"

"Adelitas," says Rosa.

"Now, ladies," says Coco, straight-faced, "you're not past your prime. There's no reason to call yourself *abuelitas* yet."

"Not grandmothers! We mean the women in the Mexican Revolution. In the morning they'd fight alongside the men, and in the evening cook dinner."

"You're no Adelitas," laughs Inti. "You can't even make tortillas."

"Neither can you." Luli thumps Inti's ample stomach. "You can sure put them away, though."

Coco looks for a cigarette, a bad habit he's picked up recently, but ends up nibbling on a strip of Scotch tape. "Fine, then. You can put up whatever posters you want."

She shrugs. "It's a start."

No sooner do they leave than Coco tears a fresh strip from the tape dispenser. "As if I don't get enough grief from you guys." He gazes at his poster of Che. "Hell, why not just put tits on Che? It wouldn't make a damn difference. He'd still be Che, even with forty-inch *chiches*." He turns to me with an exasperation that would make Freud proud. "What's their problem?"

"What the hell does De la O know about women?" Inti interrupts.

"He's studying psychology."

"So he knows about perverts. But how come women aren't all over his ass?"

"Maybe I don't want women all over my ass. At least not like they were all over yours just now."

Coco's still looking at me for an answer, and I'm tempted to tell him he'll take that question to the grave, unanswered. Instead I say, "They want the same thing we want."

Inti snorts. "You mean *pussy?*"

Gabi smiles and shakes his head. "They already have a monopoly on that."

Roque is on my wavelength. "No, they just want recognition."

"We share the work," says Coco, looking at us for agreement.

Roque nods, but not for the reasons Coco thinks. "Oh, we let Rosa and the others do more than their share of the shitwork. But the minute some outsider has a question, he'll ignore her and come directly to you. Or even me, even though she's paying for this damn office."

Before Coco can fit his other foot in his mouth, I add, "And don't think outsiders come to you because of your charisma, Coco. It's because we act like Luli doesn't matter around here."

"Except when some guy wants to put the moves on her," says Roque.

I understand Coco's reluctance. It's no different from our demands that Anglos treat us fairly. Some survival instinct tells some gringos it's the beginning of the end of the good old days.

A few days later Julia, Rosa and Luli bring by their first poster. Julia takes it out of the tube while the rest of us crowd around it. "Lolita Labon," she says, "a Puerto Rican nationalist."

Before Coco commits himself, he wants more information. "This lady . . ."

"Lolita," Julia repeats. "Lolita Labon."

"What's her claim to fame?"

"She helped carry out an assassination attempt in the House."

"What house?" asks Inti, and the Manas smile again.

"'What house?'" Julia imitates him. "The House of Representatives."

"In *Washington? Really? When?*"

"The fifties. Before anyone even knew of Che."

"An assassination plot! Against *who?*"

"Who was in the House?" says Rosa. "The same gringos we're fight-ing. She wanted Puerto Rico free."

It's hard to tell if the Paredes brothers are actually listening or only looking for a loophole. Inti finally says, "Puerto Rican? Then she's not Chicana?"

Luli groans, then points out posters on the wall. "Well, Che wasn't very Chicano either, was he? Neither was Zapata, for that matter. And that black guy in that poster, sitting on a peacock chair and holding a spear . . ."

"Oh," Julia says, "he's *raza*, all right."

The Paredes brothers raise both hands at the same time. "Fine," says Coco. "Bring anything else you want."

I'm already wondering how he'll explain Lolita's claim to fame to our middle-of-the-road fellow travelers, like the farmworker organizers who pride themselves on patriotism and pacifism. Coco probably assumes the other posters won't be as radical and will help camouflage this one. If that's his strategy, the next few days prove him right. Still, one thing puz-zles him: "How do they find so much stuff?"

"The same way we find stuff on Chicanos when teachers and librar-ians tell us there's nothing out there. We go out and look for it," I say.

Alma can't find a poster so she brings in an old photo of one of her grand-aunts and tapes it to the wall. She was a *curandera* and *partera*, Alma explains, a healer and midwife who worked in this very barrio. Other than that, she knows little else about her. The picture speaks for itself, though: There's an intensity in the gaze that makes Che's poster look like the posed publicity shot it probably was. After Alma leaves I look long and close at the photo for some clue to the old woman's per-sonality.

Finally I walk away with a feeling I've never had from those glossy posters of Che or Huey or even Zapata—a sense of awe, of knowing that she once walked the same streets I now walk. It's not until I'm out the door that I realize the most mysterious thing of all: Her tracks begin and end with that photo. Nobody thought her life important enough to record it.

Suddenly all our abstractions about oppression, about the need to unearth our own history—everything comes down to this intimate yet anonymous loss.

21
Working Within the Windmills

A week before Nacho and I leave for Michigan, Luli offers some suggestions. Her family used to do migrant work there, so she knows the area. She adds that some other Manos are working up there as well, and says, "If you run into Gabi, give him a big hug."

The bus trip lasts a full two days. By the time we reach Lansing, Nacho's constipated and my stomach's messed up from all the snacking along the way. While waiting for our boss to pick us up at the station, Nacho tries to second-guess his expectations.

"What if he's expecting a couple of really hard-core militants?"

"The guy's a bureaucrat. Getting real radicals is the last thing he wants."

Our supervisor seems overly energetic but otherwise decent. I suppose we pass his test too, since his most pressing question is, "So you guys are really migrants?"

It's a throw-away question, but we manage to screw it up. Nacho says, "Yes," at the same time I say, "No."

"I mean not anymore," I say adding, "Maybe when Luli said we'd be doing field work, she meant the real kind."

Perhaps it's too soon for that sort of humor, but he smiles anyway as he lights his pipe. His Spanish has the limits of someone who's heard it sporadically and used it even less. At first we're a little uncomfortable talking to him, especially after Nacho flubs his lines at the bus station: "Well, let's go pick up our buggage."

I barely keep from laughing out loud. Afterwards Nacho mutters, "Oh, fuck. What's this guy going to think?"

"Forget it. When it comes to Spanish we can run cirlces around his ass."

That may be true, but we're not running in the same circles. We're in his territory, doing things by his rules, and speaking English is one of them. It takes some getting used to, since mixing English with Spanish in the same sentence is second nature to us.

We'll be staying with our boss and his wife for the duration of our training, until we're assigned to the field. It's Saturday, and I intend to rest despite the numbness in my butt. My supervisor, with his overweight frame, seems the ideal host for that. I can even picture him reaching for beer and munchies in front of the TV. But he has different plans: After introducing us to the third field worker, his brother-in-law, who's our age, he takes us to a basketball court adjacent to his apartment and runs us ragged. I first figure it's some sort of initiation rite or to test our stamina, so I go along, but the following afternoon he's ready for more of the same. As far as I'm concerned, though, laying low on the Lord's day is Christianity's best contribution, so I beg off. Come Monday evening, after a full day of training and paperwork, he trots us out again.

"I can't take any more of this shit." Nacho, who's still constipated, means it literally. "It feels like I'm bouncing an extra basketball in my belly."

"Do what I'm doing, then. Sit out the stupid games."

"And make him even more paranoid? Come on . . . Don't give me that innocent look, De la O. Come on, this is Nacho. I see that young, good-looking wife as well as anyone else."

The truth is that although she's attractive, she doesn't give us the slightest come-on, which is why I feel comfortable with her. Besides, I'd much rather be around her than bumping against some sweaty idiots.

"I understand," Nacho says after hearing me out. "But when you stay inside all he does is stare at the apartment."

"Then he should spend more time with her instead of pretending he's still a teenager."

After our last training session our boss introduces us to a group of social workers we might see in the field. His speech, our going-away pep talk, is full of revolutionary bluster that would make a Black Panther blush.

"I picked these young men because they're migrants and because they're radicals." He didn't handpick us personally, we're no longer migrants, and his brother-in-law isn't even an activist. Then he ticks off for the audience all the things he expects us to do, even fighting for farmworkers and helping to organize them.

At one point his own brother-in-law whispers to us, "Say, was that on the job description?"

I don't know what's got into our boss. Maybe the audience—attractive, professional do-gooders, and almost all female—is making him exaggerate. Or maybe someone spiked the punch. Or maybe I underestimated the job; maybe Luli was right to build us up. That certainly seems the case when he ends with: "And if a few migrant camps must burn to protest living conditions, I'm sure my men will resign and do what's necessary."

Seeing the awe on the women's faces, I'm ready to burn them now. Yet I also know that if he so much as expressed that thought in Texas, he'd have to answer to a court of law. But we're not in Texas, which is why he's saying it.

Although his speech is entertaining it's also embarrassing. I keep quiet, though. Besides, a little hype never hurt anyone around the opposite sex, something that Nacho's already aware of. Toward the end he mumbles that several of the gringa social workers seem "friendly to animals."

During the mingling that follows, though, I somehow end up talking to one of the few male case workers. His name's Michael, and he volunteers for a farmworkers' support group on weekends, handing out flyers at supermarkets and such. His boycott buttons are the first thing Nacho notices, adding, "So this guy's going to help us burn some camps?"

We three become such fast friends that even after Nacho gives me a last-call look as the women start to thin out, we stick together. Actually it's not a bad move, since he's on good terms with several women there, and a new friend in a strange place can save a lot of looking around. We'll also be in Lansing every other Friday, so a place to crash other than our supervisor's apartment wouldn't hurt.

Before we're dispatched to opposite corners of the state, our boss gushes out some more revolutionary blessings. By now I'm certain someone spiked the punch. Stepping into our state cars in the harsh afternoon sun, I have an unsettling, momentary image of kamikaze pilots sent off in a glorious blaze of speeches and *sake*. Not that our state cars strike fear in the hearts of whites. While waiting for a light an elderly couple in the next lane examines the state insignia on the door with intense curiosity. I stare straight ahead, even when the old lady lowers her window for a better look.

"It's a deer," she reports. "And the boy looks Mexican."

It's not the state seal or my being "Mexican" that mystifies them, but the thought that the two don't go together. Right before the light turns green she adds: "Maybe he's from Parks and Wildlife."

Great, I think. I'm Browny the Bear.

After a few days on the job I'm almost ready to agree with her. I've been assigned to the southeast corner of the state because of its concentration of migrant workers. The countryside and cool days soften the squalor of the camps, and watching the workers pick cherries or strawberries, I almost forget how tiring field work can be. But when I visit families at the end of the day—my compromise with the growers who've cooperated—I find men lying exhausted on cots and women dragging their feet to make dinner. Even the children prefer to play indoors, having been outside all day.

My job consists of getting permission to enter migrant camps, singling out a few families and getting some facts and figures on their earnings. But I carry about as much clout as Smokey the Bear. The state car helps, but my skin color doesn't, at least not with the Anglos. Whenever I pull up to a grower's house, there's usually an initial, uneasy glance at the emblem, but the moment I step out the lines are already drawn: I look like their workers. After several attempts to ease their suspicions, I've given up trying to seem neutral. I'm exactly what they think I am, an advocate for the underdog. That's why I'm here, to see whether migrants are getting the shaft when it comes to Social Security.

The moment I mention I'm collecting data on this, most farmers start squirming, although a few are already old hands at passing the buck. "These people aren't my workers. You'll have to talk to their crew boss." Sometimes they'll add, "He's Mexican, like them," meaning that if he's fucking them over, what's wrong with an Anglo getting sloppy seconds?

If there's no crew boss, the answer goes, "I just have a few families, and the fathers contract under a piece rate, so they're self-employed. Suits them fine, too. The harder they work, the more money they make. That's how they want it."

They almost always have a grudging respect for the families, whom they call Mexican. Soon I'm calling myself Mexican too. It's easier than reinventing the tortilla by explaining what Chicano means. Those growers who don't have a good word to say are likely the owners of stag labor camps that are little more than shacks and an outhouse, as grim as anything in the Third World.

Getting past the grower is the first hurdle, but his crew boss can be just as difficult. "The boss doesn't want anyone trespassing his property."

"I already have his permission."

Suddenly the same man who disclaimed any authority says, "These are my workers. They come home tired and here you want . . ."

"Fine. I'll just report that to the state."

I don't like taking advantage of their ignorance any more than I enjoy intimidating the workers with my state credentials, but sometimes that's what it takes. At other times it's hard to tell the good guys from the bad. What do you say to a father of five who insists he can't afford to have Social Security taken from his family's wages?

"But *señor*, what about when you're too old to work?"

He points to his children. "Then it'll be their turn to support me. Besides, the crew boss tells me that all of us would have to pay this Social Security. This way we both come out ahead."

It's hard to argue when there's a good chance he'll drop dead before reaching retirement. We both know this, having attended family funerals where the deceased was barely past his forties yet where no one suggested he died before his time. You have only to look at the corpse, worn down by hard work. Those who do survive into old age, gnarled and grizzled, often end up working alongside their grandchildren in the fields. Yet for those grandchildren—young, strong, driving souped-up pickups gleaming with chrome—life could be much worse. Like middle-class kids, they believe it will always be spring. They're all wrong, but for the migrant workers there's a brutal difference: Their seasons pass much faster.

During our first weekend meetings in Lansing all three of us in the field point out how everyone passes the buck when it comes to Social Security. Our supervisor promises to do something, but soon it's obvious he's content merely to document the abuses. I urge him several times to help the elderly workers in some way, adding that my motives are partly selfish. "They fill out our forms because they think we can help them. I can't go back day after day without offering anything."

My supervisor draws on his pipe. "Well, we can't help everyone."

"I'm not out to help everyone. All I want is to help just one person. Besides ourselves, I mean."

"Well, it's your job. Take it or leave it."

His response surprises and disappoints me after his speech at the start. Later, Nacho advises me, "Let it ride. It's just a job." He insists we finish the summer with as much money and as little grief as possible: Why turn every trip into a crusade? Look, when I told my father about this job he said it was time we got something back from the cause. Besides, when they hired us, you yourself said they wanted something in return."

I decide to spend the weekend at Michael's place. I mention what's been bothering me, and he listens with a furrowed brow.

"It's not just the growers," I confess. "I'm also upset at the *chavos* who spend their weekends shining the chrome on their pickups, trying to outdo each other. I know, I know: That's the only bright spot in their lives. But if this is what they'll spend their lives caring about, why help them get it? Besides, it's hard to look a grower in the eye when he compares his so-so pickup to several new ones in the camp. He won't be joining them in the Valley after the harvest season, in the dumps they live in the rest of the year, but you expect people to make choices and face the consequences."

"Like deciding it's more important to buy chrome wheels than finishing high school?"

I nod my head firmly. "Maybe my boss is right. Maybe I should just quit."

Michael decides to change the subject. "Some friends are in charge of a Lutheran summer camp about an hour from here. They're in between sessions, so tonight they're having a dance for the migrant workers in the area. You'd like the place. Cabins in the woods, next to a lake."

I don't dance, but I accept the invitation anyway, and when we get there I'm glad I did. Michael introduces me to a slender, dark girl who's staying there and doing volunteer work in the nearby migrant camps. She could pass for Chicana if it weren't for the way she pronounces words in a pursed-up way, the English equivalent of proper, Castillian Spanish.

"She's your well-off JAP, all right," Michael explains after she's on the dance floor. "And she's the first to admit it."

Confused, I answer that while she doesn't seem like a typical gringa, she certainly doesn't look Japanese.

"I meant a Jewish American Princess, De la O."

I nod quickly to save face. I remember the phrase from magazines and television, but it's not one my friends and family would know.

"Then what's she doing at a Lutheran summer camp?"

"Looking to make life interesting."

Afterwards I walk her to her cabin. In no time at all we're into the sticky-fingers stage, but that's as far as we go. It's not until the next morning, as I'm about to leave, that she hints she's partial to guys who don't take no for an answer.

Naturally I'm back the following weekend like an eager kid at camp. Once more I can't get past her protests. When it comes down to it, getting pussy by being pushy is no better than begging for it. Maybe she thinks I'm dying to get at her just because she's Anglo, or maybe she's the same way with Anglo guys. Either way, I've decided not to find out.

But the trip is worth it. The summer camp is still between sessions, and I enjoy rowing us out to a tiny island in the middle of the lake. In one of our conversations, I find out she knows Marcos. "He and some other Chicanos from Texas and Colorado run a program that follows the migrant stream," she says. "This is their second summer in the area."

The next day I find his house and wait around for him to show up. Finally I leave a message with one of his underlings, who seems so suspicious that I doubt he'll relay the message. By the time I head back to my post, I've decided to quit my job.

22

Our Mano in Havana, Our Men on the Moon

I visit the summer camp the following weekend before going to Lansing. Having given notice to my boss, I need to turn in pending paperwork. I check Marcos' house again. This time he's there, with a different underling. We greet each other like long-lost friends; there's something special about crossing paths all the way up here.

Marcos sees I'm checking out his mobile phone, so he comments on my car. "So we're working for the state now."

"Well, only until sundown tomorrow."

I explain my reasons for quitting, but since my boss is a distant relation to Marcos, I direct my criticisms at the system rather than my supervisor. I add that my boss was a bit stunned by the news, though; he didn't think I'd call his bluff. Not that the criticism makes much difference to Marcos, who'd ostracize his own *compadre* if he let down the movement.

"Too bad it came to this, De la O. Maybe you could have helped some of the older migrants."

His assistant, who's overheard our conversation, answers for me. "He did what had to be done. By the time anyone moved on those benefits, they'd have to forward them to the afterlife."

I acknowledge him with a nod. "Too bad you weren't here last week," I tell him. "The guy I left my message with treated me like I was a grower or something."

Marcos glances at my car. "You showed up in *that* . . . the same week the FBI came knocking on doors."

For a few seconds I only stare back. I'm juggling two conflicting feelings: relief that I'm never around when these guys come calling, and a bit of regret as well—I wouldn't mind boasting that the FBI had interrogated me.

"What did they want?"

He guides me to my car, out of earshot from his assistant, then says calmly, "Information about Coco's vacation."

"What vacation?"

"Oh, just a romantic getaway, to some enchanted island." He looks away absently, as though he's already forgotten the interrogation.

"Cuba? Coco went to *Cuba?*"

"He just got back, through Canada."

"Jesus Che! You mean he crossed back through here?"

"That's what they wanted to know."

"What did you tell them?"

"I said that since they've been tapping our phones anyway, my answer was superfluous."

Before leaving I invite him to visit me at the summer camp. "I'm staying there until Nacho's ready to head back to Texas."

A few days later Marcos drops by the camp, casually surveys it and promises to bring a few of his workers to keep me company. I don't mind: without wheels I'm getting a bad case of camp fever. Lately the only exciting thing around actually happened a quarter of a million miles away: the moon landing, which I watched with several of the summer camp workers. Afterwards I stayed up with a Chicana who's from the area but not from a migrant family.

When the weekend arrives, so does Marcos, along with some people from his migrant program. They're a mixture of activists and organizers from Texas and Colorado, with a few farmworkers thrown in for authenticity. Gabi's among them, and I greet him as enthusiastically as I did Marcos. Michael also arrives for the weekend, and that afternoon the group organizes a dance and spreads the word through the local migrant camps. Marcos even lines up an amateur band from one of the camps, but they lose their way in the country roads, so that night we end up listening to some scratched *mariachi* albums in the large dining hall.

Around midnight Michael's friends ask him to take the stage and wind things down. In his eagerness to send the audience home he promises to do this again sometime. A few people in the crowd yell, "Tomorrow night, then!" and the rest second the idea with their cheers.

He does nothing to discourage them and, putting on a dazed smile, actually joins the chanting.

The next morning I explain he's set the stage for another night of even harder partying.

"I doubt it, De la O. Everyone's partied out."

"You mean we are. The *chavos* with Marcos are just warming up."

He shakes his head. "The migrant kids are in no mood. They're in the middle of the harvest."

I start to tell him that it's all the more reason to party but he's not convinced. So I keep a close eye on the activity of Marcos' workers as a barometer. In the course of my spying, I find out there's been a misunderstanding: Their idea of entertainment involves poetry-reading, skits from the *teatro campesino,* and some movement *corridos.*

But the migrant crowd that shows up that night, including *chavos* in polyester dress shirts and double-soled dancing shoes, hardly resembles a night-at-the-arts audience. Amused by the novelty, they listen politely to the first reader. After that, some start heckling, hoping that the balladeer who follows will get the hint. Others applaud at odd intervals, assuming that if enough appreciation is shown they'll bring on the *real* music. The performers, though, interpret things differently. The rowdier the crowd gets, the more they think they're stirring up cultural emotions. About the only thing most listeners catch is an occasional "*Viva la raza.*" They're cheering at the familiar, but all that does is encourage the poets to leaf through their notebooks and diaries for whatever cliches work.

Michael shows up with the Chicana I met the night of the moon landing and casually brings us together. Soon the noise inside the hall gives me an excuse to take her outside, where we find that others already have the same idea: We try a couple of trees only to find couples already there. Eventually we end up by the lake—not bad if it weren't for the mosquitoes.

She brings up the poetry readings, and I can't resist climbing my soapbox. I mention an anecdote that Borges told: When other Latin American writers criticized him for a lack of nationalism he responded that the most important book in the Arab world, the Koran, doesn't mention a single camel. A less talented writer, he pointed out, would have included camels, caravans of them, to make the work more "authentic."

"Those guys in there are trying too hard," I tell her. "The trick is in not trotting out the camels."

While she's obviously interested in our discussion, her look suggests, This is nice, but is this all?

I barely start my moves, though, when the beers I guzzled tell me I have to go. I excuse myself and retreat into the darkness, while holding my cock in one hand while the other bats off mosquitoes. It takes longer than I thought, waiting for my hard-on to make way for the beer while at the same time hoping it won't attract mosquitoes.

"Pretend I'm not here," she calls out in the darkness.

"If I could I'd already be through."

"Then let's find you a bathroom. These mosquitoes are eating me alive."

"You're not the only one. They're sucking me dry."

"Oh?"

I follow her laughter to her cabin, where we pretend to inspect each other's insect bites by moonlight, until she suddenly stiffens and stops. "Do you have a . . . raincoat?"

"Rain–? You mean *rubbers?*"

Naturally I don't. I'm not exactly running a one-man stud service out here. Besides, when you're out among nature condoms don't cross your mind unless you're sodomizing a doe, and probably not even then. She walks to her roommate's side in the dark and opens a drawer.

"Cissy usually keeps some," she whispers, then stiffens again and whispers, "We're being watched." At that instant I imagine an FBI agent spying on us from across the room.

"*Who?*" I whisper.

She whispers so close to my ear that her answer sounds garbled.

"The man in the moon?"

She turns my face toward the window. "No. The men on the moon."

"Oh, them. I think they're back home."

Soon it's my turn to play astronaut and I'm floating around, weightless and anchored at the same time, exploring her mons for the man on the moon but only uncovering a little one in a boat, then slowly entering that tight lunette, one small thrust for a man, thinking it's no wonder the Soviets call them cosmonauts, implying all the mysteries of the cosmos—as much inside you as out there.

We see each other a few times after that, but once summer camp reopens it gets harder to meet, what with her job and prying eyes. Marcos has persuaded the camp church authorities to let his group stay at the other end of the camp, so now even the woods don't offer much privacy. By then it's almost like old times: I'm sharing a room with Gabi, next to Marcos' cabin, where I spend much of my time.

The week before Nacho and I are to leave for Texas, Gabi decides to visit an organizer in a town about an hour away. Marcos lends us his car. By the time a *chavo* from Colorado tags along it's already dark.

There's little to see at that hour on country roads, so I stretch out in back. No sooner do I get comfortable than Gabi starts to pass a car at the same time that a pick-up pulls out of a rural road and into our path. Gabi barely has time to swerve onto the shoulder, where we start sliding on the gravel. Suddenly I'm tumbling and banging every which way.

The car rolls a few times then stops all at once on the bank of a levee, right-side-up. No sooner do we jump out of the car, though, than it slides back down onto the road.

At first I'm just happy to be alive. Then I realize that my glasses are gone and my face is smeared with blood. The bridge of my nose is throbbing and my eyes are bloodied, but I'm afraid to touch them so I ask Gabi's friend if there's glass in them. He shakes his head, too rattled to say anything, but I don't believe him until Gabi brings back my glasses intact.

The car's a total wreck but somehow the mobile phone works, and Gabi uses it to report the accident. He also calls Marcos, who arrives at the same time some ambulance attendants are offering to take us for a hospital check-up. By now my nose is already numb, but since Gabi and his friend aren't complaining, I turn down the offer too. I'm still staring at the car: The roof crumpled to within inches of where I lay, and a couple of chrome moldings from the window punctured the seat. One of the attendants peeks inside.

"Wow! It's like a magician's box, where they stick somebody inside then pierce it with swords."

I shiver as if the cold chrome had gone through me.

On the way back to camp, Gabi keeps apologizing to Marcos for wrecking the car, while I can't stop touching my swollen nose. Later that night, when it starts hurting like hell, I pay a visit to the young Anglo doctor who's part of Marcos' project. He has the stereo in his cabin cranked up, so after knocking I unintentionally walk in to find him fucking some girl. Or rather she's fucking him—riding him slowly and in complete control. It's not until he's outside that he mumbles something about Rachel, the Jewish Aztec Princess.

"You mean Miss Masochism?" I already sound like I have a bad head cold.

"That's only the outer layer," he says. "After that, *she* does the tying up."

When he brushes my moustache, bristled with dried blood, even the hairs hurt.

"It's broken, all right. You can have it refractured and set." I try not to wince too hard, but he still notices. "Or you can let it heal on its own."

The swelling goes down slowly, and by the time Nacho comes by for our return trip to Texas, my nose has ended up crooked. I point it out before Nacho does, even though he acts like he hasn't noticed.

"What are you talking about?" he says, trying hard to hide a smile. "It's as good as new."

Gabi doesn't even try to hide his own grin. "It's even better."

Marcos nods and adds that now it's a conversation piece.

"Right," I reply. "Then I can bring up the time we totaled your car. And how much fun we had doing it."

Marcos pretends to bop me on the nose. "A souvenir for your pains, then."

23
Jewish Aztec Princess

Nacho and I return to Texas a few days before school starts. I was sending most of my money home to my family, and the first thing my stepfather wants to know is why I didn't see my job to the end. Rather than explain, I milk the sympathy angle and tell them about the accident. If anyone deserves an apology it's Luli, who got me the job, but she either doesn't mind or else dissimulates her disappointment.

She asks my impressions of Michigan. Her family used to do migrant work there, and she's nostalgic for the climate and countryside. That's also what I miss the most, so I have no difficulty recollecting. I ask in all innocence why she didn't take the job herself.

She suggests that a Chicana wouldn't get respect from the growers and workers, but in her case I'm not buying it: As one of our best organizers she's equally effective being nice as being blunt. But no sooner do I start with a horror story about injustice and the bureaucracy than she interrupts me with a real horror story of her own.

Every summer her family picked strawberries for the same grower. Each year they asked him to repair the shack they stayed in, and each year he offered the same excuse: He didn't fix the drafts because they helped ventilate the gas leak from the propane stove, and if he fixed the gas leak then he'd have to repair the drafts too.

One evening they returned from the fields and came upon a shadow in the dusk, crouched outside the shack. It was her younger sister, who always babysat their year-old brother. In a groggy state of guilt, she confessed falling asleep then waking up to find the baby unconscious. Running inside to light the kerosene lamp and examine the baby, the father flicked his lighter, and a blinding flash left everything even darker afterwards. He was still at the threshold, so the small fireball that died out in an instant barely singed him. But at that same instant the baby's chest burst open.

The coroner attributed the cause of death to gas inhalation; the infant was already dead before the explosion.

"The gas in his lungs ignited," Luli says after a long silence.

It takes me even longer to manage a reply. "What did they do to the grower?"

"Nothing. They said it was an accident. My parents were the ones in trouble, for leaving the baby with my sister."

They brought the body back home to Texas after a crew boss offered to transport the coffin in his truck. Luli's parents rode in the cab while she and the other children huddled in back against the railings, with the baby's coffin. The crew boss had to return immediately, so they drove night and day and night. Her father and the crew boss took turns driving, and her mother was still in shock, so there were no adults in back to supervise the children. Yet Luli remembers that all that time they barely exchanged words. They spent both nights on the road watching the tiny coffin shift about and tremble slightly, as though her baby brother struggled to come back to life. She remembers too gazing up at the perfect, peaceful beauty of a starry summer night while her heart hated with a vastness that could envelop even God.

The next day I run into Adrian.

"I thought you already knew," he says. "Didn't I tell you?" I shake my head and he adds, "Last year, after a meeting, Luli asked me for a ride to visit her brother. It was late at night, but we'd been friends long enough that I figured nothing would happen. Well, something did happen. I'm following her directions, all this time assuming he lives out in the country, until we end up at a small cemetery in the middle of nowhere. I start thinking that maybe she wants me to put some moves on her after all. Instead she leaves the car and makes her way past some tombstones, then sits on the grass next to this tiny grave. She looks up at the stars and tells me about the time they brought the body back, how right after the burial she had to go back to Michigan with her father, without really saying goodbye to her baby brother." He sighs. "We stayed there almost till dawn."

The next time we see each other Luli's only mention of Michigan is a cryptic reference to someone I met there who's now in the Valley. I hunt around for a clue, until she adds with a grin: "Some *migrant*. She goes to Radcliffe. Or was going, until she took a year off to work here. She seems nice, though."

"Rachel? The Jewish Princess? She's here?"

"As far as princesses go, she looks more Aztec to me. Long, black hair, peasant shirt, sandals . . ."

I'm curious but try not to show much interest. My own guess is that she followed the doctor from the migrant project, who's also working here with Marcos.

But if she did come down with the doctor in mind, within days several other *chavos* are trying their best to take his place. To top it off, Lizard mentions that not only is she sharing a place with Julia, one of the older Manas, but that he spied them making love.

"I was taking some stuff to Julia," he says. "Her car was there, but no one answered the door. So I went out back, peeked through a window and . . ." He grins so hard he gets crow's feet. "¡*Miralas*! There they were."

I have my doubts about the story, but I'm still intrigued. The next time I see Julia on campus I make a point of catching up with her. She's attractive yet I've never been that attracted to her, and the feeling appears mutual. She gets things done, but aside from sometimes getting stoned with Lizard after meetings, she doesn't stick around for chit-chat. In fact it takes some effort on both our parts to get the conversation going, until I mention that Adrian, Gabi, Coco, and I are helping some farmworkers organize a supermarket boycott in my city.

"Oh," she says, "I should tell my housemate. She helped out farmworkers this summer."

I answer with a noncommital nod. A moment later she brings Rachel up again in a cozier context that unsettles me a bit. "By the way, my roommate and I were talking to a cousin of Alma who says she knows you. Her name's Nena."

"Hmm, small world."

"And a small movement too. She noticed my buttons one day on campus, and asked if I knew you." When she purses her lips in a way I haven't seen her do before, I know who she picked up the gesture from.

"She really impressed Rachel. We both told her she should study back East. Anywhere but here."

"What's wrong with here?"

She holds my gaze for a moment, as though asking whether I'm serious. "You tell *me*. Why are you and Coco trying to go elsewhere?"

"What? . . . Oh, we want to get out-of-state scholarships for a few Manos." Her comment catches me off guard, since the only one I've told in her circle is Nena. It wasn't confidential, and in a way I'm glad Nena's spread the word.

"When it comes to recruiting *raza*," I add, "Texas is ten years behind the times. If we find anything in California, I hope Nena comes along."

"I'll bet you do."

She's right in guessing I'd like Nena along for personal reasons, but I don't give her the satifaction of admitting it. "Whatever," she finally adds. "I just think she'd meet a better class of people back East."

"The kind you've been seeing?"

She comes out punching: "Who I see is my business."

"I agree. And where Nena goes or stays is hers. Besides, I don't hear her complaining here."

"You know us Chicanas. We suffer in silence."

"Nena's not that type. If she's suffering she'll let you know."

"You knew her well, then?"

"I still do."

"That's odd. She mentioned you like you're ancient history."

"We're probably as close as you and . . . your roommate."

"Oh, so then you do *know* Nena," she says, putting an Old Testament twist on the word.

"I know her well enough."

Julia's eyebrows arch, expecting more, but I simply wait to see how long she can keep them at attention. We reach the parking lot when she asks outright: "And how well is well?"

"Ask her yourself."

She fumbles with her car keys and opens the door. "You're right. I'll ask her myself."

Something tells me I haven't seen the last of her, but what I don't realize is how soon. That same afternoon I'm at the MANO office, having the usual guerrilla-gets-the-girl fantasy, when I'm jerked back to reality by the slam of car doors. A moment later Nena's inside, followed by Julia and the Princess.

"So, Nena," I ask, ignoring the other two completely, "what's going on?"

"Same thing I want to know, De la O." It's the first time she's called me by my last name. What's this shit you're spreading about us?"

I can barely believe my ears it's Nena, whose worst lapse in good manners was telling Coco once that he was full of *caca*. Not *shit*, mind you, not that Anglo-Saxon vulgarity, but *caca*, the sort of infantile insult my baby brother might come up with.

Julia's left the door open, and the Town Crier's already standing by the threshold. A moment later he pulls up a corner chair for a ringside seat. My hope for a bloodying behind closed doors evaporates. She insists again I tell her what I told Julia. It's useless to deny anything, but honesty won't do justice either, so I simply say, "I didn't say anything that isn't true."

When she realizes I won't incriminate myself further, she walks out in a stony silence, almost jostling the Town Crier. There's satisfaction on Julia's face, while the Princess walks out with her usual indifference.

The next day I'm even able to give myself a full accounting of my actions, although I remember my philosophy professor saying that humans aren't so much rational as they are rationalizing. If that's so, then I'm a credit to humanity, since what I said yesterday was technically true. I didn't say I slept with Nena, yet I didn't say that I didn't. So why does it still bother me? Perhaps because it's too much like the bragging that *chavos* do around each other, all half-truths and insinuations. You ask a friend, "Did you get some last night?" and you get a big grin along with, "What do you think?" Or else he pretends he's too much of a gentleman to go into the messy details. The only difference in my case is that Julia's not a guy—at least not technically.

The moment Nacho hears about the incident, courtesy of the Crier, he insists it's as much the Princess' doing. "What's she have against you?"

"Nothing, as far as I know."

"You must have done something to piss her off in Michigan," he says, even though he already knows the story, which isn't much. "Maybe you went up the wrong hole, De la O."

It occurs to me that a conversation like this is what got me into trouble in the first place. So for once I say the right thing: Nothing.

24
An Ignoble Near-Death
at the Hands of Dentists

Soon after the fall semester starts we're forced to move up our plans for a demonstration. The farmworkers' union is boycotting a chain store selling scab grapes, and it needs our numbers for a decent showing. Since the store's in my town, I list the local Manos I can get on short notice. "Let's see . . . Liz and his friends can't make it."

While Coco's not eager to have them along, he still asks why they won't be around.

"White-wing season starts that Saturday," I answer.

"Oh, great," Coco says. "They can flash back to Nam, pretending those birds are kids."

At the boycott we almost outnumber the farmworkers but they end up picketing by the curb while we cover the inner parking lot. I suspect the separation is deliberate, to minimize any accusations of "outside agitators." After a while we can pretty much predict who's driving up and how they'll respond. An old pick-up is usually rural *raza* on a weekend trip into town. The father slows down, eying the whole affair with suspicion, while the kids look out from the truck bed half-expecting a hippie parade. At that point one of the union organizers comes over and summarizes their demands in terms the parents can appreciate: Fair pay for an honest day's work.

Usually the fathers understand, but sometimes the anxiety in their eyes indicates they're leaving more out of intimidation than solidarity. I feel bad about these folks. They're moving on because they've been told to, and we're just one more voice in their lives they have to obey. I even

imagine them apologizing to their kids about why they're shopping elsewhere. I almost wish they'd tell us to get lost instead.

That's *exactly* what the rednecks tell us, easing out of their pickups
with gunracks stacked two or three rifles high. On their way back they'll
sit on the hood and stuff themselves with a bagfull of grapes. We stare
right back, waiting for them to spit out the seeds. At that point we snicker and say stuff in Spanish to unnerve them. It usually works, since
there's nothing they hate worse than seeming uncivilized in front of the
natives. The same tactic works even better with Chicanos who are there
to make points with the Anglos. They're even more sensitive about their
manners, so they'll sit there and try to swallow the seeds.

Soon we get used to the shitkickers and sellouts, but not the racists.
A few even cruise by and pelt the protesters with grapes, and I understand why they didn't put us Manos along the street. Just seeing them do
that crap makes your blood boil, especially when they target elderly farmworkers who came dressed for another day's work.

The cops told us to stay a certain distance from the street, a certain
distance from the store, and a certain distance from each other . . . otherwise we'll be arrested. Such are the boycott laws in Texas. Moreover,
we can't ask customers not to shop there since that violates some other
law. After a while, though, when the initial tension turns into tedium,
the cops and the store manager start looking the other way. For our own
part we push the limits a little at a time, redrawing the line then over-
stepping it.

As the day warms up, the harassers turn more lethargic, as do we,
until a vanful of Anglos slows down. No sooner do they yell something
than we turn it into a shouting match, just to break the boredom. Later
we find out they were out hunting white-wing when some guy shot himself in the leg, and they were simply desperate for directions to the
hospital.

Later, however, two drunk hunters circle the parking lot several
times, taunting every brown face in sight, including customers. They
cruise up to Adrian. No sooner do they park next to him than Coco,
Gabi, and I run over.

Almost everything about them seems out of synch, starting with
their convertible, which seems better suited for hunting pussy than

whitewing dove. Their outfits are new and expensive, but their thick drawl, along with their slurred speech, adds to their redneck air.

"Now what did those people want back there?" the smaller one asks his friend.

"They were saying something about grapes. So I threw that old wetback a few."

Adrian also acts like they're not there. "What brings you over here?" he asks us. "You smelled trash?"

Coco sniffs over the open convertible. "More like *mierda.*" Shit, and slang for beer.

Coco gestures to the back seat, where the men have their weapons. The larger guy also checks their shotguns so that the firepower registers in our hot heads. At the same time he practically shouts, "Hey, we're dentists, damn it!"

Adrian sidles up to the passenger's side and touches his crotch. "Then yank this out, man."

I guess the gringo next to him thinks he's reaching for a gun, because he turns to the back seat for his shotgun. No sooner does he jump out of the car than Adrian starts wresting the gun from him.

"Let go!" the guy screams.

They struggle away from the car until Adrian, an ex-Marine, pivots and whacks him hard across the jaw with the gun stock. It sounds like eggs dropped on asphalt. The gringo sinks to his knees but holds on to the gun. We're mesmerized, and don't even notice the driver jump out of the car until he grabs the other gun.

"Let go!" He sounds even crazier than the first. He pumps a shell in the chamber to show he means business and aims squarely at Adrian. "Let him go, goddamnit!"

Adrian does just that, and the semiconscious gringo slips over and forward from the waist up and stays that way, the way a baby naps with his butt raised. The guy who's standing simply stares at us, terrified to back away from what he's started.

His expression shifts from rage to horror. He steals quick glances at his friend, then prods him with his barrel like he's checking shot game for vital signs. When there's no response, he turns his shotgun at us in an ultimatum. All I can think of are the war games we played as kids. A drunk's shotgun a few barrel-lengths from my face is such a messy and unheroic way to go. But in the space of a few seconds—that seem much longer—the threat cools down into a stand-off. He's still jerking his shotgun back and forth, but now it seems he simply wants to scare us off.

Adrian is the first to test that theory. He sprints away a few feet, pauses, then adds distance without taking his eyes off him. He must figure the guy won't shoot a man with his back to him and at the same time looking him in the eyes. The tactic works. A few more yards and he's among some parked cars, where he quickly ducks for cover.

That leaves the rest of us. The guy sizes us up in his sights again, reassessing us. Coco and I follow Adrian. Gabi's the only sitting duck left. The guy has his gun pointed squarely at his chest in a wooden gesture. At first I breathe easier, thinking that his heart's no longer in it, until I realize the gesture works both ways: Maybe it was his heart that kept him from shooting all along.

Slowly and deliberately, Gabi walks away like a kid who's tired of playing a game. His walk seems determined and dragged out at the same time. I try getting his attention from behind a Volkswagen with Mexican plates when Adrian calls out, "Now what?"

He's gesturing toward a few demonstrators who dropped their banners and witnessed the whole thing. They're standing in the middle ground between the curb and us, uncertain whether to get involved.

Adrian asks again, "What the hell do we do now? When the cops get here, guess who they'll grab!"

Coco pops up his head a few cars away. Before Adrian can ask again, he answers, "It's time for Operation Our Father." He has the same look on his face as when he fantasizes about being with some guerrilla band in the mountains. "We split up, call up Father Frank, and stay at the Catholic center for today."

I'm not that crazy about the idea, but Adrian says it's safe. Gabi simply sits on a front bumper. "I have my own plan, De la O. Operation Yo-Yo."

"What's that?"

"You're on your own."

"I say we go underground," Coco insists.

Gabi stands and says, "I'm going home."

Coco invites me with a glance to join him. "Move it or lose it," he says. "Before the cops get here."

I wave him away but barely have the strength to stand. A moment ago I was burning high-octane adrenaline, but now I'm running on fumes. I look into Gabi's glazed eyes and realize he's equally exhausted.

"I came with Coco," I tell him. "Can you give me a ride back?"

"Only if you drive, De la O." He wants to add something else but can't come up with anything. "Only if you drive."

25
Overbite the Bullet

The following day, we meet in Marcos' house. Adrian goes for snacks and returns waving the evening paper. "Can you believe it? Those gringos really *were* dentists! A local guy and his out-of-town friend." He hits his own head with the rolled-up paper like a masochistic pet who'll never learn from himself.

"That's what they *said* they were," says Gabi.

"But they looked trashy."

"That's what drunk gringos look like."

Adrian reads the news item aloud. The pair was taken to a justice of the peace after someone called the police, they pleaded no contest, and paid a small fine.

"Dentists!" repeats Adrian, then imagines aloud a conversation. "So who shot those guys? Texas Rangers? *No, dentists.*"

"Oh," adds Marcos, "so then they really got *drilled.*"

"If we'd been the ones with guns . . ." I start.

"They'd have shot us like doves on the wing," says Adrian. He then points out, in another news story, how the authorities made up for that lapse in law and order: apparently another group of Manos coming in from outside the Valley arrived late. By then the parking lot was crawling with cops and security, so the union organizers decided to close shop. The lost patrol picked up the banner anyway. The police quickly hauled them to jail, but once in their cells they set fire to the mattresses, starting a small riot among the other prisoners.

Later that week someone from the farmworkers' union is interviewed by the media. It's unclear whether he's the union's official spokesman, but there's nothing unclear about his condemnation of any groups associated with violence.

"You'd think we're the ones who pulled out guns."

"Don't take it personally, De la O," says Coco. "What do you expect them to do? Organize a MANO Appreciation Day?"

"They could keep quiet," answers Adrian, "instead of stabbing us in the back. Where's the brotherhood?"

Marcos chuckles. "It's there, like some psycho cousin you don't appreciate until he saves your skin in a fight. They're embarrassed to admit we're related to the same movement. Talk to guys who organized the melon strikes here a few years back. Once they trust you they'll tell you about sabotaging railroad tracks. To keep scab melons from the market. When the growers brought in Texas Rangers, these organizers weren't about to hold hands and sing protest songs. But they also knew if they got caught no one would claim the bodies."

I turn to Gabi. "We're like those masked heroes in comic books. You try doing good and end up on WANTED posters."

He grins through a mask he's made with his fingers. "We're all a bunch of Zorros here!"

"Or zeros," I add.

I read another news story that week: The produce manager of the place we picketed claims he sold more grapes that day than the last three weeks combined. The story behind the story, though, comes weeks later, when Nacho's cousin, who works in the same store, admits that while *grape* sales shot up that day like they'd been banned, *overall* sales in the store dropped—for that day and the rest of the week. Apparently lots of people did stay away, and many of those who came in bought *only* grapes. Most customers were afraid we'd attract other maniacs and they'd end up in the crossfire.

"Great," I tell Marcos. "Pretty soon our own people will start crossing the street when they see us coming."

"I don't care if they cross themselves and wear garlic. We're not here to be popular. We're here to do whatever works."

The boycott's real impact soon trickles back to the union's headquarters, through students from the campus Catholic club who hang out with us but feel more comfortable with the farmworkers' agenda. Later the same students bring back a message from the union people: *Let's do this again sometime.*

"Tell them we'll think about it," replies Coco. He already looks like those veterans who've filed away too many war stories in their psyche. A while back a few of us went to a state strategy meeting in San Antonio, and one of MANO's founders said he was taking a leave and going back to his home town. He said he yearned to do something substantive and concrete, even if it only meant teaching an illiterate old lady to read. He added he was tired of being used, even by those politicians who furthered their careers by crucifying us. His exhausted expression then reminds me of Coco's now. He'd known for some time what we're just now discovering: While our causes sometimes overlap, the "movement" means different things to different groups.

Recently I talked to one of the farmworker union organizers, an intense and dedicated *chavo* who dreams of the day when each farmworker family owns a nice, air-conditioned home and two cars. His goal had a cozy closure to it, especially if you've worked in the fields or grew up in rundown homes without indoor plumbing. Unlike the abstract ideals we Manos fight for, I had no problem picturing his. Yet I also had to ask him whether their struggle began and ended with a comfortable home.

At first he had trouble understanding my question. Then, possibly to get on my good side, he added, "Well, once you have a nice home, you start thinking about college . . ."

"Fine, but lots of college students already have nice homes with central air and encyclopedias. Even some from former migrant families, who now want to make money off of someone else's sweat. The cycle repeats itself."

He considered this for a moment, then smiled. "So let it. That way we'll never run out of the rank and file."

26
Protests-to-Go, Pro Bono

After this last demonstration, Coco and I aren't the only ones gun-shy about giving other groups a helping hand. When Danny Moreno, my old housemate, tries to interest us in another protest, no one in the office volunteers.

"But this is a cause we can't pass up, guys," he insists.

With him it's always "guys," never *vatos* or *chavos*. I get the impression he grew up in a family where the father's full-time job was rescuing his kids from minor, weekly crises, then sitting down and explaining the lesson learned. I even tried to make him say *vatos*, but it sounded so unnatural that I let him go back to "guys."

Today he's determined to rally us around a martyr. "She's this Chicana who's doing a lot for the cause. Now they want to get rid of her."

"Who's they?" asks Adrian.

"Her supervisors."

The only thing Marcos volunteers is an ironic smile. "We all do a lot for the cause, Danny. Nobody throws us rallies."

"Come on, you guys make it sound like I'm just throwing another house party. We're talking about someone important. She's been low-key so far. You'll be hearing a lot about her, though."

"We already are," says Marcos.

"I mean once they get rid of her. She's rocking the boat."

"What do you mean, 'get rid of her'? You mean *assassinate* her?"

"They only do that to nobodies like us," says Adrian. "They simply hire a dentist hit man."

Marcos appears to give the matter some thought, then suddenly asks, "Say, Danny, whatever happened to that uncle of yours? The one we organized that protest for in Laredo?"

Danny furrows his brow, so Marcos refreshes his memory: "The one with the blow-dried hair . . . in khakis he bought just for the occasion. Plus those crocodile shoes with the cute name . . ."

"Guccis, I think," mutters Danny. "Gucci loafers."

Marcos nods again. "Those crocodile loafers fit him like a second skin, in more ways than one."

This run-in took place just before I joined MANO. Adrian gives me the details. "No sooner do we save his uncle's ass than he disappears. Not even a postcard from Acapulco."

"He took a leave. The whole thing took a toll on his nerves."

"It took a toll on everyone's nerves," says Coco. "I took a leave too. They threw my ass in jail."

"He finally came out of hiding," says Marcos, "to announce he was running for office. I heard he showed up at his fundraisers dressed in cowboy boots."

"Gucci?" Roque asks.

"I don't think they make boots," says Danny.

"They should. They'd make a fortune with our politicos here."

"The point is," says Marcos, "he never once invited us to his fundraisers."

"Well," says Coco, "maybe one day he'll ask us to throw him another protest."

I assume the matter's buried when an hour later Danny digs it up again: "So what about this Chicana who needs our help? It's not fair to hold this other thing against her. She and my uncle are completely different people."

Marcos exhales an exaggerated sigh of relief. "Thank God! I was afraid he'd screw us again, this time disguised as a woman."

Coco, though, takes a different tack. "This is a damsel in distress, Manos. Danny knows her and that's good enough for me . . . You do know her *well*, don't you, Danny?"

Quite well, it turns out. They're cousins.

"I can't believe it! *Another* relative?" Coco exclaims.

Finally Danny realizes there's nothing to be gained from the nice guy approach. "I don't *believe* you guys. Here you are, risking your ass for some farmworkers, led by guys you barely know. For all we know they're selling out to the growers and taking payoffs."

Gabi, who's an utter idealist when it comes to farmworkers, bristles at the insinuation. "You're saying Cesar Chavez is a crook?"

"Well, the growers around here say—"

"I already know the crap that comes out of the growers' mouths. I'm asking you."

"Why, you know me . . ."

"No, I don't," answers Gabi. "I thought I did, but I'm not so sure anymore."

"You know I wouldn't be with you guys if I felt otherwise." His eyes get beady; it's a do-or-die situation. "That's why I want us to go to bat for Linda. I wouldn't ask you if she wasn't on our side. But even if she wasn't, I'd still back her. That's how Chicano families are."

I almost add that this is precisely the problem. I don't, though, and apparently his appeal softens the others. Even Coco almost gets misty-eyed; he'd probably give Inti a fraternal hug if he were here. In the end they don't say yes, but they don't say no either, leaving the door open for Danny, the prodigal radical.

The next day, as I analyze Danny's performance, I admit I've under-estimated him. I often wonder why a middle-class *chavo* like him puts up with our ridicule as well as that of other Anglicized Chicanos. I'm beginning to understand. He's a political animal, biding his time, camouflaged within the movement. Maybe he's as opportunistic as Coco accuses Lizard of being, but Danny's a lizard of a different color, or rather colors: He's a chameleon.

27
Love, La Raza, and Other Lost Causes

By the middle of the semester rumor has it that Alma's ready to dump Roque. At last one day, he walks into the office and tells us Alma is no longer his.

"Whose is she?" asks Coco.

"That's just it. She doesn't want to be anyone's. She wants to be herself."

"Who else can she be?" Coco's not one to lose sleep wondering where he fits in the great cosmic puzzle.

"She wants time to see other people."

"She wants to screw other guys?"

Roque stares at no particular point, as if the answer's hiding in the air. "She just wants time to . . . stand still, I guess. She wants to discover herself."

"It sounds like *torta* talk."

Coco's referring to the clique that supposedly hangs around Julia, whom he suspects are lesbians.

"Well . . . if she's turning *torta* . . . then she's turning *torta*," Roque says. It dawns on me that Roque is clueless when it comes to lesbians. He must think they only hold hands and read poetry to each other.

That fantasy sustains him for the next few days, until he finally confesses, as much to himself as to me: "There's no question now, De la O. She's seeing someone else."

I've heard so many rumors that by now even Cesar Chavez must know, but I pretend ignorance. "Who, *Alma?*"

He says she's left him for the only child of a family that owns a local empire of Mexican food products. "Isn't that something, though? Here we are telling *raza* to be proud of our culture, and she dumps me for a tortilla tycoon . . . Why don't you talk to her, De la O?"

Tortas, tortillas, I think, *Not too far off the mark.* But I don't say it. "And tell her what? That if she marries into that tortilla family she'll put on forty pounds?"

For Roque her memory is still too sacred for teasing, and it only ends up adding to his somberness. "Be serious, De la O. She admires your intelligence."

I still don't trust myself around Alma, though, especially now. I've heard she's not only vulnerable and confused, but that she's lost weight from the crisis. Her physical resemblance to Nena doesn't help either. I suggest he find another go-between, yet I can't come up with a single trustworthy soul. Suddenly the answer comes in a flash, as if from the heavens: "Ask Father Frank at the Newman Center! I'm sure students see him about these things all the time. I'm not the one to offer advice on these things. Anyway, didn't you once say Father Frank knows her family?"

"He also knows the tortilla family. That's how Alma met the *chavi-to.*"

He then explains how Father Frank and the tortilla clan go back to when the old man brought a strange tortilla to Father Frank's attention.

"What's so strange about a tortilla?"

"One of his workers flipped over a flour tortilla on the griddle and noticed it looked like the Virgin of Guadalupe."

"You mean like someone put it through a cookie cutter?"

"No, I mean the brown spots where they burn. One spot looked like the Virgin, like those Dali paintings where hidden figures pop up at you." He glances toward his art books and I keep quiet, hoping he'll be distracted. But he simply continues staring at the bookshelf.

"So," I remind him, "the miracle tortilla caught someone's eye?"

"Imagine, one split second longer and the spot would have scorched into a motorcycle or something. She scooped it out and brought it to her boss."

"Tortilla Tycoon Senior."

"Back then he was no tycoon. He pretty much cranked them out from his kitchen. But after Father Frank blessed it, he placed it under glass next to his register."

"And began feeding the multitudes."

"It certainly fed his family. He called them Our Lady of the Flour Tortillas, and they've raked it in since. By now most people forgot how he got started, since they buy his tortillas in grocery stores. But the old man himself never forgot, and to show his appreciation he made several donations to the Church."

The story sounds a bit incredible, but I suppose that if people believe the body of Jesus is in a wafer then the Virgin can certainly inhabit a tortilla. "How does Alma fit into all this?"

"One day she asks Father Frank if he believes in miracles. I suppose she was wondering if I'd ever pop the question. He tells her about the Wonder Tortilla, then introduces her to the little tycoon." He brushes back his thick black hair. "And the rest is history."

And everyone lives happily ever after. Well, at least some do, since such is life. A woman pulls out a religious rorschach from the fire, and years later an art student pays the price of her ecstasy. Maybe destiny is simply God's inscrutable sense of humor.

28
Adelita in Acapulco

Earlier this year Roque had been sleeping on and off at the office. Later he linked up with Alma and decided they needed more privacy. Now he's back, and the hours we spend talking each night seems to be doing some good. This afternoon, though, I'm about to go up to the office when the janitor cleaning the daycare rooms guides my glance upstairs and gestures me to listen.

"Careful you don't interrupt the *parranda*," he says.

Since he's always hinting that the place turns into a den of sin after hours, I assume he's kidding about a drinking bout upstairs. Still, I decide to humor him. "It's a little early, don't you think?" Then I hear some faint guitar chords.

"When it comes to love," he says, "time ceases to exist."

I check with Luli and Sandra, who are picking up one of the playrooms.

"Is that Roque up there?"

"Him and a friend," says Sandra. "I sent them upstairs and told them to lay low until the children left. I guess they lost track of time."

Luli adds that earlier this afternoon Roque's friend showed up with a guitar and a bottle. They rehearsed for a while in our bunk room then emerged and offered to entertain the daycare kids with *corridos*. So, a bit tipsy but still in control, they sang some tunes. "The kids were all giggles," says Luli. "They had no idea what was going on. I think it did Roque some good, though."

Afterwards the two returned upstairs, where they've stayed until now. "I told them I don't want any *gritos de cantina* or cussing," says Sandra. "And that they clean up whatever they throw up."

"I thought Roque was on the road to recovery."

Luli laughs. "My grandmother says the only way you recover from love is by dying. Besides, haven't you heard? Alma's getting married."

"So that's it."

"And have you heard where she's going on her honeymoon?"

I shrug. "It's a big world, and Alma's a *big* girl."

"Acapulco. That's where she wanted her honeymoon with Roque. But the idiot kept saying, 'What's the rush? That beach has been there millions of years. It's not going anywhere.'"

I decide to check up on them, and Sandra agrees. "Just keep them thinking the kids are still downstairs."

They don't stop singing even when they hear my knock. They simply insert an "¡Adelante!" into the lyrics without missing a beat.

I know they expect me to drink straight from the bottle, so I take it at once. I'm still sharing their spittle, but this way I'm spared seeing the actual slobber.

"Say, this is some party."

"It's a wake, De la O. I'm burying my heart."

I slosh the bottle a bit. "With this much alcohol it'll last forever."

At some point in the drinking bout they've become *compadres.* They're following the bohemian ritual by the book, down to the obligatory tequila and guitar. There's even a candle stuck in a bottle with the colored lava of cooled wax, like tears of past *parrandas.* And Roque, with his paint-flecked beret, seems the epitome of the suffering artist.

His *compadre* Sosa is a music major with a so-so voice but an impressive repertoire of *rancheras* and ballads. Not surprisingly, they all deal with betrayal at the hands of a woman or death in a revolution. Any song that includes both gets sung twice. I never realized there could be that many until I sit through a string of them. They also include an amazing assortment of deaths—a hail of bullets on the battlefield, vendettas by rivals at cockfight or weddings, even the slow death of the thousand tequilas. *Compadre* Sosa knows them all, and once he taps into the public domain it's only a matter of time before "El abandonado" comes up, followed by "La Adelita," a song from the Revolution so personal that Roque insists on singing solo. Even with the anesthetic edge of the liquor, he calls up a sensitivity you only see in his paintings.

Y si Adelita se fuera con otro
Le seguiria las huellas . . .

And if Adelita ever left with another
I'd follow her tracks . . .

He pauses and shakes his head like a confused bloodhound who's lost the scent. Unable to retrieve the rest of the lyrics, he improvises: "*Le seguiria sus huellas a Acapulco.*"

He sings it in all seriousness, but Sosa stops playing and doubles over his guitar in spasms. It's a crude reaction, but it helps cover my own laughter.

"Well, Roque, her tracks shouldn't be hard to follow in Acapulco's beaches."

"Quit jacking around, De la O. You know the damn song."

As a matter of fact I do. I committed it to heart under similar circumstances, and I only have to think back to that high school heartbreak to retrieve the line he's after: "*Le seguiria las huellas sin cesar.*"

"Cesar? What the hell does Chavez have to do with this?"

"*Sin cesar*, Roque. Without cease."

He grunts his agreement and lets me help him with the next line: "*Si por mar en un buque de guerra, si por tierra en un tren militar.*"

Soza, who's even more soused than Roque, stops in mid-chord. "All this talk . . . taking a military train if she leaves by land . . . following in a battleship if she splits by sea . . . It's all fine and romantic for back then. But this is now, *compadre*. She's taking a plane."

He strums his guitar and starts testing themes out loud. "How about if the hero follows her on a jet? Or better yet, he disguises himself, boards their jet and hijacks it to Cuba . . ."

I glance at Roque. By now all he's good for is paraphrasing a plea straight out of *Casablanca*:

"Of all the honeymoons in the world . . . they go to Acapulco."

"They had to go somewhere, *compadre*."

"Why couldn't they fly to the moon?"

The idea appeals to me. "A honeymoon on the moon. Why not?"

Roque answers his own question. "I'll tell you why not. Who wants to look up at night and see where his ex is having sex?" He takes another gulp of tequila, putting the entire lip of the bottle in his mouth, what my stepfather calls drinking "a la Pancho Villa." Before he can pass it my way I say I have to talk to Sandra downstairs. That's just an excuse. I'm already getting tortilla on the tequila myself.

On the way down I hear them singing "La Adelita" once more. I think of the times I've heard groups sing it in rallies and at parties, how it seemed to bring everyone together. But now I remember what a lonely song it is. I'm sure the poor devil who composed it didn't sing it surrounded by fellow revolutionaries, before a campfire. It's a song of solitude, sung under the silence of stars, to accompany your aloneness.

29
The Bottomless Hole

One day Marcos walks into our office more preoccupied than usual, and when I ask about his migrant project he gives a distracted reply. He even manages a question or two in return, but his heart's not in the conversation.

When I return the following afternoon, dragging Lizard along, Marcos is there once more, and judging by the faces of Adrian, Coco and Inti, they've just had a serious conversation. Marcos' silence seems different from his usual reticence. When I ask him what's wrong, he asks me in turn, "You really want to know?"

It's too late for second thoughts, so I nod.

"Yesterday a farmworker came into my office at the migrant project. He was probably about our age, but you know how quickly that kind of work wears you down. He's not part of our project, but he had heard of us and needed to talk. He sounded desperate and at the same time depressed, so I asked if his problem had to do with money. He nodded then quickly added that it was too late anyway."

"Too late for what?"

"Three days ago his wife went into an early labor so he rushed her to a maternity clinic. He gave a deposit for the delivery, but the doctor demanded the rest right then and there, or else he wouldn't attend to her, saying he been ripped off once too often. So the *chavo* ran out like a madman to get money."

"Did he get it?"

"He didn't say. By the time he got back, the doctor told him the baby was stillborn."

I start saying something, but Marcos interrupts. "No, wait, that would have been a happy ending. When he finally saw his wife she was almost out of her mind, screaming that when the baby's time came, and the money was not in the doctor's hands, he forced her legs shut. He suffocated the baby inside its mother."

For a moment I'm simply at a loss for words. Even Lizard does nothing except stare at something only he can see.

"The doctor was Anglo?" I finally ask.

"What do you think?"

"We have to do something."

"That's what I said too," says Inti. "But what?"

"What do you mean, 'what'?" says Lizard. "Let's go kill that bastard."

That's probably what we're all thinking, but Coco, ever the organizer, wants the case publicized. "But it's like my *carnal* said: What can we do?"

"What do you mean?"

"You didn't hear the rest of it, De la O," says Marcos. "The man broke down so I went to get him a cup of coffee. When I came back he was gone. He hasn't been by since."

"What if we're being set up?" says Inti.

Marcos insists the man was too distraught for it to sound like a set-up, but Coco still adds that without him we can't touch that doctor.

"Maybe he'll be back."

"He should have come by already," says Marcos. "I'm afraid he thinks it's his lot in life. Towards the end he was saying that maybe it was God's will."

"How many times have we heard that before?" says Adrian.

Lizard still insists we go pay the doctor a house call. "Bury him alive. We throw him down this pit by the river. It's on a ranch where a guy lets me cross stuff. He says the hole's bottomless and had to block it with boards because his calves kept falling in. There's a guy or two I've thought of throwing in there, so I'm sure he'd have some company."

Adrian almost smiles. "It'll save the Devil a few steps."

Marcos spends the rest of the day asking some farmworker organizers for their help. After one offers to ask his members to try and locate the family, Marcos goes a step farther, asking if they can join us in a demonstration. This time the response is more guarded. "We'd have to check with headquarters first. You have our sympathy, though."

"We don't need sympathy. We need action. Any activist will tell you, 'Don't mourn. Organize.'"

"That's the point. We only organize, not bring back the dead."

We have our own rally to worry about, an anti-war protest that's around the corner. Coco's also worried that Roque hasn't dropped by the office in several days, much less turned in the posters he promised. So now Coco asks who else is available.

Adrian shakes his head. "Roque's our best silk-screener."

"He's our only one," I correct him.

"What's his problem?" Coco asks. "We're not asking for a damn mural."

"He's still taking it hard."

"Oh, so Doctor De la O's giving therapy now. Listen, we all have personal problems, but we still do our work. You yourself had a real headache a while back, right? What was it, three women?"

When Adrian senses I don't want to talk about it but that Coco does, he decides to put him on the defensive. "Just one. You remember her, Coco. She's the one who called you *Cabeza de Caca*." Coco's ready to drop the topic now, but Adrian persists. "So, De la O, if Coco ever got married, where would he go on his honeymoon?"

"*Cacapulco?*"

Coco tries to return to the task at hand. "Someone saw Roque a while back. They said he looked OK."

"I don't mean he's in a fetal position on the floor," I add. "I mean on the inside . . ."

"Tell him to take a laxative. Don't tell him I said that," Coco quickly adds.

It's a crude remark, but it goes to show that for Coco artistic effort is no different than heeding nature's call, which is why he assumes that anyone can come up with a poster.

"So what'll you put on it, Coco?"

"The usual anti-war stuff . . . Planes dropping shit and stuff."

"Shit?"

"Bombs . . . napalm . . . more bombs."

"We need something more down-to-earth." Since Adrian's a Nam vet, Coco can't argue. "Roque said he wanted to bring the war home."

"What he should bring back home," says Coco, "is his ass."

I take the task of tracking him down on campus and soon find out that his *compadre* Soza saw him working in semi-secrecy in a small studio at the art building.

"We need his poster for a protest rally," I explain.

"Oh . . . right. I've seen some rough sketches."

I'm almost afraid to ask. "How rough?"

He grits his teeth. "Did he ever tell you how when Picasso was having a hard time with women he drew them like monsters?"

As I make my way through the art building's labyrinth I keep imagining a monstrous poster: minotaurs in Marine uniforms, raping Vietnamese women. Finally I locate the tiny studio, but it's Roque who finds me first.

"De la O!" He turns to another art student. "What I wouldn't give for this guy's last name. Imagine all the idiots who'd pay for the catchy signature."

He seems in better spirits than I expected. "Any luck with Alma?" I ask.

"Lots. All of it bad. She's getting married the day after our protest. Father Frank's doing the honors."

"I just wanted to see how you're doing. Coco's worried, believe it or not."

"Tell him he'll have the poster on time."

Three days later he places it on our work table. Coco studies it then looks up, satisfied. "Let's put diapers on this baby's butt," which is his way of saying that we transfer it to a silkscreen.

"I've already done that," says Roque. "You're looking at a print, not the original."

Adrian and I nudge one another. Not only did Roque take the initiative without approval, but Coco's not complaining. When I see the actual print I can understand his self-confidence. The work itself is austere yet effective. A woman embraces a dead Chicano soldier, her son.

There's a resemblance to the Virgin cradling the dead Christ, but where Mary has a sacred suffering about her, this mother's face has been etched by everyday hardships. And yet her face shows the profound love in all sorrow.

In one corner you see the dead soldier as a child. He's nearly unnecessary, this boy with a shoeshine box, but it forces us to see his life and death through her eyes—the way she remembers him. Roque brought the war home, all right.

"What'll we call it?" asks Adrian.

I'm wondering whether words might be overkill, but after some thought I suggest a caption anyway. "Something like . . . *Una guerra gringa. Por que, nuestra sangre en esta guerra gringa?*"

"Our blood in an Anglo bloodbath." Coco doesn't even need time to mull the idea. "We knew you'd pull through," he tells Roque.

Yet looking at Roque, I ask myself whether pulling through is the same as pulling out of despair. He smiles slightly—not his usual ironic one, just the exhausted smile of a survivor who can't quite believe he made it this far. He mutters something to the effect that there's art and there's salvation, but there is no salvation through art.

30
An Act of God

After our demonstration in November, Marcos finally accepts that the farmworker who lost his newborn is not returning, but he insists we still can organize a protest against the doctor. Coco argues that we already went out on a limb with our anti-war rally and that another unpopular cause can only hurt us.

"What's unpopular about exposing an assassin?" asks Marcos.

Coco points out that people don't like to demonstrate against something so personal, and that going around yelling chants seems disrespectful to the baby. But his main worry is that the doctor could press slander charges.

"What if the publicity brings out the parents?" I ask.

Marcos wants to take the idea to the Catholic center and asks me to accompany him on campus. He's concerned that someone might accuse him of being an outside agitator, so I take him along as my guest even though I've only gone there myself a couple of times.

Father Frank, who runs the center, has helped Marcos and other Manos a time or two. He's popular with socially involved students, who see him as a rebel with a cause: a priest who drives an old sports car and infuses the movement with the catechism lessons they learned as kids. Father Frank's also popular because he's Anglo. Perhaps it's more complex than that: he's an Anglo who sides with la raza, almost unheard of around here.

On the way over Marcos hopes aloud that the incident will outrage enough Catholic students to initiate a protest on the spot. And since their reputation is religious rather than radical, they're more likely to sway the community.

Their feet, though, turn out even colder than Coco's. Father Frank keeps putting up one obstacle after another, finally suggesting that in matters like this it's God who must judge, not us.

Marcos finally loses his patience. "Whose side are you on, Father?"

"I'm not on the side of the doctor, if that's what you mean."

"Then whose side are you on? On the side of divinity, or humanity?"

Father Frank smiles. One of the *chavas* calls out, "Careful, Father, your boss is listening."

"I'm for both. I'm for divinity *and* humanity. And I'm not playing both sides. What I'm saying is, Why choose? Why not both?"

"Because you can't have it both ways, Father. How can you serve the all-powerful then say you're on the side of the powerless?"

A dozen other voices immediately protest on the priest's behalf. Marcos looks at me. "Let's get lost. If there were a Hell, this is what lost souls would sound like."

"I just had to point out the obvious," he says once we're outside. "We can't believe in fairy tales all our lives." He raps his knuckles on Father Frank's beat-up sports car. "And we can't count on any god from a machine either."

At dinnertime the next day, Gabi gives thanks for our sandwiches, like he always does when he's there. I sit there, silent, but this time I remember the bereaved father's last words to Marcos. I repeat them aloud, right after Gabi ends grace:

"There's a God up above . . . Isn't there?"

Gabi, who's been away for a while, gives a questioning glance, so I blurt out again, like a madman arguing with himself, "Well, if there is one, I sure wish he had the guts to turn himself in."

Coco's cheeks are stuffed with a huge bite from his sandwich, giving him a sorrowful look. At the same time his eyes beg me not to confront Gabi on religion. But it's too late. "I guess if I created such a fucked-up universe I'd stay away too. Hell, if it weren't for idiots like us cleaning up after him his name would be mud on this planet. The Catholic Center should give us medals."

Inti tells Gabi about the farmworker family. I'm almost enjoying being a sadistic voyeur, watching the look on his face. If I can't rub God's face in the crap he's created, then one of his believers will have to take a cowpie in the face.

Gabi doesn't even bother hearing the whole story. "How could that bastard—?"

"You mean God?"

"No! That gringo bastard!"

"You mean God's a gringo? That's what I—"

"Damn you, De la O!"

"Don't get pissed, Gabi. Just be glad. Go beyond that doctor's act, beyond his bloody hands. Go all the way to God's."

"Don't say that. At least that baby is in his hands now."

"Right. In the hands of his killer."

"Don't say another word, De la O. Don't say those things about God." He's over to me in two or three strides, and quicker than you can squeeze the shit out of a caterpillar he clamps his hand over my mouth. "Don't, De la O! Don't!" He keeps his powerful hand in place for several seconds, gradually easing his grip, but it's not until he lets go that I realize it's only his way of keeping me from blaspheming.

That night I fall asleep after everyone else does, although not for long. When I wake up the room's still dark. I wake up at once, instead of going through that sticky stage of half-sleep, and I'm crying like crazy—not sobbing out loud or trying to catch my breath, only that the tears are flowing like they'll never stop. Yet it feels as natural as breathing.

I can't remember whether I was dreaming, but the dead baby immediately comes to mind. My tears start to stir up blurred memories of other children, as faceless as that unborn one. I think of Luli's baby brother, even though all I can imagine is a child's coffin sliding around on the bed of a truck, traveling down a still, black country road. I try to see the world as Luli did then, try to see beyond that coffin, to see whether there's more to death than meets the eye or whether death is just death. I'm staring up at the heavens and seeing only stars and tears. After a while I can't see anything, as though I've entered that realm inside his coffin, where sensation ceases.

I remember two other faceless children, Isidra Loya's boys, burned when she stepped out of the house one evening to say hi to her boyfriend. They were a year or two younger than my friends and I, and we took to calling them the Tag Team Twins because of the wrestler

masks that hid their burns. They weren't twins, but the masks made
them seem identical, and I suppose that if we had dared looked underneath we could not have told them apart. On the older one's thirteenth
birthday they died in what seemed a suicide pact.

I keep crying, as much for them as for my own shame in taking part
in teasing them. My throat starts to tighten from tears of rage, for that
fucking God that didn't do shit except watch them suffer for the rest of
their hideous days, the same God that everyone credited afterwards with
a miracle, for letting the other three live, as though three out of five was
a respectable batting average for an omnipotent being.

It's starting to get light outside, when suddenly I decide, like a religious revelation in reverse, that I'm wasting my time and tears on
someone that either doesn't exist or doesn't care. The moment I decide
that, the moment it truly sinks in, the tears stop.

I lay on the floor until well past daybreak, then get up and examine
my pillow. I expect it to be soaked, but it's barely damp. I suppose some
people would call that a miracle.

31
A Disabled Deity

Lately I've been going back to the old man's house on weekends. My stepfather feels more secure knowing that I'm keeping an eye on the old man, and he in turn keeps an eye on me. For all his bluster my stepfather worries when I'm away from home, the same way my paternal grandfather worries about my wayward uncle. My mother's more like her mother—caring, but able to stand her ground when she has to.

I still stay at the MANO office much of the time, so I haven't seen much of Nacho, who's staying with his family and putting in as many hours as he can at work. Coco, Gabi and I are still talking about our out-of-state trip to get scholarships for Manos, but when I suggest we invite Nacho along Coco's somewhat cool to the idea.

I ask him anyway. He's for it, and in turn invites me across the border on an errand. It's been a while since I've been to Mexico, so I take him up on the offer and bring back a bottle of liquor for my grandfather. Their cramped, wood-frame house was already lopsided when my mother and I lived with them after her divorce. During those two years, the three rooms and the yard with the twisted mesquite trees were the center of my world, but nowadays only my grandmother's garden shows any signs of upkeep.

It's early afternoon, time for my grandfather's *radionovelas*. I often wondered why he prefers this ritual to the small television my mother left them after she remarried, until I realized he couldn't follow the plots once I wasn't around to translate. He's sitting on the bed in profile, with his eyes closed and his better ear to the old radio he's had since before I was born. Occasionally he nods in silence, as though taking confessions from the other side of the speaker cloth. My grandmother's at the opposite end of the room, trying to sleep while a north wind hums through cracks in the clapboards. I remember the bedroom from my childhood, but not the cracks. Such things don't matter much when you're a kid, but they matter now.

During a break in the *novela* he makes a point of staring silently at my long hair, but the moment I hand him the bottle of Oso Negro he grins and tells my grandmother, "Who needs a heater when there's this?"

I start to say something but stop in midsentence—just as I did as a child—when the *novela* returns. Instead I start leafing through his Mexican police gazettes, which I used to teach myself to read Spanish. I see that some things haven't changed. One cover showcases a confessed child molester, another a "self-made widow" who chopped up her husband and served him as *carnitas* to her in-laws. I sometimes wonder about this continual diet of inhumanity in a man who sees the hand of his celestial father in every aspect of life. Yet like most God-fearing men, he's convinced this world can be no other way.

I wait for the *radionovela* music to fade away then mention aloud the molester's victim in the tabloid, pointing out how the neighbors said she kept crying "¡*Diosito mio!*"

My grandfather shakes his head and answers softly that the Devil is forever afoot in the world, always ready to tempt us.

I point to the cover photo of the molester. "Seems the Devil's doing all the work. I wonder where God was for her. Why he didn't answer her cries for help."

"He was where he's always been. He's everywhere. *We're* the ones who try to turn our backs on *him*."

I already know I won't get anywhere. Instead I put down the tabloid and turn my attention to my grandmother, telling her about the infant who was forced to suffocate inside his mother. Yet I know he's listening.

"You're angry," he says softly. "That's why you and those others are out in the streets."

"I'd say there's enough injustice in the world to justify it."

This time instead of sternness there's only sadness in his look. "I wouldn't know. I only know what life is like without a father. We both grew up like little animals."

I hear his remark as though I were two separate people. A part of me can't take seriously the idea of anyone growing up like a wild child. I remember the articles in his police gazettes about finding wild boys in the jungles of Guerrero or Yucatan, and I remember reading them aloud to my friends: "Shit, I know this guy! He goes to my school!"

And yet when he links his childhood to my own I feel a sentimental bond as strong as the blood we share. It doesn't matter that I remember having him and my stepfather by my side as I grew up. He sees his own childhood reflected in mine.

"God didn't turn his back on you. Do you have any idea how tiny you were when you were born?"

"What's that have—?"

"You weighed three pounds," interrupts my grandmother, widening her eyes as though she can still see me back then. "Three pounds, zero ounces. You had to wear handkerchiefs for diapers. No one thought you were going to pull through."

She gets out of bed and pulls out a box from under it, then opens a smaller box within to show me the back of my birth certificate. "Look at your footprints."

I've heard countless anecdotes about my premature birth, but looking at those tiny impressions no bigger than adult thumbprints, I have to share her wonder that I'm still around.

"You asked me where God is," says my grandfather. "You're living proof he's around."

My grandmother can't resist remarking that it's also because my father paid a pretty penny to keep me hospitalized for several weeks. My grandfather gives her a look suggesting that if she can't help then to keep quiet. She's right, though. I may begrudge my father other things, but as my mother's the first to point out, he put up their fieldwork savings. I manage to tell my grandfather that if it hadn't been for that sacrifice, my fate would have been no different from that baby's.

"You say I'm proof there's a God. I see it different. The fact that some of us start out with one foot in the grave is proof he's nowhere around."

"We don't know what God's plans are."

He says nothing more. Turning his good ear to the radio he tunes in another *novela* that's already begun and turns up the volume. I assume he's angry, until I see the sorrow in his eyes, the same one he gets when talking about my younger cousin Oscar, who's had nothing but trouble with the law since his mother died.

Oscar is the only other grandson who drops by to see the old man, with an occasional gift. My grandfather had also written him off as another "*animalito*" after his mother died. Oscar's done his share of mischief since, but he's a kindhearted kid, which is more than you can say for some of my other cousins. Take Niche, for instance. After some *chavo* burned him in a drug deal, he and his buddies burned him back, literally: They took him out by the river, doused him with gasoline and watched him go up in flames. Niche even bragged about it until a few other De la O's advised him to disappear.

Oscar's soft-spoken and unassuming. Lucio claims he steals from the church poor box. I'm sure if my grandfather knew where he gets the cash for his gifts he'd bar him from his house. Not that his other grandchildren are beating a path to his door. The grandson he raised hasn't seen him in years, and my grandfather claims it's because he's ashamed of the shack he grew up in. So other than Oscar, I'm the only grandson who bothers to visit regularly, even though my motives are mixed. I appreciate his taking us in following my mother's divorce, even though he showed us the door afterwards. But my visits are also a perverse reminder that it's the feral grandsons who still bother to see him.

There may not be much justice in this world, but the little there is can turn out downright poetic.

32
Cities of Silver and Gold

The fall semester is almost over when we return to our plans for out-of-state scholarships. Like many other good ideas, it ended up mothballed. Later we heard that schools from the East and West coasts were eager for minorities, so we asked about sending several Manos there. But the Eastern leads we tracked down sounded noncommital, the available slots were too few, and even these were mostly for blacks.

By early December Coco insists that if we're going to move on the idea, the time is now. I couldn't agree more. I'll be a junior after next semester, and since most colleges require two years of study to graduate from there, I'll have to apply within the next two or three months.

Gabi, Coco and I finally decide to check out some campuses in person. We settle on California rather than the Eastern schools because we'll have more *raza* to relate to. We also decide there's no point in visiting campuses once the semester's over. So we leave on a Thursday, after my last class, which should put us in California by the weekend. My finals start the following week, but by then we should be back.

We're not even out of Texas when Gabi's car starts giving us trouble, minor things which still eat up our time and budget. Coco makes some quick calculations and decides we have enough money to reach California but not enough to return. "Let's head north," he says, "to Colorado." Marcos once introduced Coco to a Denver leader with a following among the more militant nationalists. We've all read his newspapers and his ideas on Aztlan. "Up there he's bigger than Cesar Chavez," says Coco. "He has a large cultural center, and I'm sure he'll help us with the rest of the trip."

"It's Denver, then. Besides, De la O is dying to see snow."

But coming from a place where we can wear short sleeves nearly every day of the year, we're ill-prepared for the cold. Soon we're noticing gaps in the car's floorboard that we weren't aware of, so that even if the car's heater worked the bitter cold can't be kept out. As we're crossing the Texas Panhandle, Coco asks through chattering teeth, "Say, De la O, doesn't your father live around here? Maybe we could crash with him till we fix the heater."

"It's too late to turn back," I answer, as much to myself as anyone else. As far as I'm concerned, he might as well live a million miles away.

We huddle in the front seat to keep warm the rest of the way and take turns scraping ice from the inside of the windshield. "So, De la O, you'd never seen it snow, eh?" Gabi's words come out in small vapor clouds, like speech balloons in a comic strip.

"Not inside a car."

We reach Denver at night, and at the first gas station Coco quickly slurps down six cups of hot chocolate. Minutes later he's curled in the back seat with stomach cramps. For a while Gabi and I tease him in the hopes he can come around and help us find the Chicano center.

"And all this time I wondered why they called him Cocoa."

"No, De la O. Coco, like in *coconut*. Hard and brown on the outside, soft and white on the inside."

"Well, I've never seen any part of him that's brown." I glance back. "If anything, he looks even whiter now."

We finally find the Chicano center, where they're wrapping up a conference of some sort. *Raza* from all over is still around, but we're too exhausted to talk, so instead we grab some blankets and some badly needed sleep.

By next morning the participants have thinned out, but we manage to track down some Chicano students from California. They're recruiting for the Claremont Colleges, a group of private schools, and encourage us to pay them a visit once we're in California. We also link up with a character of indeterminate ethnicity who calls himself Vidu. He entertains us with anecdotes of his brushes with government agents. I say *entertain* because that's how I take his tales, even though they're serious stuff.

"*Tortured* you?" asks Gabi. "You mean here in the *U.S.*? But why?"

The more outraged Gabi gets, the more casual Vidu becomes. "Oh, I know one or two things I shouldn't."

Actually it's difficult to say what he does know, if anything. But if sorting out fact from fiction bothers me, Gabi's enjoying the conversation immensely. I hate anyone insulting my intelligence to my face, but Gabi doesn't mind in the least, and Vidu is happy to oblige. He pauses only upon hearing we're headed to California, then practically invites himself along. Coco and I glance at Gabi, since it's his car. He says yes, so the matter's settled.

That evening, after Coco touches base with the center's leader, one of his security people tells us to drop by his office next morning for our travel money. Now that we can breathe easier I suggest we go see *Easy Rider*, showing a few blocks away.

Gabi agrees. "Let's buy popcorn too."

"But no hot chocolate," I add.

Coco isn't that crazy about going—despite his long hair and political ideas he's opposed to the drug culture—but afterwards he walks out in shock. "They blew them away," he keeps saying, as if he'd seen a documentary. "Those rednecks just blew them away."

"Well, they had long hair." It's Gabi's way of hinting that Coco and I tuck in ours till we're in California, but I remind him ours was short when those gringo dentists nearly shot us.

Back at the center we bunk down with several others in the huge basement. Vidu wraps himself in an Army blanket only to start inching towards an attractive Chicana from California in a sleeping bag. He rolls and drags himself toward her like an oversized snake, and even though he's not good-looking, he's soon whispering sexy Marxisms in her ear. I'm a little envious, but I also see it as a good omen: If this guy can score with Chicanas from California, there's hope for us all.

The following morning, waking up in unfamiliar surroundings, I have a momentary disorientation. I notice two *chavos* talking to Coco about the antiwar rally we held last month. It turns out they just had one of their own, except they've been billing it as a first for Chicanos. The problem is that ours came first. It's a hot potato that Coco's eager to toss elsewhere, which he does as soon as I stir. "I was just telling them about the rally." He turns to them. "Ask De la O, he gave one of the speeches."

"Oh, we believe you," says a slender *chavo* with black, very lanky hair that lashes about when he gesticulates. He asks, though, whethered we bothered filming the rally.

"They're just rallies. No big thing."

The slender guy, already testy, answers otherwise: "The issues we addressed are *life and death*."

That may be true, but I suspect that the real issue is the rally's place in the record books. It's not just that we got there first by a few days. In the map of Aztlan that exists in his mind, we're from some dark, unexplored terrain. Maybe that's why his friend keeps digging for details, as if to uncover a technicality.

I hadn't thought that much about the rally, but now I realize such things mean a lot for some people. Yet the last thing we need is bad blood between *tejanos* and *californios*, so I actually end up arguing on his behalf, that his Los Angeles. rally was much larger than ours. And since it had the publicity ours never had, for all intents and purposes it was the first.

"For all we know," adds Coco, "some other group did one before both of us."

The idea of adding yet another footnote to their accomplishment only disturbs them further. Finally the slender guy announces that he organized a demonstration even earlier than ours. It sounds more like a one-man protest at his university, where he burned his draft card in front of some other students, but he did record the event on film.

I congratulate him and once he's saved face, he extends a sincere invitation to stay at his house in Los Angeles.

Shortly before noon we meet in the leader's office. I like him at once, and his informal style makes the seriousness of his underlings almost unnecessary. He asks about the movement in south Texas, even though it's no secret he and some of the MANO leaders have their differences. In the meantime, watching his foot soldiers carry out their everyday duties, I can't help but compare them to our own hangers-on. Perhaps it's the honor of working for someone important that makes them seem so formal, and perhaps their discipline is one reason they have a large center and we don't. Still, I almost miss the occasional chaos we have back home.

Afterwards one of the security guys approaches Coco and hands him some money, which we don't count until later. It's a small wad, but its gravitational mass still makes Vidu's eyes bulge. "We could double that in Nevada in one afternoon. We wouldn't even have to go out of our way."

I'm thinking, *We could also lose it in five seconds,* when Coco responds: "We're going to California, period. Are you with us or not?"

33
California Cousins

On the way west Gabi's car drives like it's ten years younger, and the northern New Mexico sky is such a deep blue that we take a side trip through a snow covered forest. The trip reminds me of a Kerouac road novel, and for a while I almost wish Lucio were here. I quickly come to my senses, though. There's an enjoyable innocence to traveling with Gabi that goes beyond the worry of getting busted. Coco is loosening up, too, whereas Lucio in the end always misses out on the heart of the matter: the sheer pleasure of being aware and alive, without dope, theories, or any other opiates.

Even Vidu is behaving. I expected him to torture us with nonstop tales of torture, but the countryside seems to soothe him, although I suspect if I pulled out a joint he'd turn out as big a dope fiend as Lucio. Once we reach Los Angeles, though, his paranoia antennae go up. No sooner do we call the anti-draft activist to let him know we're here than Vidu decides it's time to part company. Gabi gives him the activist's number in case he needs to contact us, but he simply hands me his fleece jacket and disappears into a crowd of *barrio* pedestrians.

Our dinner at the draft resister's home is my first taste of *californio* life. His parents ask about his activism that day as though it were just another extracurricular activity. They not only tolerate it but actually encourage it. After we leave the next day, though, Coco points out that the parents were liberal, middle-class, and well-educated—not your typical Chicano family. I argue back that in some ways they come closer to the ideal *raza* family than our posters of farmworker parents with stoical, sensitive faces and a child equally drugged on sanctity.

"So you'd rather have this guy's family on your wall."

"I'm just tired of my own family putting me down for trying to do a little good in the world. It's not like I'm asking for understanding. I don't even understand myself much of the time. In this guy's case, though, it's nice to know he can turn to his family in times of trouble."

"For us it's always a time of trouble," says Coco. "If I waited for support from my mom, I'd still be clinging to her skirt."

"That's not what De la O means."

"What then? Asking them for bail after you're arrested at a protest?"

His sarcasm puts things in perspective for Gabi, who shakes his head. "My folks don't have that kind of money."

"You said the magic word," says Coco. "*Money.* It's easy to put your ass on the line when your parents can buy it back."

I disagree. "Actually it's easier to do nothing. Look, imagine us having it that good. We'd probably spend our days in Disneyland, relating to Peter Pan instead of Pancho Villa. Anyway, it's not the size of his parents' pocketbook that counts. It's the size of their hearts."

"Right. The bigger they are, the more they bleed."

"I don't know," Gabi finally says. "That house felt all right. And I liked his folks for the same reason De la O did. Not because they're a lot like mine but because they're different, in ways I wish my life had been different."

I expect a sneer from Coco, but he's almost sympathetic. "What I couldn't understand was how we could come from such different backgrounds and still be fighting for the same thing. Then I realized we weren't fighting for the same thing. He's a pacifist who happens to be Chicano, while I'm—"

"A Chicano who happens to be communist."

Coco's old man is a political animal of a darker stripe, a dyed-in-the-wool socialist who dismisses our protests as tantrums. So while my stepfather criticizes me for being radical, Coco lives with not being radical enough.

That same afternoon we follow up on the names of some UCLA students and administrators that the activist gave us. Our first contact, a Chicano student leader, has an office on campus, something that surprises us so much that he almost apologizes for having it so good. "Actually it's in the basement, so you could say we're still underground." But when we discuss bringing over several Manos as students he tells us the doors are closed. "This is a state university, meaning you'd have to pay out-of-state tuition. That means putting up two scholarships for each *tejano* we bring in. Personally I like the idea, but the Chicano community won't go for it."

"What's their problem?" asks Gabi.

"The money comes out of state taxes they pay for their kids' educations. There's no way they'll pay extra for out-of-staters when their own kids have a hard time getting in. Don't take this the wrong way . . . but why not just transfer to another campus in Texas?"

"Because our state doesn't give two shits about Chicanos. And even if you get into the better schools, Texas is still Texas."

He smiles and gives a slight shrug. We're disappointed, but we can see his point, which also shuts the doors at the other state schools.

Before returning to Texas we touch base with some Brown Berets in L. A. Most of the *chavos* barely speak Spanish, yet they smirk when we explain that the MA in MANOS stands for Mexican-American. It bothers me a bit, but it bothers Coco and Gabi even more. Other than that they treat us well and even assign us a guide for a tour of East Los.

The barrio houses look a lot better than the ones back home. I suspect the problems of Chicanos here are not so much material as psychological. I'd like to know more, but our guide prefers to point out the lowriders and the ugly graffiti along the way. "You should see this place Friday nights. Lowriders as far as the eye can see."

I can't get excited over *chavos* who spend their energies fixing up cars for leapfrog contests. He even introduces us to a few. They're alright, although several act hardcore after learning we're *tejanos*. Even their Chicano handshake seems like a fad, as much a *raza* ritual as Zapata's face staring fiercely from the door of a '56 Chevy across the street. These *chavos* are more concerned with the color of their car's tuck-and-roll upholstery, and the *chavas* want eye shadow to match that upholstery. I guess Gabi's on the same wavelength, because he asks our guide: "What else do these guys do besides cruise around?"

"You mean like for their community?" We nod at once, as though we're finally talking the same language. "Well, some join car clubs."

I still give the guy the benefit of the doubt. "And these clubs do things for the barrio?"

"Oh, sure. Dances and stuff like that."

Before I can turn to Coco he's already asking, "I'll bet there's hard partying at those dances." Our guide gives us a wide grin while Coco continues baiting him. "Lots of chicks, lots of Coors . . ."

"And lots of dope! But you *tejanos* know all about that!"

I stay quiet for the rest of the ride, unable to work up any enthusiasm for the occasional van with Aztec artwork. The same goes for a wall mural of a muscular Indian warrior carrying a curvaceous but unconscious maiden. A couple of years ago I would have found all this fascinating, but now it even pops up on calendars from the Our Lady of the Flour Tortilla factory. It's become as ordinary and overdone as a burnt tortilla.

"Say, De la O," Gabi says suddenly, "didn't you once say someone stole Pancho Villa's head from his grave? Well, I just found it." He points to some decorated hubcaps on a parked car. "Four, in fact."

I'm not about to defend the artistic tastes of lowriders, but I still point out, "At least here they acknowledge him. Back home the *raza* is just ashamed."

It's a weak excuse, and Coco pretends to contemplate the hubcaps to keep from laughing out loud. "I always figured Villa's head was rolling around somewhere."

As a last resort, we call the Claremont recruiters we met in Denver. The *chava* who tried to sell us on the idea back in Denver convinces us to drive over at once, before the holidays start. She adds that since the Claremont Colleges are private schools, out-of-state tuition doesn't enter into the equation.

When we reach the first campus we have to put up with the same put-down we met in L. A. "MANO? Mexican-American? Where have you been? You should change your name to MEChA."

"MEChA? What's that stand for?" Coco knows, of course, but he also knows most of the Chicanos we've met here speak Spanish with difficulty, so he lets the guy struggle through Movimiento Estudiantíl Chicano De Aztlán, then coldly corrects his pronounciation.

I point out that back home MEChA is seen as a college club, organizing car washes and dances, while MANO, because it organizes in the barrios, is seen as more militant. "In fact, some Manos at my school want to change over to MEChA just to be accepted on campus." After adding that there's not much in a name, I can't help but throw another barb: "Besides, most of the *raza* we've run into here have Anglo first names."

One of the *chavos* interrupts: "That's because our teachers changed them."

"Who's more important?" asks Gabi. "Your teachers, or your parents who named you?"

We've touched a nerve. When someone else insists he used to speak Spanish like a Mexican until the schools left him with a mental block, Gabi answers that our teachers also punished us for speaking Spanish at school. "After that we spoke English in front of them. But we spoke Spanish everywhere else."

It helps our credibility that the *chavos* who keep up with the national scene are aware of events in Texas. The state leader who went back to his home town this summer organized a major school walkout in his community. News of it is getting around to other barrios in the rest of the country. We describe how even though that area was overwhelmingly *raza*, Anglos almost always ended up as class officers, cheerleaders and the like. As we're saying this, and as most of the *californios* listen attentively, I can't help but sense an undercurrent of competition. The itemizing of injustices becomes a sort of scorecard, comparing the scars of oppression from our respective regions.

Still, I'm impressed how Chicanos here have managed to get college courses and programs relevant to *la raza*. When Coco insists it's a lot easier to get those things in college than in the barrio, I answer back, "If it's so easy, how come we're still outcasts on campus?"

"It's like you said the other day, De la O. Texas is Texas."

The following day we tour Pitzer and Pomona College, and later that evening we attend a Chicano Studies get-together before the holidays. It's going well until one *chavo* wonders aloud why they'd want to admit outsiders. When a couple of MEChA members let him know they're originally from Texas, he tones down his rhetoric. What's strange is that when he introduced himself as Roy Aztlan I assumed he'd be more openminded. Gabi even wonders aloud why instead of adding an ethnic nickname he simply doesn't go by his real name. "He should just call himself by his real name—Rogelio—and leave it at that."

"Maybe Roy *is* his real name," I answer.

His claim to fame is being an ex-gang member and an ex-con, and he's stressing his street life to make a case for his application. Several women are part of his audience. A few are eating it up, but the rest listen with an amused expression. Most of the guys around them, however, are listening for the same reason he's talking—to impress the *chavas*—and their earnest nods suggest that he's describing their own *vidas locas*, even though most of them appear Anglicized and middle-class.

His remarks remind me of those convicts who don't see the light until they're behind bars, insisting they're political prisoners, never rapists or robbers. They spend their days writing letters to movement newspapers, congratulating us for the work we're doing and eager to join us in the struggle. Usually I feel sorry for them, because once they're out they'll realize not much has changed.

This Aztlan character says he's an ex-con too, but mentally he's unable to leave his jail cell. Other than his exploits of blighting the barrio with graffiti, all he talks about is his time in the joint, although one of the more street-wise students mumbles that the guy was only in correctional school, not prison. He also senses that Coco, Gabi and I are not impressed by his anecdotes and singles us out. "So what group are you guys with?"

When I explain the acronym the guy grins as though the answer were worse than he expected. He tries to upstage us, saying he's with the Movimiento Estudiantíl Chicano De Aztlán. At least that's what he tries to say. "So you're the *tejanos*." He gives us a condescending smile, but there's also a trace of nervousness. Maybe that's why he takes the offensive again, asking whether we think we're the only real *raza*. He suddenly changes the topic: "You ever been to prison?"

Gabi gives him the same unfazed smile he gave to Vidu and his horror stories. "No. Have you?"

He must be wondering whether we're aware he was only in juvenile hall. "I've been locked up."

"So has this guy." I point to Coco. "They threw his ass in jail during a demonstration."

Earlier I heard a *chava* say the guy was in for rape. I turn to Gabi, but speak loud enough for the group to hear. "Remember the Zamarripa brothers, who tried that jail break? They say that compared to Texas, state prisons here are like a trip to Disneyland."

Gabi picks up on the sarcasm. "What about reform school?"

I think for a moment. "Oh, that's Neverland. They say the only *pintos* who reminisce about prison are the 'broads.'"

There's a moment of tense silence. Suddenly he shoves my shoulder, and only his loud laugh keeps me from jumping out of my skin.

"He's right! We say the same thing!"

We have a nice chat after that, considering the uneasiness. It's too bad except he pisses away his good points on his *vato loco* image. When he leaves I turn and tell Coco: "I guess *raza* is the same everywhere."

"No, it's not," he says with a stern air.

"Sure, it is, Coco. These *chavos* are Chicanos, just like us."

"They're Chicanos," he finally admits, "but they're not like us."

34
Great to Be Home, Can't Wait to Go Back

We leave after only two more days at Claremont in order to be home for my final exams. On the way back, we have plenty of time to sort out our impressions.

For instance, one afternoon a Chicano Studies class screened a Bunuel film with subtitles, *Los olvidados*. During the very last scene, in which a boy's body is thrown into a trash dump, suddenly I realized I had already seen this movie as a kid in a barrio theater. I even had a gut memory of myself squirming in my seat, stunned that even in movies children could end up dead and discarded.

Several of the *californios*, however, either could not relate to it or did not want to, and a couple even complained that the movie was about Mexicans, not them—an odd gripe since they eagerly dressed up their own ethnicity with Mexican symbols. Another said that showing movies about Mexicans proved that Chicanos themselves had no actors or films to relate to. He was right about American movies, but it was obvious he didn't grow up on a diet of Mexican movies like my friends and I. But his comment made me realize that we're an invisible minority partly because we've been absent from the big screen. Blacks, after losing their languages, had to create home-grown talent, while Chicanos simply imported the mother culture, including movies from Mexico. While Mexican artists helped us preserve our roots, we've paid a price: We didn't develop that much home-grown art because all we had to do was turn southward.

Reflecting on that, I fall asleep until dawn, when our car breaks down just as we reach New Mexico. It's the fuel pump, and we hitch a ride from an Anglo farmer who carries on an intense conversation with

Coco in the pickup cab while Gabi and I freeze our butts in back. I can't hear what they're saying, but when he suddenly pulls out a revolver from under the seat I have a weird, hybrid image of *Easy Rider* and the duelling dentists. Yet Coco himself seems calm, and it's not until we're at a gas station that Coco says the guy was just showing how paranoid people here are about long-hairs, especially after the Manson murders.

We're in luck and get a fuel pump—for a steep price—but on the way back we can't get a ride to save our lives. Coco has to take off his old boots by noon, and all I can think of is downing ten soft drinks in a row. We don't reach our car until almost dusk, and by then Gabi's so thirsty he drinks from a reservoir bottle under the hood before fixing the fuel pump.

Once more we're back in Texas low on gas and money. Coco contacts some Manos in El Paso, who feed us, then take us to a nearby college. By now we figure we can work a campus like the guys in Claremont who passed themselves off as Black Panthers and took up a collection for the Party. The pair was as pimpled as Coco and I, but since the L. A. Panthers had recently shot it out with the cops, the college crowd coughed up a bundle. We don't even come close with the contributions from our sympathizers, but it buys enough gas to get us home.

Now, back on the road, decisions must be made.

"So when are we going back?" I ask.

"Take it easy," says Coco. "We're not even home."

"I'll tell you when I'm going," says Gabi. "Not till the Southwest becomes Aztlan. Maybe not even then."

"Don't get us wrong, De la O. Califas has a lot going for it. But all this stuff about gang graffiti and *vatos locos* . . . It's not for me."

"But we have our own hard-core guys. Much worse, even."

"That's just it. We see them for what they are. And one thing they're not is part of the movement. Over there the crazies get all the attention."

Gabi agrees. "We have guys like Lizard, but we don't go around saying he's a revolutionary."

Coco seems worried they might discourage me from applying. "You could get a lot from their colleges, De la O."

"You mean 'you' as in 'us' or as in 'I'?"

"I just mean there's a lot there for the right person. It's just that Gabi and I don't fit in."

"You do," adds Gabi. "I heard you talking to those guys about writers and film-makers. You belong there."

"You make it sound like I was kidnapped by California gypsies and taken to Texas."

"Migrants might be more like it," says Coco. "But like I said, De la O, you could learn from them, and they from you. God knows they're naive."

"The problem," says Gabi, "is that they don't know that. They think they're perfect."

"That's why we need someone who can go explain how we see things."

"Which is where I come in."

"Don't sound so negative. I'm just not right for the place."

"What'll I do there by myself?"

It occurs to me I'm talking like I'm already there, and Coco adds to the illusion. "Don't worry. We'll talk some other guys into joining you. I know two who'd be perfect."

"But you can't get others to go if you won't."

"Of course I can. I'm their leader, remember?"

True to his word he arrives home promoting the place like he's selling paradise plots on commission. If his audience assumes he's signing up too, he does nothing to make them think otherwise. Those who do ask outright are simply told, "You'd be a fool not to go."

But the fact that he's not going makes me wonder whether it's the fools who'll end up there—a fool's gold rush. MANO, no matter how primitive, is a political organization with its power struggles and rivalries. As an organizer I've made it a point to stay in the background. I don't feel comfortable around the power-brokers, much less being one of them, and Coco senses this. He knows I'm not a threat, since someone who's serious about setting up a local empire wouldn't leave the area. I'm also fairly certain that while he'd like a group of us to study in California, he really can't see himself a part of it.

Yet there's a good chance I might not make it either. I missed a final exam in my science honors course and the professor refuses to let me take a make-up, leaving me with an "F." Later I get more bad news: Lizard and Nano were busted. The cops didn't realize they had busted two Manos, or else their arrest would have made news. Not that Lizard's kept quiet about the episode, but in truth he's not that involved anymore. Coco doesn't miss him one bit, and those who do, like Roque, see him less as a Mano than The Good Humor Man. He still has his sense of humor; when Nacho and I finally bring up the bust he pretends to swagger down the cell corridor and greet the other inmates with his trademark "¡Míralo!" There he is!

Nano's recollection of the incident is less heroic. "We get in the cell and find the cots all taken. So Lizard scrambles up a wall, catches a few bugs and says, 'I'm bunking right here.'"

Not to be outdone, Lizard insists that Nano put out during the night. "I wake up the next morning and his underwear is backwards. That front slit for taking out your cock—it's covering his ass. He's still asleep, but there's this big smile on his face."

"Well, shit," Nacho asks, "why not just take them off, Nano?"

"I was sh—sh—shy around all those guys."

I had left hoping Lizard might get into a school in California along with me, but even overlooking his grades, his arrest pretty much seals his fate. "Damn, you idiots should have waited till we were in California to get busted."

"What difference would that make?"

"Because it's no big thing over there, Liz. Everybody smokes dope."

He gives me a look of disbelief. "So then why do it?"

35
Ivory Tower of Babel

During the holidays I get my grades and confirm what I already knew unofficially: I flunked my honors science class. I didn't return in time for the final exam, and the instructor would not give me a make-up test, which was his right. I wasn't about to beg for a break either, but since the grade is bound to affect my honors scholarship, I take the next step and burn my other bridges.

I have a long talk with my honors advisor, first pointing out that the "F" wasn't due to incompetence. I admit it's ultimately my fault but also add that I had my doubts about the class early in the semester, when several times the instructor criticized the poor for trying to get a fair shake from society. The comments were uncalled for and irrelevant to the course, and since I was showing up for class with political buttons, I knew what he thought of me. I add that I should have seen trouble coming and not given him the chance.

Since I'm on the subject of grievances, I add that last semester I took another honors course with a teacher with conservative ideas. He was interesting in his own way, and while I took his lectures with a grain of salt, I also looked for some wisdom in his remarks. Besides, he would go on and on about Plato's political philosophy, then afterwards I'd see him checking out the co-eds outside his classroom. I'm sure those weren't platonic ideas going through his head, but somehow the quirk made him likeable.

This time, though, I mention an incident from that time that trespassed good taste. It was the day after a television special on Indian reservations, and there was a lively discussion going on before class. A few Anglos looked my way, expecting me to mount my soapbox—the same ones who once had the audacity to comment in class that Chicanos had never known real discrimination.

Listening to those same guys lamenting the plight of the Indians, I suspected the sole purpose was to suggest that this was paradise by comparison. The conservative professor listened somewhat bemused until someone asked his opinion. "Well," he said, "the solution is obvious. You fence in their reservations . . . poison their water holes . . . wait a few days . . . and the problem takes care of itself."

"Are you serious, sir?" This from a gringo who never lost sleep over the lives of the less fortunate.

"Certainly. It's obvious that contact with our culture has only led to chaos in theirs."

He fielded some confused protests from the class and dismissed them as the outpourings of bleeding hearts, but I also sensed from his glance that he hoped to draw me into the argument. Finally he smiled directly at me. "The young man with the shades . . . I'm sure the class would appreciate your feelings on the matter. What's the solution?"

I tried to untangle a reasoned argument from my rage but gave up. "The solution," I finally said, "is for red, brown, and black people to get together and kill the whites."

There was a collective, nervous laughter. He took a step or two towards me and said softly, "Seriously, though."

"I am serious. As long as people think like you . . ."

He blinked as though I had given an idiotic answer to a throwaway question, then mumbled something else and wandered toward the day's lecture. By that afternoon the same students who earlier had sat there aghast were already excusing him. "He didn't really mean what he said," said one.

"Then why did he say it?" I didn't give him time to answer. "Sure, he added a little smirk so he could say afterwards it was all in the spirit of satire."

For me that episode was a turning point in the program. I tell my advisor all this to get to the real news: I'll be taking a regular course instead of the second required course with the conservative instructor. It amounts to dropping out of the honors program. My advisor sighs, adding that my "F" in the science course doesn't help matters either. He'll see if I can keep my scholarship through this next semester, provided I take the other honors courses. It's a compromise I can live with, since I enjoy the other honors classes.

In place of the class I'm boycotting, I substitute a regular require-ment that meets in a large lecture hall. Most of the students don't bother to attend, and of those who do attend, a small core complains they can't follow the lectures. The instructor's not a native speaker, so his pro-nounciation takes a little getting used to. The complainers also panic when he reminds us our first test will include a magazine article he placed on reserve.

One of those lost souls is the wavy-haired guy I met in Nena's liter-ature class, the same one who warned me against encouraging the instructor to have them read Cervantes. Now he's upset that I find our reserved readings insulting.

"For Christ's sake," I tell him after class, "they're from *Life* magazine. They're not for reading, they're for looking."

"Anything wrong with that?"

"Not in my book," his friend answers for me. "More pictures means less words."

I happen to have something that overlaps with our assignment, a paperback by Norman Mailer on Kennedy and Johnson. It's more inter-esting than the instructor's article, and I even brought it to class hoping to get his opinion.

"Listen, I'm reading this book on Kennedy . . ."

"Shit! We have to read that *too?*"

I shake my head and explain my plan, which is to summarize the magazine article at the start of our essay, then focus on the book. Yet they seem aghast, as though I'd pulled out a *Playboy* inside the student Catholic center.

"Put that thing away, man! Don't do anything foolish."

"Yeah, don't give him ideas about real books. I thought I made that clear last year." The wavy-haired *chavo* stares at his friend. "Remember what I told you about this guy? Now you believe me?"

"But how will we learn anything," I insist, "when this prof won't give us anything worth reading?"

"You want to learn? Go back to your special classes."

"And do us a favor. Don't tell your MANO buddies he treats us like highschoolers. Whenever the *raza* gets a break on something, you guys come and screw things up. Anyway, while you guys are demonstrating, the rest of us are too busy working." He says "the rest of us" and "working" as if we Manos spend our days lining up for surplus cheese from the government.

"If you want to work," I tell him, "go ahead and work. But if you want a real education . . ."

He glances at his watch. "As a matter of fact, I'm running late. Just take my advice. Don't do anything cute."

Naturally I ignore his advice. During the exam I answer the essay with a token reference to the so-called readings on Kennedy and Johnson, then move on to *The Idol and the Octopus*. It's a show-off gesture, but I want to show him that at least some of us can jump higher than the junior-high hurdles he sets for us. When I finally get my exam back I can only stare at the big, bright "D-" in secret, hoping my two classmates won't sneak a peek. By the time I pay the instructor a call, I already anticipate several scenarios—that my argument were obscure, or that I misinterpreted Mailer. Instead he tells me what to him is obvious: I'm an idiot.

"You don't read book on right topic," he tells me.

"It was the right topic, sir, only a different source . . ."

"No, no. You read animal book."

For a moment I assume he means *Animal Farm*. "Animals?"

"You say Johnson an octopus . . ."

"No, no, that's what . . ."

He enunciates as slowly and carefully as his foreign accent allows, as if talking to someone barely human. "You . . . know . . . what . . . octopus . . . is?"

I can't believe I'm having such a surreal conversation, with a college instructor to boot. I don't know whether to laugh or scream, but somehow I manage to keep a straight face. But even as I start explaining the author's argument, I suspect he thinks I'm some sort of an alien. In the end I abandon all arguments except the one based on survival: I concede that while I screwed up that essay question, I still shouldn't get a low "D." But by now he's not only upset that I still can't tell the difference between a president and an octopus, he's wondering aloud why I'm not satisfied with a "D" when so many others are.

He finally gives me a "C-" to get rid of me. By the time I reach the student center I'm angry, not only at him for acting like he did me a favor, but at the school for not giving enough of a damn to find us better teachers.

I consider complaining to my honors advisor again, but if I were in his shoes I'd simply say, I told you so. Another irony is that the problem's not really about a language barrier. A couple of times some students next to me even made fun of his pronounciation but I reminded them that as Chicanos we shouldn't talk. And while the instructor's insensitive, he's not a bad person. He reminds me of other teachers who can be quite nice provided you stay in your place.

At the student center I search for sympathetic souls. Actually I don't much care whether they're sympathetic or not, which is why I don't mind that Baby and Steve, the future attorney, are among them. I simply want to unburden myself.

I'm so caught up in the injustice that I expect moral outrage from those at the table. Instead, except for Baby, everyone else has a good laugh at my expense. They say I should have seen it coming, especially after my classmates warned me.

"They were right," says Steve, who still can't stop smiling. He repeats a popular *raza* phrase: "*Para pendejo no se estudia.*" You don't need a degree to be an idiot.

"The only thing going for you," he adds, "is that you're applying elsewhere."

He's right. My plans to transfer are quickly turning from an option to a necessity.

36
Yosemite Zapata

At the start of the semester Marcos and his friends moved into an abandoned Catholic seminary out in the country, almost a stone's throw from the Rio Grande. Marcos informed the press that it's the site for an upcoming conference on Chicano education. It's actually part of a larger, state-wide strategy meeting for MANO, but the smoke-screen keeps the authorities at bay. Located on a low man-made hill, it looks large and mysterious, with enough rooms for spending an occasional evening there. It's also the ideal place to get loaded, a fact that's not lost on Roque and Lizard.

We still keep our other office in case the authorities decide to re-liberate the place, and it's there that we get a call from a MANO chapter in San Antonio. The Town Crier takes the message, as cryptic as it is blunt: "Zapata arriving on 5:30 bus."

The mystery's solved when Franky drops by the office. "Remember that Sananto organizer I told you about? That's his *nombre de guerra!* He's finally coming down!"

Last year Franky spent a few months in San Antonio and met this Zapata guy, who's been his hero ever since. He's even a bit insulted we haven't heard of him. Coco suddenly nods, searches through a stack of statewide MANO newspapers, then throws one in my lap.

"Oh, the guy who rips off Che."

"What do you mean?" says Franky.

I quickly track down a quote. "Listen. *Wherever death may surprise us, in an alley, at a demonstration . . .*"

"Che said that?"

"The first part. As for alleys and demonstrations, he wouldn't have been caught dead there. I think he had mountains and jungles in mind."

Franky's not listening, though. "They say he's survived two assassination attempts."

"Who says?" asks Adrian.

"Wait until you see him, then decide for yourself. He's like a revolutionary coming down from the mountains."

When we pick him up at the bus terminal he looks at Rocinante like it's some kind of bad joke, so Adrian explains, "It's our camouflage car. The surfboard rack turns into a missile launcher."

When Gabi tries to lighten him up by asking whether the bus line lost his luggage, he answers in a low voice that matches his mood: "I don't trust buses. My men are bringing my equipment by car."

The first chance I get, I whisper to Adrian, "You mean there's more like him coming over?" I also wonder why anyone would even travel by bus for security reasons, unless he figures his enemies are less likely to blow him up alongside innocent passengers. By his estimate those enemies exist in abundance: the obligatory cops; rivals in the movement who envy his "commitment and charisma," to use his own self-estimation; and Army Intelligence. Given all that, you'd think he'd at least travel undercover instead of wearing camouflage fatigues and a Che button on his beret. But the most conspicuous part of him is his mustache, even larger than the original Zapata's. Since he's as small as Zapata too, the mustache seems nothing short of enormous, reminding me of a portrait of Nietzsche in one of Lucio's books. With this guy, though, you get the impression there's little behind it. If someone snipped it off I wouldn't be surprised if it walked away on its own.

Most of us keep quiet for Franky's sake, but the minute Lizard lays eyes on him the *chavo* immediately becomes one of his walking caricatures.

"De la O, you still catch cartoons on Saturday morning. Who's that angry little guy with the six-shooters?"

"You mean Yosemite Sam? The one with the handlebar mustache?"

"¡Miralo! Yosemite Zapata!"

From then on even Coco calls him that, and when he informs us he's here to provide armed security for our upcoming conference, he only confirms Lizard's six-gun caricature. Adrian explains that we appreciate the offer but that it's not necessary, an understatement if I ever heard one.

Coco also agrees. "Yeah, thanks, but we won't need the security."

"You need it." He says this as though he knows something we don't.

We try putting up a united front of indifference, but Gabi takes the bait anyway. "We do?"

"My intelligence reports say you need it. That's all I can say."

He probably can't say anything else because he doesn't know anything else. I even doubt his "intelligence," yet he manages to set off alarms in several heads. Coco's, though, isn't one of them. "I'm not saying things won't get tense. But guys with guns would only add fuel to the fire."

"My men are *men*, not guys. They're handpicked, and trained in the martial arts."

But once his handful of men arrive they leave a lot to be desired— except for their berets and fatigues. Most of us wear an occasional khaki or camouflage shirt, but I've always felt silly wearing a beret. These guys, though, not only wear them day and night but color-coordinate them with their camouflage-pattern fatigues. They also carry canes with them constantly. In fact, by the end of the week Yosemite Zapata is criticizing our lack of martial arts training.

"And you guys call yourselves urban guerrillas?" he asks Gabi one day.

"Say, De la O, have we ever called ourselves that?"

"It's usually others who do the calling. But now that you mention it . . . no, they've never called us that."

From then on it becomes his personal mission to turn us into Aztlan warriors. Since his men will be our instructors and we their human breaking boards, the training seems more to keep his own guys in shape, so with the help of Rosa Rosales I cook up a counter-attack. We tell their karate instructor that his training's not necessary because Lizard is already offering boxing lessons. Technically that's true, even though Lizard's lessons take place irregularly, if at all. Rosa says she's heard Lizard brag that martial arts experts are no match for boxers. When she mentions this to the karate instructor, he not only insults Lizard's sport but his hero as well: "Why, Ali couldn't last one round with Bruce Lee!"

The next day they arrange a grudge match in the day-care playground. There, in full view of the staff and the kids, who expect either pulled punches or comical, cartoon maneuvers, Lizard puts the karate instructor in his place, alternately punishing and playing with him. He finishes with a brutal flurry of punches that leaves the instructor with black eyes and bee-stung lips, and the children with saucer-sized eyes.

Even Coco, who's a bit upset because we hatched the match without his go-ahead, can't resist savoring the victory. After helping the instructor to Yosemite Zapata's room, Coco pauses at the door. Finally he goes inside.

"One of your guys—I mean men—picked a fight in the playground. He'll be OK. Just keep him away from the big boys."

It continues that way until the conference starts. During that time we keep the uneasy truce of an alliance based on a common enemy. It's times like these that I can't help but think, Thank god for gringos. Otherwise we'd be at each other's throats.

37
Wherever Death May Embarrass Us

The conference starts on schedule, with Manos arriving from throughout the state. Yosemite's men map out and enforce a parking perimeter on the front seminary grounds to keep the curious away from the old burial grounds in back.

In the same corridors where seminarians once sought serenity and spiritual guidance, the more militant Manos walk around in the colors of Aztec priests, arguing about revolution and unrest. The official agenda, though, is quite different: electoral politics. Voter registration and the *raza* vote as a fulcrum of power are the order of the day. The words are blowing in like a changing breeze. You can't argue with success: The state leaders who went back to organize their own communities pulled off their school boycott, and now they're campaigning to take over several school boards and city governments.

Outside you can still smell pockets of border weed, but with the new push on working within the system even Roque is turning on clandestinely. They've even scheduled a dance at the end of the conference, something as conventional as a tamale sale. Marcos says the dance symbolizes the new agenda, a political debutante ball. That leaves me out, because I never even bothered to learn to dance. Yet I show up anyway, even if just to sit this one out. Maybe I'm desperate for a bit of excitement. Yesterday I even talked Roque into spray-painting an outside statue of the Virgin Mary. She was plaster white, and now she's bronze, and naturally that made the local news.

My interest in the dance was also sparked by Roque's comment that Alma's cousin, Nena, might be there. When I get there the basement crowd appears intent on disorienting a local band, demanding corridos and rock music. I can't find Nena, but The Jewish Aztec Princess is there, and when our glances meet I get the feeling she wants to talk. Then again it may be the beer buzz. I don't find out because a high school Mana who's already beyond a buzz insists I tell her all about my tour of duty in Nam. Perhaps it's the loud music, but I can't get it through to her that although I said a few words at our anti-war rally, it was Adrian who talked about his tour.

No sooner do we find a dark spot outside and start getting it on than one of Yosemite's guards comes snooping around. I'm reluctant to sneak into the seminary graveyard because Roque swears he's heard a baby crying out there at night. He was probably stoned at the time, but this is not the time to find out. I can't take her to the bedroom I've liberated either because Yosemite's men are keeping the second floor sealed off for a meeting of the state leadership. I can go upstairs, but she can't. My remembering the meeting finally puts a stop to our awkward messing around, which is just as well. This one's barely sixteen, and so woozy she still thinks I'm Adrian.

We promise to track each other down after my meeting and the dance, but I have a feeling the latter will last until the wee hours. Upstairs, as I search for the meeting room, I notice Coco enter a room down the hall. He waves, and since he leaves the door ajar curiosity gets the better of me. One of Yosemite's men is standing guard, but since he saw Coco greet me he lets me through.

Inside I immediately recognize a few of the state leaders. Everyone's sitting on the floor, alongside two facing walls, and the moment I enter they turn towards me. One of the leaders waves my way to reassure the rest that I'm one of them. Someone by the door makes room for me.

At first glance the discussion seems informal and unfocused, almost trivial, until I realize they're addressing the one audience they can't bullshit—each other—meaning that there's less posing and pretension. At one point a husband-and-wife team monopolize the discussion, along with an ashtray they've almost filled. Their comments aren't about ideological issues but about nuts-and-bolts matters: contacts, money and the occasional palm to grease or ass to kiss. I can follow what they're saying but it takes my entire concentration, the same way I'd force myself to listen to certain college lectures. It's not the beer or anything intellectually taxing, yet somehow I feel dumb as a dodo and just as extinct.

The moment the couple pauses to inhale at the same time, Marcos interrupts to summarize their views. Almost in the same breath he starts to rip apart their arguments using their own inconsistent quotes. But afterwards no one reacts to his argument, not even with the cliche that times change. It's just that no one wants to hear. Instead they stare at each other like they're carrying on a telepathic conversation, then continue as though the interruption had never occurred. Suddenly Lizard comes down the hall, calling out an all-aboard for anyone wanting to go back to town.

"Nacho!" he yells. "Where the hell's De la O?"

He's not going away, and when Coco signals he's disrupting the meeting I'm forced to pop my head out the door.

"¡Miralo!" says Lizard. "Listen, Franky here says he'll give you oral sex, but don't tell his boyfriend Yosemite." When I point into the room and gesture him to keep quiet he lowers his voice. "What?"

"They're having a meeting."

He clamps his mouth with one hand but seems more amused than apologetic. "So are you staying or going?"

We're heading towards the stairs when Yosemite's guard approaches us with his trademark cane, raising it just enough to get our attention. Lizard still walks straight toward him, like someone certain he has the upper hand. At the last moment his greeting lets the guard save face and let us through.

It's been so long since I did dope that the moment I open his car door I start getting stoned. "Shit, Liz, the smoke's spilling out like dry ice!"

"They can't bust you for possession of smoke, so don't worry. And you won't find any seeds inside."

Nano, who stutters when he's stoned, nods. "Yeah. They all—all went up in smoke."

As luck would have it Yosemite's men not only have a checkpoint going in but another on the way out. To make matters worse I recognize the guard's swollen lip: the karate instructor Lizard punched out. It occurs to me that maybe it's his fate to keep running into Lizard, the same way I bump into the Jewish Aztec Princess at the most unexpected moments. He points something at us which I take to be another walking stick. I don't realize it's a rifle until it's inches from the windshield.

"Nobody said they could carry guns," I tell Franky, hoping the guard hears.

He does, but it doesn't make a difference. "Nobody said we couldn't. We're making sure no one liberates anything."

I have to smile at the irony: Here we liberate the place, then worry about other *chavos* liberating things from us. Lizard suddenly says, "Let him play with his toys, De la O. This guy never saw real combat."

The taunt is meant to shame him, but instead he looks at each of us unnervingly hard and slow, the way Border Patrolmen try to unmask illegal aliens and smugglers. Suddenly he recognizes us—or at least Lizard—and cradles his rifle to show who has the upper hand now. When he leans in for a closer inspection a part of me panics that he must have smelled the dope a mile away. At the same time another part reminds me that he's no cop. Lizard suddenly floors the accelerator. I'm in the back, on Lizard's side, and the guy's face streaks past the window in a blur, along with his garbled shout.

"Liz! He's ordering us to stop!"

By now Lizard's laughing like a maniac. "Ordering, *shit!* He's screaming! I ran over his foot!"

I'm dying to look back, but I'm also certain that if I stick my head up I'll get zapped. So I duck to the floor along with Nacho and Nano, piling on top of each other like we're already dead and stacked. Now instead of yelling at Lizard to slow down I'm praying he'll go faster, even though no matter how fast he goes a bullet can reach us faster. Suddenly he makes a hard turn, and I'm jerked back to a sitting duck position. But it doesn't matter now. We're on a country road, home free, and we're yelling at him all at once, cursing and congratulating him in the same breath.

Nacho rolls down his window and the cold air revives us. But the night's chill, the beer and the fright we just went through make for an uncomfortable brew, so I ask Lizard to stop beside a field for a piss. He ignores me, and when Nacho asks him too he slows down but continues cruising, just to show who's calling the shots, so I simply say, "Never mind, Liz. Nacho decided to pee in his pants."

He pulls over at once. Outside I can't see anyone, but I know Nano's close to Lizard because I hear him ask softly, "Jesus, Liz, what if you broke the guy's fuh—foot?"

"So what? He has a walking stick."

I take my time taking my leak, gazing up at a cold, starry sky. I'm shivering but I'm also warm inside, as if the moment is branding into my brain in ice fire.

"I thought I'd never get to pee again," sighs Nacho.

"Like the gringos say, it's so *organic*."

The starry country sky makes me feel so alive that my sudden howl makes Nacho jump.

"Damn, De la O! I almost . . . !"

"It's the call of the wild!"

"Damn right! I thought a coyote was about to bite my cock off."

Lizard suddenly jumps back in the car and turns on the lights. "Hurry up! I hear a car coming."

I don't care. I think about the leaders back there on the hill, plotting the trajectory of our lives, while I'm pissing it away with Lizard and my other friends. Suddenly I start yelling at the top of my lungs: "Wherever death may embarrass us! At a dance! At a strategy meeting!"

Nacho joins in without skipping a beat. "Taking a piss! In a lettuce field!"

I stop in mid-stream. "Jesus, you're right! We're pissing on someone's lettuce field!"

"It's oh—oh—okay, De la O." In the dead of the night Nano's stammer sounds soothing, as though everything's right with the world. "It's oh—oh—okay. It's non—non—union lettuce."

38
Martyrs Don't Matter

Before receiving last semester's grades I mailed my application to Pomona, hoping to send out my transcript before the "F" could be added. I have only two possibilities now: Get into Pomona or continue here as a regular student. If I end up here I'll need a loan, so I make an appointment with the financial aid office.

On the morning of my meeting I'm the only student there, but I still have to cool my heels until the secretary takes my folder, opens it and calls my name as if the place is full. She starts shutting the folder and asking me to follow her, but I glimpse a newspaper clipping attached to the inside. I don't catch the whole headline, but one word in capital letters stands out: MANO. I immediately wonder what it's doing in my financial aid folder, but I don't want to tip my hand. "Excuse me," I say in an offhand way. "Could I see that for just a second?"

"I'm sorry," she answers with the firmness of a loyal secretary. "It's personal."

"I know. I'm that person. It's about me."

She smiles weakly but continues ahead, holding the folder close to her chest until she hands it over to the man reviewing my case. He studies it for a moment but also keeps it close to him.

He immediately wants to know why anyone would give up an honors scholarship. I'm not about to discuss my differences with the two professors. Instead I complain vaguely that the program's philosophy isn't right for me.

Finally I point to the folder. "If you really want to know, it's all in there." When I mention the news clipping he pretends to peek in and gives me a puzzled look, so I try to reach across the desk. "Here, I'll show you."

He pulls back to keep the upper hand. "What makes you think there's anything like that in here?"

"There's one way to find out."

He doesn't even bother with his secretary's excuse but shifts the conversation back to financial aid. I still can't quite believe what's in the folder, but my being a Mano is no secret by now, so I too turn to the original reason I'm here. "You're asking why I'm here. I need a regular loan."

No sooner does he set me up than he lets me know it's too late for one. "At least for a government loan."

"What do you mean? Are there other kinds?"

"Well, bank loans. But no bank around here would give you one. Not with your . . . long hair."

I'm ready to leave but insist once more on seeing my folder. It's hopeless, of course, just like the scenarios going through my mind. Even if I take the folder by force, what then? Run out and show it to someone I trust? This guy would simply say I put the clipping there myself.

"I think you're just paranoid," he says, as if he can see the scenarios in my head. I finally stare him in the face and see the enemy incarnate: the ugly gringo we talk about in the abstract, except now he's here in person.

I walk out of the building and into one of those aftermath moments you'd like to blame on drugs or a bad dream, anything to wish away the harsh facts. Part of me can't accept that such blatant blacklisting could happen on campus. But another part tells me this is what the struggle's been about all along, and it's this part of me that's left with nothing except a fierce pride. I stand under a tree and watch other students go by. I wonder why I even bothered risking my hide for them, while they spend their days either aping the Anglos or worshipping them. Perhaps a few years ago I wasn't that different, but there's a point in the road where you make a choice, and that's where I took a different path.

Standing there, it occurs to me that there's no law that says they *should* care. The thought also crosses my mind that I'm not indispensable, not to the movement, not to anyone. It's not a happy thought, but it's not a sad one either.

Later that evening I gather the courage to drop in on Nena. I haven't talked to her since the incident with Julia, but she's asked Roque about me once or twice, so I'm hoping we can be friends again. On the way to her apartment I'm trying to figure out the best way to tell her what happened this morning, but when I finally get there I don't feel much like talking. Instead I try to pick up where we left off and ask her to show me the novel she read from the last time I was here.

"It's been so long," she says. "Which one was that?"

It's an awkward beginning, yet it helps break the ice. "Christ, I was hoping you'd remember. I thought I was the only one you read to."

"Oh, you are, you are." She manages a sly smile to suggest that others don't settle for so little, then adds, "Was it *Cien años de soledad*, by Garcia Marquez?"

"That's the one."

"You said you were going to read it."

"I am. I'm just waiting for the translation."

"I heard it's already out."

"Then I'll wait till it's out in paperback, so my friend Lucio can get it for me."

There's one chapter I remember, and I ask her to reread it, about what goes on through a rebel's mind as he faces a firing squad. I hint that today I'm having similar thoughts. She tracks down the part, then describes in a soft, steady voice the rebel's rage, about how in the end, after fighting so hard, a few *maricones* line up to shoot him and he can't do shit about it. I ask her to read it once more, then a third time. Afterwards she waits awhile before bringing up what we've both been avoiding. "About that falling out we had . . ."

"Forget it. What's past is past." I can afford to be forgiving. After all, it was my fault.

"That's good, because Julia asked whether Rachel could stay here for a while."

Suddenly I realize that what's past is still very much in the present. "She's here now?"

"Yes." I make an involuntary glance toward the closed bedroom, and she quickly adds, "I mean, not at the moment. She's out visiting friends."

I stay a while longer to give the impression I couldn't care less, but actually I'm anxious to leave. I'm sure she notices, because she says something about turning in early.

I drop by during spring break but find out she's gone home. Since there's not much happening at the MANO office, I too go home for the week and run into Lucio, also in town for spring break. He seems more somber. I guess marriage isn't quite the way he imagined, not even with his father footing the bliss. Even his wife seems different, putting on the airs of poor people who move up in the world.

For once he lets me do most of the talking, so I tell him about how the movement is changing—but not for the better—and how the students don't give much of a damn except for getting their degree. He's not surprised, though.

"What do you expect? You're part of a cult."

"A what?"

"You've heard of the peyote cult?"

I try to recall the little I've read about what happened after the Indians were defeated and had nowhere to turn. Some thought that their ghost dance would destroy the whites and return things to the way they were before. Others looked to peyote, using its visions to lose themselves or find their way.

"But we're out there fighting, Lucio. We're not retreating into drugs."

"So you're not secretive. But to the rest of society you're just as crazy as any cult. You have your rituals, your heroes . . . your own way of seeing the world that sets you apart from the rest of the raza. You're on the fringe."

Afterwards I give his comments more thought, and they don't seem that farfetched. After all, I decide, Christianity started as a cult, one that caught on. It's the same with Quixote: Most people who admire his ideals would never dream of actually putting them into practice.

That night I dream about a march that's at once strange and nostalgic. Coco and Marcos are there, and so is Gabi, and many others who drifted into the movement then drifted away. They all have vaguely familiar faces, the kind that only appear in dreams, and where, even though you know their identities, if you look too closely they'll dissolve into strangers. I'm watching from a distance, like one of those curious bystanders at our protests who anticipates a passing freak show. Leading the march is the old don himself, carrying a lance and banner. They remind me of Picasso's scraggly outlines, except that now both rider and horse are stripped down to their skeletons, like those Posada prints from the Revolution. Following them in the distant shadows, a trail of protesters carry their own banners from the movement. I can only make out one of the slogans: *Viva la muerte*.

The next morning I visit the seminary and find it's almost abandoned again. Marcos is there with some out-of-state *chavos* helping him get the alternative college off the ground. He asks about my own plans, and when I mention that everything's up in the air, one of his friends makes a pitch for their extension college. "The way you talk and think, *carnal*, you could get your B.A. with us in no time. After all, the knowledge you got in the barrio should count as much as the one from books."

"De la O already turned me down," Marcos warns him. "He says he wants a real education."

I add that you shouldn't get college credit for something you already know or already are, but Marcos and his friends can't keep from grinning. I feel like a kid from the Catholic center. I wait until his friends leave, then ask Marcos whether he can get me a trip to Cuba, like he did with Coco. Maybe I'm trying make up for my remarks. He says he's lost his Cuban contacts, but he *can* put me in touch with some terrorists looking for recruits. "They have a first-class training center. They're international, but they want people for domestic operations."

Maybe it's his turn to outdo me, but I don't call his bluff to find out. I only say I'll sleep on it, adding that I'm flattered by such a hard-core offer.

The following week I receive an acceptance letter from Pomona. I'm ecstatic but at the same time nervous, since now there's no turning back. When I tell the other honors students, most are happy for me, except for one who always complains about the breaks "we" get.

"I'm not surprised," he says. "These days minorities are in." He mentions the proverbial brilliant friend who was turned down for college in favor of a mediocre minority. Every Anglo has one, although no one ever admits being the brainy specimen himself. It's like a rumor, always something that happens to some faceless friend. When I try to corner him as to specifics, the guy simply says, "I can't say much more, even about the minority who got his slot. It wasn't a Mexican, though."

I reply that I know of lots of average Anglos who got excellent breaks. "That sort of shit has been going on for ages, but all that time I never heard Anglos complain."

"Oh, really? I wasn't aware of it."

"That's because it's so common that no one ever questions it. But I can prove it, and without fictitious friends. Let's take you and I. Tell me your high school GPA, and your scores on your college entrance exams."

"Well, it's not that important."

"Of course it's important. That's how your friend was discriminated, right? Someone with a lower score . . ."

"I never said you were one of them."

"Sure you did. You implied I got into Pomona because I'm a minority. The truth is that if we lived in a world where we were judged by our abilities—if we lived in a *socialist* society—you wouldn't even be here. And that's not even counting the hurdles you never had to jump."

A month before school's over, after I've sent my letter of acceptance and agreed to Pomona's financial aid package, I find out I almost didn't get in. I had applied through a special program for Chicanos, but since I didn't fit their profile of an at-risk student, the committee turned me down, saying that my qualifications were too high. Luckily one of the Chicanos on the committee picked my application from the reject pile and personally walked it to the regular admissions people.

After I tell Coco and Gabi the good news, I can't help but contradict Coco's image of California Chicanos. "Remember Alex from Pomona, the guy who was going to law school? He picked up my paperwork and took it through the normal channels."

"So you're going in as a regular student?"

"Right," adds Coco. "Tell everyone you made it on your own."

"Of course." I answer with a decent impersonation. "I'm even changing my name. From now on call me 'Of the Oh.'"

39
Old Turks Never Die,
They Just Turn Into Eunuchs

The successful school boycott upstate is followed in April by even more impressive gains under a third-party banner. Chicanos in several towns manage to take over school boards, city councils, and mayorships. Officially MANO didn't organize it, but everyone's heard of the Manos who did. It's only a matter of time before Coco's contacted by a *raza* politician from a nearby town.

"He wants a dialogue," Coco tells us.

"That's what they said in sixty-eight," I say, "when the Mexican government asked students to meet in Tlatelolco Plaza."

Marcos adds, "A dialogue is something you set up with your enemies."

"Be serious," says Coco. "What can this guy do to us?"

"What can he do for us?" Adrian asks back.

Several other Manos have their misgivings about the proposed get-together, but by the time Coco tells us, it's beyond tentative: He's already set up a meeting, insisting all the while that we at least hear the guy out.

Adrian for his part can't understand what politician in his right mind would want us as allies.

"One with re-elections guaranteed up to his deathbed," says Marcos. "Once these old guys get their foot in the door they're harder to kick out than the Pope. The only problem is that the state Democrats take them for granted." He adds that the old guard is pretending to bolt to a third party to make its own party jealous. "And if a Chicano third party is the wave of the future, they'll already have their foot in the door. In the end they'll either use us and leave us, or else stay and compromise the hell out of us. Either way we lose."

I already have an idea how these south Texas bosses run their constitutients' lives from cradle to grave. One year they're godfather at some baby's baptism, the next year pallbearer for the kid's grandfather. Some families would even let them bless their crops and livestock if they asked. None of us care for their kind, even if they are *raza*, and Adrian sums up our feelings on the matter of an alliance: "What do we get from joining up with this guy?"

"What we get," says Coco, "is a little legitimacy. I'm sick and tired of everyone using us then running for cover whenever we draw heat."

"How do we know this guy won't do the same thing?"

"We don't. But I don't see anyone else offering to sit down and talk. All he wants is a meeting. Sort of like in public."

"Sort of?"

"Sure, like holding hands in the park, but out in some secluded corner. Don't worry, the news people won't know till afterwards."

Arriving at the county courthouse auditorium, Roque remarks that we should have worn three-piece suits. Fortunately it's a weekend—nobody's being arraigned and the rest of the building is closed—so the press doesn't get wind of the meeting. It's just as well, since neither side seems anxious to publicize the affair. And since we outnumber the other side, we also stand to lose more if the get-together boomerangs. We stand out in our fatigues and political buttons, unlike the rustic *raza* in cowboy hats hanging around their boss.

Still, he's not the typical gladhanding politico. Since the hangers-on who surround him are also his mouthpieces, he hardly talks to anyone outside his circle. Sitting on stage, he's sandwiched between Coco and what seems like a survivor from a Viva Kennedy group. I can't tell why the second guy's there, but Marcos guesses it's a tactic to throw the curious off the scent.

I point out the flunkies buzzing around the boss. "They never leave the old man's side, like those pistoleros from the old days."

"What do you mean 'old days,' De la O?" says Marcos. "The tradition is alive and well."

"But who on earth would even bother the old . . . ?"

"Haven't you heard? We're anarchists. One of us might show up with a grenade up his ass, ready to pull out the pin."

When he finally welcomes us from the podium, it's clear that he's used to dealing with two groups: his voters, few of whom have more than an elementary education and whose needs revolve around basics like garbage collection and street lights; and his backers, who talk solely in dollar signs. So he relates to us in the same way he relates to the rabble, as a champion of the oppressed. But that's hard to pull off when you run your own political machine. You can't play Robin Hood and Sheriff at the same time, at least not around us.

Nacho, sitting next to me during the long-winded speech, suffers in silence until he hears, "And now my time is coming to an end . . ."

"About time," Nacho murmurs in a raspy whisper that nonetheless carries.

". . . But I suppose that's the fate of old Turks."

One of the flunkies in front turns and glances back at us with a face that could earn him ten years in any state prison.

I whisper in Nacho's ear, which immediately implicates me. Nacho nods, then adds a little louder: "Oh! Old *turds!*"

Great, I tell myself, now I'm on their hit list.

The old man finally takes his seat to energetic applause from his camp. Coco's about to take his turn at the podium when Marcos, who's sitting among us in the audience, asks to make a comment or two. He begins in his usual disarming way, remarking how before the meeting an older man asked one of the Manas about her Che button. He wanted to know whether Che was the lead singer of some rock band, or else the band's guru. The Manos in the audience snicker.

Marcos then explains, "for those of us ideologically deprived," that Che helped lead a revolution. He carefully omits any mention of Cuba and communism, though. When he concludes with Che's burial in an unmarked grave, several men listen closely. But after that build-up Marcos says that it's unnecessary to mourn Che or anyone else for that matter. He hopes that if future generations remember us at all, it will only be to ask why we didn't do more.

The old man gets up again. He's worked hard to carve out his own little kingdom, and not just for the money and power that comes with it. He also wants the worldly equivalent of an afterlife: a street named after him, or perhaps a park. Marcos' talk of burying cadavers—in unmarked graves yet—has struck too close to his tired, old bones. So he informs us how a few years ago he participated in a U. S. Senate subcommittee on hunger and poverty here. He describes how the testimony was taken in this very auditorium, dropping a few names while gazing at particular spots in the auditorium, as if he can still see the lingering ghost of each luminary.

Finally he adds in Spanish, the tongue we were chastized in as children: "Maybe I've said more than I need to about myself. But if we're going to stand here and talk about some rotten rebel from God-knows-where, then let's honor our home-grown heroes." Then he holds his ground at the podium until Coco takes over.

Coco starts out on a conciliatory note, observing that the subcommittee the politico took part in concluded that the diet of the average migrant worker was comparable to a Guatemalan peasant's. The old man nods in appreciation: At least one young Turk knows his history.

Then Coco lets the other *guarache* fall. He asks whether anything's changed since the subcommittee left town, urging us to check out the migrant *colonias* in the old man's backyard and see what his generation has done. He points out how our *raza* politicians have stood out by their absence at our demonstrations. "Our old Turks," he says, "may as well be dead Turks. And like Marcos said, they're best left buried in unmarked graves."

I almost feel sorry for the old guy. But since he's not the type to take this lying down he has no choice but to answer his accusers. By now the routine resembles one of those musical duels in old Mexican movies, where rival *mariachis* take turns belittling each other's *machismo* through song. He grips the podium, then proceeds to put us in our place, dismissing our protests as infantile tantrums and reminding us he was dirtying his hands in political mud when ours were still in Play-Doh.

"Our parents couldn't afford that," Adrian pipes up. "We played in the mud of the fields we worked in. The same fields owned by you and your grower friends."

From then on the old man's speech turns even more personal and bizarre, but instead of acting insulted, we pretend we're thoroughly entertained. His speech becomes increasingly nasty until, his catharsis complete, he abruptly takes his seat.

As we file out I can sense an invisible line dividing both sides. Even when he and Coco go through the motions of an elaborate and obligatory *abrazo*, the act resembles more a mutual search for concealed weapons. When his flunkies clear the way he briefly looks past Nacho and me, as though we're not even there. The two flunkies who flank him also look right through us, but it's intentional, like when the Princess and I cross paths.

"They're just assholes," says Marcos afterwards. He looks around as if wondering why he wasted an afternoon here. "We should have showed up with grenades up our asses after all."

40

New Uniforms for a New Ballgame

A few days later I drop by the office to go over unfinished business with Coco. He starts with his nervous tic, cutting slivers of tape from the dispenser and chewing them, then finally says: "I hear Lizard did a number on one of Yosemite's men."

"You mean busting the karate guy's lip? That's ancient history. Besides, you already knew."

"No, during the conference."

"Oh, that. That's ancient history too. He had a run-in with the guy outside the dance."

"Run-in is right. He broke his *foot*."

"Well, now the guys in Sananto know better than to mess with us."

"I think they got the point. Now let's keep Lizard at an arm's distance."

That won't be much of a problem since Lizard hasn't been that involved lately. I don't admit it, though, since it only adds to Coco's argument. "For how long?"

"For good." Seeing my reaction, he searches for a phrase that's less final, but tact has never been one of his strengths. "Like for the good of the cause. We're going into real politics, and the rules say you don't mix politics and dope. At least not up front, and definitely not when you're starting out."

"So Lizard's a liability."

"He'll never change, De la O. I take it back. He's gotten worse. Now he's into harder stuff. They're talking about a third party, eventually statewide. If we do that the gringos will be checking every hair on our ass. Look, Marcos and I disagree on some things, but he's right about one. We can't pull out our opponents' skeletons unless our own closet is clean. We can't have Lizard popping out when we least expect it."

He's right again. Lizard's a fun friend, but that also means that when he hears 'party,' it's not politics that crosses his mind. Still, I can't just write him off altogether. "He's committed to the cause, in his own weird way."

"Nowadays who isn't?" He hesitates, as if deciding whether to continue. "And speaking of commitment, when's he start doing time?" He catches me by surprise, and he knows it. "The guys from Sananto told me. I guess it was their way of getting back."

"How'd they find out?"

"They asked around and turned up some dirt. Lizard's not the only *vato loco* around, you know."

"I guess it is a small Aztlan."

"And it's getting smaller. There's no room for dinosaurs. Like Marcos said, we'd better bury our own skeletons before they bury us."

"What *about* Marcos? How's he fit into this new strategy?"

"I don't think he does, do you? You heard him the other night. He didn't have much to say."

"He had a lot to say, but no one wanted to listen."

"Same thing." He starts on a fresh wad of tape. "Look, De la O, I'm tired. I'm tired of being that guy we watched on TV as kids . . . The one in black . . ."

"Zorro?"

"No, no. The gun for hire."

"*Have Gun Will Travel!*" That's not his name, but that's what we barrio kids called him. I even remember his card. "Paladin! His card used to say 'Wire Paladin.' Imagine. I was the brightest kid on the block, and I still thought 'Wire' was his first name."

"That's the one, the 'knight without armor.'" For a moment he's lost in some childhood fantasy. "We're the same way. Someone needs our help half-way across the state, and off we go. Only we're not even for hire, we're for free. And like anything else free, nobody appreciates us."

"That's what Nacho's father says."

Coco glances down as though embarrassed at both our innocence and our insignificance. "This being everywhere without belonging anywhere gets old. We get old. In a political party, you belong. It's like a home you can go to."

"Listen to yourself. We're ready for an old folks home. One day we're day care radicals, the next we're retired. Coco, it hasn't even been two years."

"I feel old already." He smiles. I almost confess that if it weren't for the fact that I'll be leaving, I'd feel burned out too. Instead I bring back our conversation full circle. "And Lizard, he's getting old too?"

"Around here he is."

"And what about Marcos? Is he headed for the history books?"

"Come on, De la O, don't flatter us. Anyway, every book has to end."

"What'll you leave, Coco? A footnote?"

He smiles as if to say he could live with the idea. "It could be worse."

"I suppose. You could leave your foot, period, like that karate instructor Lizard ran over."

I look around at the posters on our walls. I try hard to imagine Zapata as a politician, and his poster as an election placard. I can't pretend that hard.

41
Witch Hunt

It's not even the end of the semester when Lucio returns home. By now I'm staying at the old man's house, spending time with my family before I leave, so Lucio starts dropping by like the old days, as if he didn't have a wife and a newborn to look after. He's still doing dope, but his moments of hipster humor are a thing of the past. Now he's making references to religion, insisting that most great thinkers acknowledged some form of spiritual life.

But since this is Lucio, it's not that simple. Soon he leaves the garden-variety religion behind and starts exploring sorcery. Lucio keeps talking about something I heard a lot about in childhood: *lechuzas*, witches who turn into nightbirds to harass their victims. And he's insisting that there's one after him.

It's hard to tell if our conversations are helping him any, so I decide that my getting lost for a few days will do us both a world of good. I know he won't go looking for me at the MANO office. I haven't been there in a while myself, and since I'll be leaving this summer, some of the other Manos are already writing me off. I drop by that Thursday, but as soon as I walk in I realize it's not the best day for a visit. Coco, Franky and Roque are in the middle of an animated argument, and as usual Coco has the floor. He sees me and for a moment he stops talking, and I somehow sense I'm already an outsider.

"It comes down to one thing," he continues. "What's this damn movement coming to? Where are we headed?"

Coco turns to Franky. "You saw what happened. You tell him."

"Remember that *chavo* from Laredo? The one who's been helping Marcos set up their Jacinto Tijerina College?"

"Didn't he stay here when we had that conference?" When Franky nods nervously, I add, "Is he all right?"

"Well, some guy came looking for him this morning."

"What? FBI again?" He shakes his head. "Undercover?"

"You could say that. He was dressed as a woman."

I'm still locked into an infiltrator fantasy. "You mean this guy showed up in disguise?"

"He showed up *in drag*. You know, De la O, a guy who likes to dress up as a woman."

"A *transvestite?*"

"See?" says Coco. "I *told* you he'd know."

I'm not sure what that means, but now is not the time to ask. "You're sure it was a guy?"

"Well," admits Franky, "I didn't get a real good look at her."

"Him!" says Coco. "You said it was a *he*."

Things for me are getting fuzzier than Franky's memory. "So you really don't know for sure . . .?"

"I couldn't find my glasses. I was napping when the knock woke me up." Roque grins and makes a jerking-off gesture behind Franky's back.

I ask why, if he couldn't see that well, he thinks she was a guy.

"It was her voice. It sounded sort of breathless, like your friend Baby's, but at the same time low . . ."

I look at Coco, who's been smoking quite a bit. "Sounds like someone we know." But before he can sidetrack the conversation I turn back to Franky. "So who else saw this . . . guy?"

"I did," says Roque, "and a friend from the farmworkers union. We were down the hall, and when Franky let her in we went back to talking."

Coco compares their eyewitness accounts to the blind men describing an elephant, but Franky draws the line.

"Wait a minute, I'm not that blind. Anyway, next time he shows up I hope you're here. Maybe you can grab his trunk and find out for yourself."

"Don't even *think* about a next time," says Coco.

Franky apologizes and quickly agrees. From behind his thick glasses, his eyes still seem as huge as when he first told me about the incident. He's worried it can damage Marcos' efforts to get Jacinto Tijerina going.

His fears are founded, because by the following day some Manos are already referring to the future college as "Jotito Tijerina."

"I didn't tell anyone," swears Franky. "And I'm sure Roque didn't either."

"That leaves Roque's friend. Or Coco."

His eyes become as large as last time's, and suddenly I flash back to an episode of my childhood. I was at my uncle's house the night my teen-aged cousin came home in shock. My aunt was about to scold him for the late hour when his strange color stopped her. He finally stammered out how a woman in a see-through blouse had lured him to the alley behind the theater then turned into Satan before his eyes. My eyes turned as huge as his, and even though I always walked back to our house by myself, that night my uncle walked me home.

Franky's eyes before me look just like my cousin's the night the Devil almost seduced him: a chaotic mixture of terror and denial.

But when I run into Coco that afternoon and search his own eyes for a sign of betrayal, there's nothing obvious, so I ask outright: "Have you heard about Jacinto Tijerina college?"

"You mean Jotito Tijerina?" He smiles, but only for a moment. "Listen, right now it's still just an inside joke. But if the word gets out any further . . ." He sounds like a doctor trying to downplay a prognosis but only scaring you further.

For my part I hope it's all a bizarre comedy of errors. "Has anybody told Marcos about it?"

He gives me an incredulous smile. "You want to take a shot?"

"It's like my father says whenever we come out losing," he continues. "*Ya son hombrecitos.* We're men already, or at least we should be. This guy from Laredo knows what to expect if he hangs around certain kind of people. It's like you and Lizard. You either hang around with him or you help the movement. But you can't do both, because if you're caught you only hurt the cause. Listen, De la O, there's lots of groups out there getting screwed. But in the end each one only wants one kind of justice: *just us.*"

Afterwards I mention my conversation with Coco to Franky and Roque. When I think back to the odd mixture of concern and vindication on Coco's face, I remember once more my cousin's alleged encounter with the Devil. More precisely, I remember my uncle's strange demeanor that night, so I describe the episode to them, including my uncle's smugness, which reminds me of Coco's.

They follow my story, but afterwards Franky wonders aloud whether my uncle paid someone to teach my cousin a lesson. His reading between the lines throws me off guard for a moment. "I really hadn't thought of that . . ."

"Oh, I thought that's what you were getting at. That maybe something like that happened here."

"Something like what?"

"That somebody set this guy up with that tran— . . . with that other guy."

At the moment the scenario seems farfetched it, but once I'm home I start to reconsider. But no sooner do I get back than Lucio comes around with his own paranoia. I already figured he was having problems with his wife or, more likely, with drugs. He takes psychedelics so often that he claims he hardly hallucinates anymore. But now he claims there's a sorceress out there trying to get him.

At first I suspect he's fucking with my head. When I realize he's serious, I end up frightened too, but what scares me is that he truly believes it. I'm betting that his mind's overdosing on psychedelics, so I try using his paranoia to get him off psychedelics. "If it's true that someone's after you, then all the more reason to stay straight."

The advice certainly makes sense to me. With witchcraft haunting his days and nights, you'd think the last thing he needs is to derange his senses even more. Yet he insists that the psychedelic trips have done him good.

The entire topic makes me nervous, so I ignore it for the next few days. Lucio even disappears altogether for a while, but when he shows up again his obsession's taken a new twist: "I think it's Nicky's older sister. She's studying sorcery."

"Oh. Not at my college, I hope."

I think I'm starting to figure things out: He's interested in her, but can't bring himself to admit it. Like a good amateur psychologist I even trot out my theory of what's going on, but with a bait he might swallow: "Maybe she likes you."

"Oh, she's crazy about me. She wants to make sure I feel the same way." He lets me think I'm on the right track, only to add, "I'm just target practice, De la O. She was flying every night for the last two months over our apartment."

"But you were several hundred miles away. How could she fly all the way out there?"

"If I had all the answers I wouldn't be like this."

I remember hearing as a kid about this married man or that one being bewitched by his mistress, but all you had to do was take one look at the evidence—her face and body—and the real reason was obvious. Everything else—the purloined lock of pubic hair, her *Siete Machos* perfume—all that was superfluous. Like my stepfather says, *La panocha estira trenes.* A pussy can pull trains. But in Lucio's case I can't see the driving force that's driving the locomotive.

For a time I dismiss the whole thing as one of his chemical experiments carried too far. Then one evening we're about to drop off his wife and baby at her mother's house, when she comments, out of the blue, that they're finally getting a good night's sleep. "There was this animal back home," she tells me, "clawing at our screens every night. Even the neighbors were complaining. They thought we kept a cat in the apartment, and that it was in heat." She looks at their baby and adds, "She was even losing weight, right, Lucio?"

Afterwards Lucio drives around for a while. I'm gazing out at the dusk when all of a sudden something flies directly into our path, coming so close and so quickly that by the time I startle it's gone.

"Shit, Lucio! Did you see that?" He stares straight ahead and merely nods. It seemed too large for a hawk, so I ask, "What was it? Some sort of a shadow . . ."

"What do you mean a shadow? It had to be a shadow of *something*." He's absolutely right, he saw it too. I can't chalk it up to drugs, either, since I haven't done any in a long time. I'm panicky, but Lucio seems composed, almost serene. Then I realize why: I've seen the *lechuza* for myself.

"So that's what's following you!"

He merely nods.

"But it's just a large bird, right?"

"No, De la O. It's not a bird. It's Superwoman."

What's just as strange is that Lucio strikes me as the last person to be going through this. He grew up middle-class and educated, insulated from the superstitions the rest of us were raised in. He looked forward to summer vacations while for the rest of us it meant picking cotton or else suffering inside our homes with only a small fan to share. I always assumed he'd never heard of *lechuzas*, which I considered a sort of lower-class *raza* archetype.

Once the semester winds down I do a little more checking up on *lechuzas*, asking my older relatives about them. Some suspect I'm trying to have a little fun at their expense, but eventually they open up, prefacing their remarks with, "Now, I'm not saying I believe this, but once . . ."

Even the recollections that don't include the supernatural have a certain spookiness. Lizard mentions the time he was driving home before dawn when he hit a nightbird. "It flew right in my path, just like you say happened to you. Only this one didn't get away. From the jolt you would have thought I hit a person. I got out to check and there it was, right in my headlights. It had a wing-span this wide." He stretches his arms almost their entire span. "But what was scariest was its face. It was creased and almost human, like a cross between . . . a wrinkled newborn and . . . a shriveled old lady."

Lucio's also found out his grandfather had a similar experience, so he asks him for help. I suppose if anyone can, that old man's the one. He's a tough old bird, every bit as eccentric as Lucio. He wears vests even in the hottest weather, and one day during my adolescence I found out why. I was in the bathroom of El Cine Rey when he walked in. I didn't know him then, and neither did the *pachuco* who zeroed in on his vest watch. The *chuco* muttered that he'd always wanted a gold pocket watch— that he'd tear out his own old man's heart for one. When the old man immediately opened his vest, I assumed he was surrendering his watch. Instead he pulled out a small but lethal-looking semi-automatic, chambered a bullet and aimed it at the *chuco's* crotch. Lucio's *abuelo* took his time finishing up at the urinal, shaking his last drops on the guy's shoes. Not that it mattered much; by then the *chuco* had already wet himself.

So when Lucio tells me his grandfather agreed to help, I almost imagine him taking potshots at the *lechuza*. Instead he shows me a frayed copy of *The Twelve Truths of the World*, saying it's the most powerful weapon you can use against *lechuzas*.

"What's this do, exactly?" I remember hearing adults mention the ritual as a kid, but I had never given it much thought.

"Whenever a *lechuza* whistles past, you say the first truth and tie a knot on a length of cloth. That ties it to a certain perimeter. Then you go down the list, bringing it closer to earth, until it falls to the ground."

"Then?"

"Then you struggle and hold her down until she promises to leave you alone."

"Her? You mean the *lechuza* or the witch?"

"They're one and the same, De la O."

"But someone once told me the *lechuza* actually turns into a woman. Did your grandfather say that too?"

"He wouldn't go into that. He just said that if I chickened out—if I couldn't hold it down—I shouldn't even fuck with it. That's why he had to think hard about giving me the book."

On my way home I'm carried along by a nervousness that's both scary and exciting, like whenever I discover some disquieting fact that makes the world at once understandable yet more mysterious. The most fantastic part is hearing about the *lechuza* from Lucio. I could accept the account coming from someone older and more superstitious, but hearing it from Lucio is even harder than believing in sorcery. In fact, as he struggled with the old, formal Spanish in his grandfather's copy, my first thought was that Lucio has enough trouble reading ordinary Spanish.

Maybe there is a method to his madness. Perhaps it's his way of going back to his culture, like the *californios* I met who lost their language and went looking for it far in the past, beyond Spanish, to the ancient tongue of the Aztecs.

42
A Far Journey

The semester's over but Lucio's not doing any better. He doesn't seem as obsessed with the sorceress, but maybe that's because he's not saying much about anything. That's cause for concern, since the one thing Lucio likes as much as drugs is conversation.

With Lucio keeping to himself I've been hanging out with Nacho, who's looking for another summer job up north. He's convinced Danny, the honors student who joined us in Del Rio, to join him in a job search up there, and he's inviting me along. I'm considering it, partly as a way to get Lucio out of the hole he's in. My plan is to go along for the ride then hitchhike back. After clearing the plan with Nacho and Danny I ask Lucio, who immediately agrees.

Danny takes us as far as Illinois and drops us off. Lucio and I hitch-hike into Chicago, where a Puerto Rican who stocks vending machines takes us to Indiana in his van. A few more rides and we reach downtown Lansing, and from there we walk the rest of the way to my ex-boss's office. We chat for a while, but it's obvious he's not thrilled to see me.

I mention that we need a a place to stay and ask if Michael's in town. He suggests instead that we stay with some Chicano college students. "They live close to MSU. Good kids, active in the movement. A couple of *tejanos* are staying with them, so you'll fit right in. Both worked for Marcos last summer." He describes one. "A handsome guy with a nice mustache, like Zapata's. Always wears khaki pants."

"Gabi!"

"Yeah. That's his name."

"Great! But what's he doing here?"

"Attending a migrant workshop. You know how we love workshops around here."

He offers to take us there after work, and I spend the rest of the afternoon telling Lucio about Gabi. He listens, but his mind's somewhere else—perhaps on the *lechuza*, perhaps on drugs. That's another reason I'm glad Gabi's around. He disapproves of getting stoned, yet he's protective when anyone's under the influence.

Gabi and I greet like long-lost war buddies. Half a dozen other *chavos* live in the large house, and Lucio immediately sniffs out the resident dopehead. In fact the kid's been clean for the better part of a year, but the clothes and demeanor of the rehabilitated are probably what alert Lucio in the first place. Within an hour he's cornered him by the stereo, in a hushed exchange they've both practiced in similar circumstances.

"Tell your friend to watch out," whispers Gabi. "Rudy has a history of drug use."

"It's Rudy you better warn. Lucio's drug use is prehistorical."

Lucio waits until Gabi's in the kitchen to reassure me: "It's taken care of." He nods towards Rudy. "Rimbaud says he'll come up with something." He makes it sound like *I'm* the one desperate for drugs.

Rudy makes good on his promise. That evening four Chicanas show up, one toting a purse with chemical goodies. Gabi excuses himself when they pass around a jumbo joint, and I turn it down too.

The students alternate between gossip about the other *raza* on campus and more political matters. It's only a matter of time before the stoned talk takes on cosmic dimensions. Gabi and I try to show an interest out of courtesy for their letting us crash here, but since we're not getting stoned we're ignored.

Lucio doesn't say anything—his interest in the movement is at best abstract—and the Michigan students do little to draw him into the conversation. What impresses them is his tenacity with a toke. "This guy's a human vacuum cleaner!" says one.

Lucio dims the glow on his joint just long enough to correct him: "An industrial vacuum cleaner."

By now even those of us who weren't smoking have a contact high. But while everyone else is turning mellow, Lucio's circuits are just starting to crackle. Chemicals that tranquilize most brains only give his a jump start. Without them he's almost in hibernation, like the Burroughs junkies he likes to read about, but seeing him make that leap from lethargic to loaded is an experience to remember.

That's what happens to these students. At first he interrupts tentatively, asking questions as if he has difficulty following their discussion. But soon he's off on several existentialist tangents. And while the other students are ripping off someone else's ideas as their own, Lucio gives credit where it's due. "I don't like being the fly who sits on the ox and says, 'We are plowing,'" he explains. And the more he downplays his intellect, the more they're impressed.

Suddenly he takes off his windbreaker, as if he's barely warming up to the conversation. His t-shirt sleeves get rolled up in the process, and for an instant everyone stares at the screaming skull on his bicep.

"Jesus! Is that thing a tattoo?" one of the *chavos* asks.

"No, it's a birthmark."

Soon the others turn timid, leaving him to dominate the discussion. Only the Chicana who brought the dope keeps up with him so effortlessly that they seem two of a kind.

I keep an ear on Lucio, concerned he'll make good on an earlier threat to score psychedelics. For now, though, he's content with a cerebral firtation. He even gives her his profile and listens with his eyes closed, and when she asks what's wrong he answers, "Nothing. I'm concentrating on what you're saying." Soon I realize he's less after her body than what for Lucio passes for the spiritual: her stash. He quietly recites a list of hallucinogenics until she answers, "I have a couple of hits of that . . . But I'm saving them for the right occasion."

"Your wait is over, then."

"But I don't even know if they're good any more."

"If they're not, then nothing happens. Besides, you don't want your cat accidentally eating them."

"Wow! How did you know I had a cat?" Then a more important consideration crosses her mind. "I wonder what would happen if he took it?"

Lucio grins like a Cheshire cat on psychedelics and turns so quickly that I can't even pretend I wasn't overhearing. "We already know how that experiment turns out, eh, De la O?"

He's referring to a street study he and Nicky carried out on a barrio alleycat. But rather than protest my innocence, I simply say, "Yeah, afterwards he ended up like those cats drawn by a schizophrenic artist." I describe some series of pictures from one of my psychology texts, where the artist's cat drawings mirror his own mental disintegration. Lucio returns to the psychotic cat.

"After the acid trip he was a changed cat. He'd lie in the middle of the street and refuse to move. People would honk, rev their engines, but he'd just stare at them like he'd been reincarnated as a lion."

"Wow! Is he still alive?"

"If he is," says Lucio, "he's down to his last life. Unless he turned schizophrenic and doubled them."

As she gets ready to leave I'm hoping she'll invite Lucio along, but she's either not that stoned or else has more sense. Our hosts spread some sleeping bags on the living room floor, and I crash almost at once. When I wake up later that night something tells me Lucio hasn't gotten any sleep. He wonders aloud with a hoarse whisper, "So what do you think, De la O? Is there hope for these guys? Can you and your friend turn them into Chicanos?"

I'm not sure he's serious. "They're already that."

"I guess you're right. Where there's dope there's hope."

I'm hoping he'll let me go back to sleep, so I keep quiet. I'm almost there when he calls out again: "De la O, remember I once told you about Van Gogh's friend, Gaugin?"

"I don't remember. But tell me tomorrow . . ."

"He once wrote about taking a long journey, only to find the very thing he had fled."

"Lucio, your first problem is you read too much. Your second is you remember all of it."

"Only the things I can connect to."

"Well, try connecting with your pillow."

"She's here, De la O."

"Who?"

"Nicky's sister. She followed us."

43
Acid Indigestion

The next morning I wake up to a discussion the students are having in the kitchen. By the time I walk in, Gabi's asking, "So how much of the coalition budget are Chicanos getting now?"

"Ten percent," says one.

"Ten percent?"

"Maybe a little less," admits another. "And that's not just for Chicanos. That's for all the minority organizations that aren't black."

"So you tell the black students you want a fair slice of the pie," says Gabi.

"We've told them already. They say Chicanos aren't that important in this state."

By now I have an idea what the discussion's about. "Then tell them you're dropping out of the coalition. Ask the other minorities to do the same."

"But then it won't be a real coalition."

"It's not a real one now," says Gabi. "They're using you, that's all."

"What if they won't go for it?"

"What have you got to lose?" I point out. "They need you more than you need them."

"But we're all brothers in the struggle."

"Some brotherhood. All you get are crumbs from your Uncle Sam's banquet."

"Besides," says a third, "these guys are from the ghetto."

"Some are," I add, "and some aren't. Just like some of you are from the barrio."

Something tells me I'm being generous with the statement. They remind me of Danny, nice but naive. They discuss the issue some more then leave, but not before telling us that the Chicana with the psychedelics dropped by earlier and left two large capsules, along with a note: "I don't know if this is acid, mescaline, psylocibin or what. Maybe it's all of the above. I do know it has speed, so be careful. If I don't see you again, have a nice trip."

"So," Lucio says after reading the warning, "Lucy in the sky got cold feet."

She also has common sense, something I could use at the moment. "Too bad. You would have made a perfect pair."

I'm referring to their love of drugs, but Gabi reads something else in my remark. "That's right! Lucy and Lucio."

The capsules intrigue me. Yet my survival instinct isn't completely gone, since I offer Rimbaud, the kid with the haunted look, as a sacrificial lamb.

Lucio won't buy it. "He's a burned-out case."

"Even better. There's nothing to mess up."

"Don't think of it as something to mess you up, De la O." He's already taking for granted that I'll join him on the trip. "But giving it to Rimbaud's a waste. It's like giving it to The Chief or the *pachucos* back home. They end up tortilla, but that's all."

He's trying to flatter me, and when I call him on it he changes strategy and mentions an anthropologist, Carlos Castaneda, who took psychotropics with a Mexican Indian *brujo*. "He wrote a book that makes what the hippies are doing look like kid's games."

"Is this guy *raza?*"

"With a name like Carlos he doesn't exactly sound Anglo, does he?"

In the end, after a whole day of debating, we each take a hit after dinner. No sooner do I swallow the capsule than Lucio adds ominously, "Remember, De la O, no matter what happens it's just a chemical."

Gabi takes us for a ride downtown, to a head shop we saw when we first came into Lansing. Some windchimes by the entrance catch the breeze whenever the doors open, and their notes are the most beautiful music I've ever heard. My reaction catches me by surprise. An instant ago I wasn't even aware I was stoned and suddenly I realize it's stronger than anything I've taken before. And of course, the trip's just started.

Lucio feels it too. "The stuff is doing its stuff."

By now Gabi knows we're high but can't figure out how. He sniffs my sleeve for a clue, like a bloodhound that can't pick up a scent. "So what did you *vatos* smoke?"

"It's acid," says Lucio.

"*LSD?*" Gabi practically yells it out. The straight customers stare our way. Lucio dismisses them as weekend hippies, and we start enjoying some psychedelic posters on display. One catches my attention, a cross between a Biblical scene and a psychotropical paradise, and before I know it I'm on my hands and knees for a bug's-eye view. Gabi gets nervous, so he takes us outside and to his car, concerned but at the same time curious. "What's it feel like, De la O? Are you okay?"

Suddenly I hear a soft whistle high overhead, solitary yet stark, as if we were out in the country instead of downtown. I end up responding to Gabi's question by glancing up at the heavens.

There's barely a swath of sky due to the buildings on either side, and it's turned a twilight hue. But on the skyline across the street I catch the silhouette of a huge bird. The creature moves its wings once or twice, just enough to keep it aloft, yet not enough to call it flapping. It slowly glides over us in a diagonal, from the skyline on one side of the street to the next. Then it's gone, but I stay rooted to the spot, fascinated and terrified at the same time.

"My God!" says Gabi. "What was that?"

His question sobers me up enough to answer: "You saw it too?"

He's so unnerved that at first he can't even nod, and when he does he can't seem to stop. Instead of answering I step up my stride to catch up with Lucio, who hasn't bothered to stop or even glance up from the sidewalk.

"That's . . . the thing that's been after you, right?"

He pauses without raising his eyes.

"But what was it, Lucio? A nightbird?"

"It's whatever you want to make of it." He finally glances at me, and while I seem to be staring at my own terror, there's something else: an immense relief, the certainty that now I can't doubt him.

I'm also glad that Gabi saw the creature. Even he seems changed. He guides us to his car and drives us towards campus in absolute silence.

Lucio suddenly stares out into a patch of blackness and pounds the window. "What the hell do you want?" In shattering the silence he almost shatters the glass as well. He asks again, this time in Spanish: "*¿Que chingados quieres?*"

I offer the advice he gave earlier: "Remember, it's just a chemical."

He stares out so intensely, like a guard dog sensing evil in the night, that I also start looking out against my will. Gabi's trying to return him to the world of reason, but I doubt Lucio hears any of it. He's still staring out the window, concentrating so hard on whatever's out there that I'm certain he's drawing it closer.

"*¿Que quieres?*" He shouts so suddenly that he startles me. "*¿Quieres chingazos? ¿O quieres coger?*"

It's the ultimate challenge: Do we fight, or do we fuck?

Seeing that there's still some sanity in my eyes, Gabi tells me, "We can't go back home tonight, De la O."

I only nod and let him drive us to my friend Michael's. No one's home, so Gabi lets us in and stays as our shepherd. By now Lucio and I are conversing on a telepathic plane: I close my eyes and describe his movements and gestures. Gabi's amazed, but I can only wonder why I hadn't done it before.

Later Lucio and I take to crouching a few yards from each other and facing away. Then suddenly, out of eyesight and without warning, Lucio leaps at me at the exact instant I'm jumping out of the way. It's so synchronized that Gabi insists we've played the game countless times before. By that time he wishes aloud he could have gotten stoned too; he's all but forgotten the episode with the *lechuza*.

I thought I had too, but a moment later I feel weak and weirdly quiet, like when I laugh too hard and for too long. All the terror I felt earlier gathers momentum like an avalanche, and I bolt for Michael's bedroom without excuses or apologies. Inside the bedroom, standing before a mirror, I gaze at my eyes for the longest time, trying to pinpoint and stare down my own nameless nightbirds. I stand there until my eyes are the only part of me that seems sentient. Everything else has turned into an afterthought.

44
The Nightbirds Return Home to Roost

Michael lets us crash at his place for the next couple of days, giving us space to recuperate. In fact, he gives us a *wide* berth. Later Gabi explains that on the night of our trip Michael came home late, stoned on tequila. When Gabi told him I was visiting, he decided to impress me with a demented, drunken entrance. But I apparently upstaged him with a spectacle that sobered him up on the spot. Gabi won't say exactly what I did, but it's made Michael cautious around us ever since.

They say that corpses and houseguests start to stink by the third day, so I decide to head back home. Lucio, though, is in no condition to hitchhike. He seems even more withdrawn than when we got here. Maybe it's the thought that he couldn't outrun whatever's haunting him.

Michael hasn't any money to lend, but he takes me to my ex-boss, who heads a local *raza* organization that might give us an emergency loan. It's not until I'm in his office, in the middle of my sales pitch, that I suddenly ask myself what I'm doing here. Everything seems familiar: his desk, his placards, the pipe he's puffing on. But in truth it's a totally different world than last summer, for the simple reason that I no longer work here.

Still, he gets us a loan the following day. Maybe his group really wants to help out, or maybe they're giving in to guilt, like those California kids writing out checks to the Panthers. I'm sure he knows they'll write off the loan as a bad debt, but perhaps it's a small price to see us gone.

We're barely airborne when Lucio makes his first spontaneous observation in a long time, after I wonder aloud whether his father might make good on our loan to the organization. "*Se la quieren maderear con chi-*

canos," he says shaking his head. There's a price for the privilege of know-ing us.

Lucio's tranquil in a resigned sort of way. I almost say to him, *Don't look out the window now, but guess who's following us.* It's just as well that I don't stoke up his paranoia, though, because by the time we land in the Valley he's back to his secretive ways.

Once home I go out of my way to stay out of his, only to end up run-ning into Lizard. He's driving a different car now—not brand new but still expensive—and as I get in I'm thinking that compared to Lucio, Lizard's the lesser evil. With him I only have to worry about grass. Then I get a good look and realize that the rumors of his shooting up must be true. Lizard's lost so much weight that I can't resist teasing him.

"Say, Liz, I'll be leaving some old pants I can't get into. Let me know if you need them."

"I've got enough money to buy Boy Scout uniforms for every Mano in the Valley. Besides, I can still kick your ass with one arm tied . . ."

He doesn't finish the sentence. I suspect we're thinking the same thing—tying up an arm to pop up the veins. We drive around in silence for a while, then I say, "Haven't seen you around. Nano either. Nacho says you guys are shacking up."

"Nano's going to be shacking up soon, but with some other guy." He pauses, smiling, but adds in utter seriousness, "He got busted again, this time for dealing. He sold grass to some undercover feds."

"He must be shitting in his pants."

"He should, but he's not, and that's what's strange. He says only a fourth of the load was dope. The rest was alfalfa."

I try to think like Nano would. "And he figures the feds will take the time to weed out the dope from the other stuff."

"That's what I told him too. But he's not that worried, and that's what worries me. My hunch is he'll be doing time very little, if that much."

"I don't follow you, Liz."

"Look, he should be doing time *already*. Remember, we both got busted once, and this is his second bust."

I'd forgotten about that, and add aloud that I'm amazed the feds for-got too.

"They didn't, De la O. They're just hoping his friends did."

It takes me a while to say it out loud. "Think he's setting you guys up?"

"You said it, I didn't."

Nano's a nice guy, and he and Lizard go back a long ways, yet Lizard's convinced he's trying to get him busted. In fact the only reason Lizard's telling me this is that the narcs don't have me by my short hairs. Besides, I'll be leaving soon.

I bring up my trip to change the topic, but Lizard links even this to his dealing. "Well, let me know if you need a connection. I hear almost everyone out there smokes dope."

"That may be true, but you'd think they'd have their connections by now. Especially since they also have the border in their backyard. What we need to export is Manos, not marijuana. I'll try to get a couple of you idiots up there to California."

"You'd just end up babysitting, spending your spare time helping us out. And we'd end up being dead weight. And if we still didn't make it, I'd bet some of the guys would blame you for talking them into going. People don't appreciate the shit you do for them."

"Is that why you quit MANO? I don't mind much."

"Well, you should. The people who used to put us down are now going around acting like they're the original Chicanos. Then there's our own guys, like Coco, who get paid by community programs while we work for free." He catches my confusion and adds, "Don't tell me you didn't know about Coco?"

"I sort of suspected it." It's a lie. I didn't suspect a thing.

"I suspected it too, but I did more than that. I found out the truth."

"Well, if they are paying him, it can't be much. Besides, Nacho and I got paid in Michigan. But all that's history now. From now on I'll try to bring some of our *chavos* up to California."

Lizard remains unconvinced. He stops at a store to pick up a six-pack, and by the second can he's again dragging out other people's skeletons. "So did you guys ever find out about Loza?"

I don't remember seeing him in quite a while. "Why? Something happened to him?"

"No, not to him. But you guys got screwed. He was spying on MANO."

"You're fucking with my head, right?"

He shakes his head and has me think back to the time someone from the FBI wanted him to keep tabs on us. It was after one of our first meetings, and at first we thought Lizard was joking, especially when he wouldn't tell us his answer. But he stuck to his story, and he had the right credentials for recruitment, what with his Green Berets background.

"He probably figured you guys weren't that smart. After all, he used to tell you those stories about Che, and no one lifted an eyebrow."

He has a point. "So he told you he was also spying?"

"No, not right then, but he did get me suspicious. Back in Nam I ran into guys like him all the time, old-timers who didn't seem to have any business being there. They usually turned out to be spooks."

"So when did you find out?"

"Remember that party at my place?"

"Where I met that *chiva y muerte* chick. Whatever—?"

"Never mind Tita. The thing is that after you and Nacho left, Loza showed up. I'd invited him but never expected him to come. And if you thought you guys were out of place, you should have seen everyone's antennae go up the minute he walked in."

"So why did he stop at your place?"

"Maybe he wanted to know if I was still interested in surveillance. Or maybe he wanted to find out about my friends in the business. The point is he wanted something, and he wanted it bad enough to show up."

He adds how another *mafioso* who suspected Loza of being a narc slipped a couple of "godfathers" in his beer. "By the time he left he was quoting from his Army Intelligence manuals."

"Did you see him afterwards?"

"Sure, but he didn't remember a thing. That's the good thing about *padrinos*."

"So why didn't you tell anyone?"

"I did. I told Coco the first time Loza approached me."

"What did he say then?"

"He just gave me that little smile of his. When I finally got Loza to admit it, I felt like going over and telling Coco, just to see him swallow that little chickenshit smile. Then I figured, Fuck it, the best revenge is to keep quiet."

"You should have told us, Liz. He's been digging up dirt on us all this time."

He gives that special smile whenever he senses fear in others. "What dirt, you little coyote? I dug up enough dirt on Loza that night to bury him all the way to Nam."

After he drops me off I realize I'm grateful for the information, but also disappointed he didn't tell me sooner. He's right: We were so caught up with Loza's Che stories that we couldn't see the obvious. We assumed that anyone who went to our meetings saw the light, and that if he repeated the right cliches he had to be one of us. Armed with our posters and buttons, we were as superstitious as peasants using garlic and crosses.

The next day I make it a point to drop by the center and check out the matter with Coco. By now it's not much of a center anymore. He and a few others are still there occasionally, but now that the leaders are taking MANO down a well-traveled road, the political donations are coming in. Most of the books and equipment have been moved to an office across town. I hear they even have a staff.

At first we make small talk to keep our feelings from surfacing. It's not until he starts organizing his papers for a meeting at the other office that I suddenly say, "Liz found out Loza was an infiltrator."

He barely raises his head. "That's an old rumor. He told me that over a year ago."

"Back then he suspected it. Later he got Loza to admit it."

Coco puts down his folder and looks up with disbelief. "What did he do? Torture him?"

"Something better. Stoned him out of his mind."

This time the smile melts from his face. I add: "Liz says he didn't bother telling you the second time because you blew him away the first."

He doesn't say anything else. In fact I don't hear from him until the following week, and even then indirectly. I run into Adrian, who says they confronted Loza. "He practically packed up and disappeared that same night." Once the word spreads everyone reacts as though Loza's background had been obvious. We're like the neighbors of some nondescript nobody arrested for multiple murders, who end up saying they suspected something all along—he seemed too normal.

Even Coco's saying that pieces of the puzzle he couldn't figure out before are now falling into place. For my part I wasn't even aware there were pieces lying around, much less a puzzle to be solved. In the end, though, more questions are raised than answered, because once you fall victim to that sort of thinking you never again sleep in innocent bliss. Soon all the Manos I run into are finding spooks and gremlins in everything but their refried beans. Coco implicates Loza in a screw-up we had with some political buttons earlier this year. We ordered a batch that should have read LA RAZA UNIDA—The United Race—but what we got was LA RAZA UNDIDA—The Sunken Race.

"You're saying Loza was behind it?"

"Judge for yourself, De la O. Loza was in the know about that order."

"So was I. How do you know it wasn't me? He could have sabotaged the job altogether. But substituting *undida* for *unida*? That takes creativity and a sense of humor."

"But that's what makes him so good. You'd never suspect him."

"Anyway, that's not the first time it's happened. Remember our RAZA COSMICA buttons? Instead of Vasconcelos' cosmic race, we ended up with LA RAZA COMICA. So now on top of everything else, we're comedians."

Coco furrows his forehead. "I'd forgotten about those!" he says. "And Loza knew about that shipment too!"

A few days later I run into one of Nacho's neighbors. Like a lot of other *chavos* in the barrio he attended our meetings a couple of times. Then he realized things wouldn't change overnight and that there was a price to pay, so he stopped going. I give him the same story I give everyone else: how I'm hoping that once I'm in California Nacho and a few other friends can join me.

"Just make sure Lizard's not one of them. Last night he was telling some friends that you're going off to become a narc."

For a moment I wait for him to laugh out loud. After I realize he's not kidding, even after I realize that Lizard might indeed have said that, I still have trouble taking it seriously.

"I'm disappointed. I thought he gave me more credit than that."

"You still don't get it, De la O. Last year they were saying the same thing about Beto Menchaca."

"Didn't someone put a bullet in his leg?"

"Three." He tattoos three taps on my leg with his index finger. "Here . . . here . . ." On the last one he digs a fingernail deep into my kneecap. "And *here*. They fucked him up, *carnal*, and all because a few beers made someone suspicious."

"But Beto's still around."

"Oh, he's around, but now he's a lot slower." He does a cruel caricature of Beto's shuffle. "Now he walks sort of sideways, like a crab."

We talk about other matters, especially fantasies of California. But an hour later, as I walk away, I can still feel that fingernail lodged in my knee.

45
Mosquitos Waiting in the Wings

I've been staying at the old man's house the past few days. My mother's worried about my leaving but backs my decision. At least it's California instead of Cuba. My stepfather's just glad that MANO will be making local headlines without my help.

I get a call on Tuesday, and since I'm a late sleeper, my family has to rouse me out of bed. "It's a friend of yours."

Even before I answer, Nano's already babbling on the line. He finally calms down enough to explain: "It's Lizard, *carnal*. He's dead."

I'm wait for more, but there's only silence. I don't say anything either because I have this image—so certain it may as well be real—of Lizard listening in at the other end. A strange noise, like a strangled laugh, cinches my suspicions.

"Is he just dead, or deader than shit?"

My mother gasps but I dismiss her concern with a quick smile. Any second now I expect Lizard to come back with, "Watch it, motherchicken!" But no one answers. The line seems dead, then there's that strange noise again. It's Nano sobbing.

I'm too astonished to apologize.

"Overdose. He's gone, *carnal*. Gone."

I want more details, as though I'll find a technicality that'll cancel everything, but these insignificant images of Lizard get in the way, the laugh and the gestures that were his trademark. If I push my imagination I can even imagine him convulsing or whatever happens when you overdose, but that's as far as I can go. I can picture him dying—fighting death—but I can't picture him dead.

Nano says the family insists it was an accident, but others aren't rul-
ing out a deliberate overdose. I remember how down Lizard was the last
time I saw him. "You mean suicide?"

"Shit, no, Lizard would never do that. They're saying someone gave
him a pure batch on purpose." He starts asking me about the strange
lady Lizard introduced me to at his party. The tattooed one.

"You mean Tita?"

"That's the one."

I know what he's thinking. "No, Nano, she's not. She was just hus-
tling a little something for herself, like everyone else." I add that she's no
angel, but neither is she an angel of death.

Then he's off on another tangent, an almost incoherent account of
the time Lizard kept him alive during an overdose of his own—shaking
and taunting him, walking him around. I'm hearing him, but I'm also
wondering how they could have lived through that without my having
been there or at least without my having known about it. Then he stops,
as if none of that matters anymore. "Lizard's dead, *carnal*." He says it
again with the stubbornness of someone trying to get it through his own
head.

I'm having a hard time accepting it myself. But as Lizard himself used
to say, "There it is." Reality, now deal with it.

Used to say. I can barely think it, much less accept it. It's as though
you're walking down a road with someone, and occasionally you glance
at him, because you take it for granted he'll be at your side, if not infinitely at least indefinitely. Then suddenly he's gone, and you can only
measure the loss by everything you see and feel after that, the adventures
or even the ordinary moments you'll never share with him.

Nano asks abruptly, "When are you leaving, De la O?"

For an instant I take it to mean I'm next, and I get a sudden shiver.
Then I realize he's referring to California.

"I don't know, Nano. Soon. Pretty soon."

"You'll be at his burial, though."

"I'll be there. And I'll contact the *chavos* at the new center."

"Well, since they barely remember you, what makes you think they'll
remember Lizard?"

"Who could ever forget Lizard?"

"Coco and a few others were trying to, even when he was alive." He stays silent so long that I wonder whether he's still on the line, until he adds, "You're the last, *carnal*. The last of the Mohicans. All those motherchickens we helped out, they just wanted a bone. You're the last."

I call up the new center and ask for Coco, but the *chavo* who answers doesn't know anyone by that name. "Peredo," I tell him.

"Which one?"

"The ugly one." But he's not in the mood for jokes, and it takes me a while to remember Coco's real name.

"He's not in," says the guy.

I ask for a few other *chavos* by name, until he wonders aloud how I know them. In the end I simply leave a message for Coco about Lizard's death.

Nano was right. The *chavo* has no idea who Lizard was: "So this is personal."

"It's both."

"I mean it's not about the party."

"No, it's not about the party." Even as I say it, I know what he's thinking: If it's not about the party, it's not important.

Besides Nacho and myself, Adrian is the only other Mano at the burial, and he found out through the obituaries, not the center. After the service we run into Nano, in the company of two other *chavos* who, like him, seem heavily sedated. Whatever they're on, they didn't bother with a prescription.

They turn out to be Lizard's cousins, and Nano introduces me to them. "I want you to meet a friend. He was a friend of Leo's too."

Hearing Lizard called by his real name only adds to my sense of unreality.

Physically his cousins seem just as strong as he was in life, but they shake my hand with the timid grasp of the bereaved. Nano adds that I'm the last of the Mohicans, even though they have no idea what he's talking about. The minute Nano takes me aside I tell him as much. He gives me his why-worry smile, as though we're sharing an inside joke. He adds, as quickly as his drugged reflexes will allow, that he's been busted a second time, glancing at Nacho and Adrian every so often to make sure they can't overhear. I act like it's news to me.

"A second bust? That's hard time, for sure."

My grimace isn't just for show. Spongy, gentle guys like him end up on the wrong end of a cock there. Lizard would have been the first to remind him of that prison lore that *pintos* bring back to the barrio—how another prisoner will come up behind you, press a knife to your neck and his cock to your ass and ask, *¿El de fierro . . . o el de carne?* Naturally most guys take the carnal choice.

I let him lay out his alfalfa defense. "But Nano, what makes you think the narcs will take the time to pull out every blade of alfalfa?"

"We'll do it for them." He whispers like a man with a foolproof plan. "My lawyer's hiring this expert on plants . . ."

I let him finish, even though we both know it's a lost cause. Now I know why he's calling *me* the last of the Mohicans. Where he's going, he won't count, at least not for a few years.

For the next couple of days I try to work up the will to go say good-bye to Nena. I'm leaving for California in the next few days and time's running out. Besides, there's nothing like the death of a friend to remind you of the friends you still have.

I also try my best to remember Lizard as Leo, out of some vague respect for the dead and because, when all is said and done, that's the name etched on his tombstone. I remember telling him once about another Leo—Tolstoy—hoping the namesake might get him interested in literature. We were driving around aimlessly that afternoon, when I mentioned a Tolstoy novel I was reading, and the central idea behind it: Life is everything. It suddenly struck me then how we were taking that drive just to kill time, as if we had all the time in the world. Afterwards we continued driving around aimlessly, but at least I started to savor the luxurious laziness of it all.

The comment got him to thinking, too, but in another direction. "So this *tocayo* Tolstoy says we should try everything."

"Not exactly, Liz. Life is still fragile. What he's telling us—"

"Don't worry, De la O. I won't make you do anything dangerous."

There it is, as he liked to say.

That Monday I find out Nena's in summer school, so I make it a point to go say goodbye. She's not at her apartment so I swing by the student center, and after a half-hour's wait she shows up. We barely start talking when our old classmate Cervantes comes over.

"So," he tells me, "I hear you've gotten too good for us."

"No. I've *always* been too good for you guys."

"I told you," he tells Nena. "He just pretended to be one of us." He turns back to me. "Anyway, you're not the only one leaving. Heard the latest about Esteban?"

"Who's Esteban?"

Nena tries to help. "Isn't he that friend of yours who acts like he's already a lawyer?"

"You mean *Steve*! He's always going around telling people to call him Steve."

"Well now you can call him anything you want," says Cervantes. "Even Esteban. Or I should say, *especially* Esteban. He heard some schools back East wanted Chicanos. He threw out a line to some out-of-state law schools and got a bite. One place even invited him to visit their campus, so he figures it wouldn't hurt to show he's . . ." He turns to Nena. "What's that word?"

"Ethnic."

"That's the word. In fact he wanted to talk to you. He'd like to help you guys out sometime."

I shrug. "I'm not plugged much into MANO anymore." I don't add what bothers me the most: that Coco would welcome him with open arms.

Cervantes says nothing for a while, content to let the irony sink in. "I don't see any happy faces. Besides, isn't that what MANO's all about? Helping Chicanos make it?"

"Who said Steve's a Chicano?" Nena responds.

"Who said he isn't?" asks Cervantes. "That's what he's calling himself now, and it's good enough for that law school. That's about as legal as you can get."

"But he's not," says Nena. "At least not a real one."

She's surprised when I side with Cervantes. "Then he's an unreal one. And like our friend here says, that's good enough for the Anglos."

Nena stares at me. All I can see is our born-again Esteban rubbing elbows with gringos who tell themselves, *Why, they're just like us.* I can almost hear him going back to his old habits, insisting they call him Steve.

"Well, he says he's Chicano," says Cervantes, "and who knows him better? That's the trouble with radicals. They keep saying they're for all *our people*, then they close rank like some country club. I can already imagine him up there. *Hello, just call me, uh, Eh-steven.*"

He laughs long and hard—they way an outsider enjoys both sides of a feud—until the emotion exhausts him. After an awkward silence Nena suddenly asks us whether we ever read Azuela.

Cervantes glances at me for a clue.

"He was a doctor who joined the Mexican Revolution then wrote about it." I turn to Nena and add, "I read *The Underdogs.*"

She smiles and nods. "Have you read *Las moscas?*"

"*The Flies?*" I shake my head.

"Well, that's how Azuela viewed the opportunists who followed the revolution. They switched to whichever side was winning."

"That's Esteban all right. Well, maybe *mosca* is giving him too much credit."

"Let's call him a mosquito, then," says Nena.

"*Moscas*, mosquitos, whatever," says Cervantes. "You still have to give flies and mosquitos credit for surviving. They outlived the dinosaurs."

I shrug. "If you don't mind eating shit or sucking someone's blood to survive."

"They didn't seem to mind. The point is they survived."

"You remind me of something my papa always says. 'You chase the hare just so someone else can step in and catch it.'"

"Speaking of fast animals," Nena asks me, "how are you getting to California? A Greyhound?"

"Actually, I'm getting a ride."

"Who with? Some migrant family?" Cervantes jokes.

He's not that far from the truth. "No, all the migrants here already left for California." I really should leave it at that and avoid the inevitable teasing, but I suppose it's my perverse pride on doing things differently that makes me add, "A *mexicano* who knows my family is driving close to

Claremont, and he offered me a ride. My uncle's giving me a ride to his place, across the river, and we'll cross back into the States a few hours along the way."

Cervantes sits up straight in his seat. "A *mexicano*, you said? Christ, you guys always do things the hard way."

"Is there any other way?"

"There is if you happen to be Steve. He says there's a good chance that law school might fly him up for an interview."

After a while Nena gets up and says she has a class. She adds, "If you're still around here this evening, drop by my place."

After she leaves, Cervantes explains my luck with another rural pearl of wisdom. "It's like papa says, 'The hog with the longest snout always gets the best ear of corn.'"

46
Adios, Dulce Nena

It's been a couple of weeks since my psychedelic trip with Lucio, yet I still don't feel I'm all here. I'm not having hallucinations or flashbacks; instead there's an absence: I've lost my enthusiasm for things. So I revisit the healer from a couple of years ago.

Even though I don't mention the episode in Michigan, she decides I'm suffering from *susto*—a strong shock or fright—then sweeps me with some branches from a shrub. The strange sensation of the leaves barely brushing over me, plus the unusual murmur of her ritual, is extremely soothing. Afterwards I feel relaxed and alert at the same time, as if I've awaken from a much-needed rest. I'm still not as good as new, but it's a step in the right direction.

From the healer's house it's a twenty-minute walk to my grandparents' place. It's a visit I've put off even though my grandfather wants to give me his blessing before I leave. Since our last disagreement was over religion, somehow the blessing seems like I'm giving in. Finally I tell myself that the *curandera's* ritual was also religious. Besides, I'll miss my grandfather's anecdotes.

I find him in a good mood, to where he even congratulates me for staying out of jail, despite taking part in several protests. Before I realize it I've asked him about the time he himself was locked up. "Mama told me you once protested some law or other."

He's silent for a moment. "It was in Karnes County, near your grandmother's hometown. That was the year of the great dying, the worst epidemic I've ever seen. I didn't realize how many *mexicanos* lived around there until I took my own *compadre* to the quarantine camp." He tries to remember the stench and decay of that summer day, "like a dead dog on a wet morning." The agony of the dying taken prematurely to mass graves to make room for replacements. He closes his eyes and adds, "I can still see the scraps of flesh stuck to the cot canvas, and I remember thinking how desperately our bodies cling to the world of the living. The authorities said my *compadre* and the other *moribundos* would be cared for, but I didn't know anyone who made it back. So when your grandmother came down with smallpox, I knew she might very well die. But I also knew she would not die in a quarantine camp."

So he broke the law and hid her in their shack, tending to her for days. In the end she lived, but when the wife of a neighboring sharecropper caught the disease and died, her husband blamed him for not alerting the authorities. The sheriff who came to investigate took one look at the fresh scars on my grandmother's face and took him away.

"How long were you in jail?"

He takes a long time to answer. "Almost long enough to walk out with a clean conscience. I'm sure I did what was right. And yet . . ." He moves his hand gently, as though stroking my grandmother's face across the room. "She had such beautiful brown skin, as smooth as your cousin Bibi's." He makes a second stroking gesture, except that this one suggests a farewell.

This time I'm the one who's silent. I had heard vaguely about his jail sentence, even how it had to do with my grandmother's smallpox. I had assumed she had come down with the disease because he had simply refused to bring her a doctor—that's the sort of man he is—and whenever I looked at her gentle face whose scars only added to her tenderness, I had blamed him. Now I knew otherwise.

There are many things I'd like to ask them about the quarantine camps and the premature graves. But this is not the time for such talk, and in the end I simply ask for their blessing.

Walking back home, I think about how these rituals are as close as real life comes to storybook endings. In the real world you move because you want to or because you're forced to, or out of some push-pull combination. Maybe you leave or else you die, or someone close to you does, and you end up crossing bridges that leave loved ones behind. That's where I am now, ready to cross, knowing I can't bring along the people I care for any more than Lizard can. But you can try to bring that part of your life to a close and possibly set things right, either by settling old scores or else deciding that some aren't worth settling. That's what I've come to conclude about my father. I've come to accept that the only way I could ever please him was by failing, because then he could claim that I was nothing without him.

Yet there are other relationships where nothing else except an apology will do. Such is the case with Nena, so I go see her one last time, ready to admit my mistakes. Of course, no sooner am I in her apartment, angling toward an apology, than I realize that it means nothing to her. She simply says, "Fine, but is that the main reason you're here?"

I was prepared to admit my mistake but now I can't admit my real feelings. "I was thinking about you and your love affair with Quixote. I stopped by to see how it ends."

"Oh," she says smiling, "we lived happily ever after . . . No, I take it back. His real loves were his horse and his sidekick."

She opens a bottle of wine she was saving for after her summer finals and adds, "I suppose it ends like everything else you read. The more you find out, the less you know." She barely touches her lips to the glass. "A while back I even read that these days we have it all wrong, looking at Quixote like some hero. Some say Cervantes saw Quixote as ridiculous and out of touch, which is how people in his time saw him too. All that stuff about noble causes and fighting against all odds, all that's what we want to believe now." She makes a pained yet comical expression. "Isn't that the most unromantic thing you ever heard?"

I want to touch her, and perhaps she also wants me to. But we've been friends for too long without taking it further, and that only makes things harder now.

"Well," she finally adds, "I hope you learned a thing or two here."

"I did, maybe more than I bargained for. In fact, the most radical thing I learned—"

She pretends to cough up her wine. "Take it easy. I didn't ask about radical things."

"Well, I'll tell you anyway, even if it sounds naive. Besides, it's the sort of lesson you don't learn in a classroom."

Maybe it's the wine talking, or maybe I feel the occasion calls for a word or two of unsolicited wisdom. I announce: "If there is a god, he doesn't give a shit about us."

Nena gives me that smile whenever she thinks I'm trying to provoke her—there's a sadness behind it. "Well, if you live long enough . . . you'll find out it was only the second most radical lesson you learned."

"Oh, really? So what's the most radical?"

"When you finally come to your senses, and realize you were wrong the first time."

She takes the sting off her remark by describing my deathbed scene. It sounds straight out of *Quixote*, as I, bleary-eyed and with a white beard, clutch the family Bible to my chest. I let her finish the scenario, then offer one for her: I describe her forty years from now, with blue hair and a hymen.

"In your case, though," I add, "you'll regret the most radical thing you *never* did."

"I think I can live with that. I expected something about how wrong I was to stay here."

"Now that you mention it . . . ." I'm glad she brings it up, because I want to give my California recruitment pitch one last try. "Look, it's too late for this year, but once I'm there—"

"But I'm fine here."

I pretend not to hear. "If not Pomona, maybe one of the other schools there. There's Pitzer, there's Scripps . . ."

"But this is where my roots are . . . . Why are you smiling? Roots are important."

I empty my wine glass. "There's nothing wrong with them if you're a tree. In fact, that's the only way you'll live. But that's why people have legs. If you aren't getting nourishment in one place, you up and leave."

"But you guys go around talking about *culture* all the time. Well, that's part of your roots."

I try to have the last word. "My culture is more like . . . internal roots. It's something you carry with you wherever you go. You don't have to stay in one place because it's already inside you. And you can always add to it or take parts away."

"But your family's part of all that. That's what I mean by my roots. If you go, where does that leave them?"

In a sense she's right, I think. Unfortunately the family is also where it *ends* for lots of us. Save your family and screw the rest, let their own families take care of them. I'd like to tell Nena that I want to go beyond that, but something holds me back. Maybe my wanting to take her and some of my friends along proves her point. Or maybe I'm somewhat envious of someone who doesn't have to go away to find answers, who can cover the perimeters of her universe in an embrace.

She seems to intuit my thoughts. "My family's very important to me. And I don't just mean my parents. I'm close to all my brothers and sisters, even my cousins."

I think of my own parents, bewildered in their own ways over the uncertain path I've chosen. I think of my younger half-sister and half-brother, too young to understand why I've hardly been home; and my older half-sister, who'll never understand at all, even though in our own way, from our own worlds, we share a parallel craziness that baffles the rest of the family. I think of my cousins: those who thought I was doing so well until I strayed down a strange path.

"Come to think of it," adds Nena, "you hardly ever talk about your family. All you talk about is your MANO friends."

"That's because for me they're like family."

I'm hoping that a brotherhood-of-man speech will do her one better and that she'll drop the whole subject of family. But I don't sound that convincing.

"Some family. When I walked into that place where you guys live, I felt sorry for you. I mean, here you have posters of this anonymous farm-worker family, and there you are living apart from your own flesh and blood. If my own family wasn't so far I'd be staying with them. Alma once told me how you guys lived on the same diet for days, or else ate the leftovers of whatever the day-care kids had. She said how on weekends, when there was no food at the center, you sucked on cough drops to kill your appetite."

"That's because I give most of the scholarship money to my folks." I don't say it expecting a medal, or even to emphasize my family ties, but it's the truth and it impresses her. "Besides, I wouldn't feel right sneaking out of the center to feed my own face. Like I said, they're like family."

"Well, all I can say is, some family. You remind me of the Lost Boys."

"You've lost this boy. What do you mean?"

"Peter Pan's friends. Didn't your mother ever read you bedtime stories?"

"She can't read."

"Oh, really?" I nod, and she's embarrassed. She's quiet for a moment, then finally asks:

"Then tell me, lost boy, care to spend the night here?"

The offer catches me off guard. I'm about to say yes, then decide to play it shy. "But I'll ruin your roommate's sleep."

Actually it's my own I'd be ruining. I can already see myself trying to sleep in the living room while I wonder what unnatural acts are going on behind their closed door.

"Rachel's not here."

I wonder whether she's not here anymore or whether she won't be here for tonight, then I realize it doesn't matter. My days around here are numbered anyway. She's still waiting for a response, so I try to turn my indecision to my advantage. "I don't know. I was thinking of sleeping at the center . . . and between this floor and the one there . . ."

"Who's talking about the floor? You can bunk on the bed. That's a lot better than the center, right?"

I didn't expect her to be so blunt, but that surprise is replaced by a second one when she opens the bedroom door: twin beds. If there's a lesbian love nest here it's not obvious.

I take off my boots cautiously, expecting her to change her mind at any moment, then I notice she's still by the threshold. "Don't tell me you're the one sleeping on the floor."

"I need to do something first," she says, shutting the door on her way out.

I'm fantasizing about what that means as I take the bed closer to the door. The seconds turn into minutes until I open the door an inch or so and peek out: She's typing on the kitchen table.

Expecting the worst—an all-night term paper—I return to bed and fall asleep. Sometime during the night I feel her groping in the dark. She touches my chest and I stir to let her know I'm still waiting.

"How did you know this was my bed?" she whispers.

"Sometimes this nose comes in handy."

We embrace and wrestle around in bed for a while, until I wonder whether I have another Jewish Aztec Princess on my hands. I even ask myself whether her roommate's pillow talk included my lack of assertiveness back in Michigan. Maybe I'm trying to convince myself that if you want sex bad enough it justifies getting a bit tyrannical in bed. In the end

I realize that's not how I want Nena, but since my body can't take no for an answer either, I decide it's best to leave.

I calm down long enough to make sure she's asleep. I'm lacing up my boots when she says in the flat voice of the freshly awakened, "Wait till morning. I'll drive you back."

I realize I didn't really want to leave, that I was doing it out of some vague, misplaced pride. Besides, it's not even dawn yet. So I plop back in bed, this time without bothering to take off my boots. A moment later she hugs me without a word. We're embraced too tightly to undress, but it doesn't matter. It doesn't matter either whether she prefers women or men or both or none. It doesn't even matter whether she's wondering why I'm no longer trying to undress her. We've made our peace in the next-best way possible.

The following morning she takes me to the center. We don't talk much, yet we're so comfortable that I don't take offense when she teases me that men will never understand women.

"Maybe. But what makes you think you'll ever understand us?"

"How could we, with half a dozen guys sleeping under one roof, and never stopping to wonder what the neighbors might say?"

"What might they say?"

"That you're having orgies every other night."

I have this feeling she's hinting at something more personal, but it doesn't matter now. Instead I mention the time we liberated the old seminary. "Remember that place? Way out in the middle of nowhere? Anyway, during our conference some out-of-town Manos suggested it was a great place to party. So Lizard tells them, 'Oh, man, there's sucking and screwing from wall to wall every weekend. Right, De la O? Listen, next time we'll give you *chavos* a call, if you don't mind driving all the way out here.' He waits for the guys to take the bait, then adds with a dead-serious look, 'Shit, we'll even invite some women over next time.'"

Having said this, I realize Lizard was the only Mano who could say that without worrying about his reputation. But now I also wonder whether Nena thinks I told the anecdote on purpose. If so, she doesn't show it.

"Well, listen, if you want a break from the orgies, you can have my place after Thursday. I'm going home for a few days after summer finals."

I thank her but turn down her offer. I don't bother adding that I haven't stayed at the MANO center for quite a while now, nor that by then I'll be in California.

She drops me off at the center where, as luck would have it, Roque and Adrian are already up and about. Seeing me this early with a *chava*, even the guard's eyes widen. Before she drives away, Nena waits until I pass around her side and lowers the idle so that her gentle voice travels just far enough to reach me.

"It doesn't matter if you lie that you were laid last night, as long as you tell them you were loved."

47
The Man From Nowhere Hitchhikes Home

Walking up the stairs of the daycare center I notice Rocinante's tail end out by the alley, piled high with books and boxes. Upstairs a *chavo* who's packing odds and ends mentions that Marcos was here earlier and might still be around.

Since I'm returning a couple of books, I couldn't have picked a better time. I found them a few days ago during my own packing, considered taking them along, then figured it was a good excuse for dropping by the center one last time.

Nano was right about the changing of the guard; even if I weren't leaving it would still be my last visit here. Coco has moved most of the equipment to the new center, and Marcos has decided to put some books and posters in storage until the alternative college opens its doors. So while his helper sorts and boxes books, I sit in a corner and sort through my own feelings. Marcos and Coco are going in different directions, but it's inevitable. Still, I always assumed the center would outlast us, that reinforcements would replace us. A while back one of my honors profs pointed out that the more things change the more they stay the same, and while that may be true, maybe there's another side: The more things seem to stay the same, the more they change.

Even though I don't know Marcos' assistant by name, I've seen him here before, and as he fills boxes and moves them to one side of the room or the other, he seems like someone dividing up possessions after a divorce. "So I suppose Coco gets custody of the Town Crier."

"Nope," he answers. "The Crier just up and left last week."

"Where did he go?"

He shrugs. "Back where he came from, I guess."

"And where was that?"

He shrugs. "Who knows. Marcos says we should have packed him in a box and stored him for the time being."

Wondering about the Crier's origins and whereabouts, I'm reminded of Lucio's anecdote about one of the Dadaists, "the man from nowhere," who upset the art world by pulling words out of a hat to create poems. The approach bothered me because I felt it was an insult to other artists. But what bothered me more was his apparent indifference to his origins. I still don't care much for his on-the-spot poems, but now I'm starting to understand where he's coming from, or more precisely, where he's not coming from. In a sense being from nowhere is like being from everywhere. Watching Marcos' assistant, I can't imagine that old Dadaist bothering to sort through books, or even owning any, since he could always create his own art on the spot.

Roque and Marcos suddenly appear in the hallway, perspiring and a bit out of breath. I can't say what surprises me more: seeing Marcos in town, or seeing him sweaty and disheveled, far from his usual universe of traveling and thinking. "Well, well!" he says, indicating some boxes. "Now that you're leaving let's put you to work one last time. Kevin's stashing some boxes in the station wagon. I'm taking some things I had here to our college. We'll need everything we can get our hands on."

"In that case . . ." I hand him the books I borrowed. "I don't know if they're yours . . ."

He looks at one with Che on the cover. "This one's Coco's. But he won't be needing it in the new office. Not unless they set up a wing for a museum."

Roque, who's still helping out both sides, seems uneasy with our discussion. "So," he tells me, "you're going after that West Coast wool."

I don't like to admit it, but I guess pussy's part of the package. "Let's call it love."

"What's wrong with here?" asks Marcos. "You've been unlucky in love?"

"Unlucky? I can't even place a bet. The women here want guys with money."

"Can you blame them? Most of them are poor, just like us."

"It's not a matter of blame. I just don't want to go through that shit. The ones I met in California were different. They already have enough money."

Nena's still in my thoughts, but already she's turning into a nostalgic ache. Then I think about the last thing she told me. I try to strip away some of the bullshit *chavos* attach to being a lover, until I simplify it to its essence: someone who's able to love. "On second thought, maybe I haven't been that unlucky."

"At least you're lucky in school," adds Roque. "Maybe you can bullshit your way through classes over there too."

Marcos glances at me then looks away, leaving me to wonder whether he's still bothered that I wouldn't attend their college.

Kevin and Adrian arrive, each carrying a large box with smaller ones nested inside. Kevin's sweating worse than Marcos, and when he regrets aloud not being home to pull out a few beers, Roque runs out the room and returns with half a bottle of tequila.

"Since we're cleaning out old memories . . . I hid this a while back. I swore I'd wait until Alma came back."

"Let it age some more," says Adrian, "till it's amber. There's no better tequila than *añejo*."

"I could, but it wouldn't make any difference. She's not coming back. And soon we won't be coming back here either."

"Then let's kill it," I say.

Naturally the tequila does nothing to cool them off. If anything it aggravates the heat. But Roque's not the only one eager to close a chapter in his life. Kevin starts his toast: "Here's to the best of times . . ."

"And the worst of times . . ." says Roque, passing me the bottle.

"And for the times we were too stoned or stupid to tell the difference."

Afterwards we take the last boxes downstairs and load them. I wait for Kevin to take the wheel, but instead Marcos dangles the car keys and tells me with his typical seriousness, "Didn't I tell you? Kevin sold me his wagon."

I can't decide what's more incongruous—Kevin selling his car or Marcos buying it. I'm searching Marcos for the hint of a smile when Kevin calls out, "I'm just loaning it."

Marcos turns it on then remembers something. "So how are you getting to California, De la O?"

I'd rather not get into a long story, so I simply stick out a thumb.

"Hitchhiking?"

I'm tempted to leave it at that, to add to whatever little legend I might leave behind.

"Then maybe Kevin could lend you Rocinante. How about it, Kevin? This way he'll have to return."

"I'll never get her back!"

"He brought back the books," says Adrian.

Kevin can sense they're kidding but won't take any chances. "Listen, I know De la O's always lusted after my Roci. When you said you'd bought it I could hear his heart break all the way over here."

"No offense, Kevin, but it's not my kind of car. Besides, up there I'll have plenty of surf woodies to choose from . . . Now look whose mouth is watering."

"What we can do is offer you a ride home." When I nod, he tells Marcos, "Go on, give him one last ride on Rocinante."

Adrian gets in back so I can ride shotgun, then yells out, "Someday he'll be back, bragging about how much he's learned! If I'm not here, give him the *guarache* test!"

Kevin comes closer. "Which one's that?"

"You just ask him to say *guarache.*"

"I don't think Kevin's the one to give it. Hell, he still calls me *day-law-oh.* Anyway, I'd end up with an incomplete."

"That's the best we can hope for," says Marcos.

I grin and nod, remembering what he once told that old politico—that if we've done our job those who come after us will see a better world and wonder what all the fuss was about.

He guns the accelerator as Kevin yells out.

"De la O!" I can barely hear him. "Don't forget!"

"Forget what?"

He yells something else as Rocinante starts moving, but by now I can only see his mouth move. I look closely, but I can only guess. I think he said, *Guarache.*

I take one last look at the neighborhood around the center, regretting that I never got to know the people, knowing that it's already too late. Yet it's also like my own barrio, with its peeling paint and its families sitting on their porches. As we leave the center behind, an interesting garden catches my eye, the chaotic kind you only see in barrios. For a moment I even wonder why I hadn't noticed it before, and I turn to Adrian.

"Was this here all along? Or is it that it's just now blooming?"

Marcos turns and says, "How soon we forget."

As we drive away, the gardens and the people tending them begin to blur, already becoming memory, and I tell myself, Perhaps, but we can always remember.